REQUIEM'S HOPE

REQUIEM'S HOPE

DAWN OF DRAGONS, BOOK II

DANIEL ARENSON

ISSARI

A white dragon, she flew across the wilderness, a thousand demons of the Abyss flying in pursuit.

Issari panted and her wings ached with every beat. Jabs of pain shot through her belly, and fire blazed in her maw, blasting out smoke that blinded her. She had been flying for days, barely resting, as they drew closer behind her—shrieking, roaring, clattering, hissing—the creatures of nightmares.

Heart thudding, struggling for every breath, she looked over her shoulder and saw them. Three days ago, they had been only a shadow on the horizon. Now she could see their eyes blazing, their fangs glinting red in the dawn, their claws stretching out toward her. Creatures of rot. Creatures of scales, of slime, of disease, of leather and of mummified flesh. Demons. Beasts of the underground. The unholy army her father had summoned to kill weredragons, to kill her kind.

Issari turned her eyes back forward and blinked away tears. The wilderness of the north spread before her: hills topped with patches of snow, plains of frosted grass, and forests leading to distant mountains.

My kind, she thought, her scales clinking.

She was eighteen years old, and she had never known of her magic, had never shifted into a dragon, until only days ago. All her life, weredragons—the cursed, diseased ones who could shift into reptiles—had been people to pity, to protect from her father's wrath.

And now I'm one of them.

She didn't know how she had become a dragon after all these years. Had praying to the Draco constellation given her this magic? Had she inherited it from her parents and only seen it manifest now? She had lost her baby teeth late, bled late, grown to her adult height late; had she simply discovered her magic late too?

"Catch the reptile!" rose a shriek from the southern horizon; it rolled across the plains like thunder. "Break her spine! Tear off her wings! Pull every tooth from her mouth, and snap her limbs, and drag out her entrails, and make her beg for death!" The demons jeered, their voices rising into a single cry, a sound like shattering metal, whistling steam, and collapsing mountains. "Slay all weredragons!"

Issari growled and flew harder.

No, she thought. *No, I am no weredragon. Weredragons are monsters.* She howled and spat fire across the sky. *I am Vir Requis.*

She picked up speed and streamed across the world.

"Make the sky rain the blood of dragons!" rose a screech.

"We will feast upon dragon flesh!" bellowed a deep voice.

"We will crack their bones and suck sweet marrow!"

Issari ground her teeth, narrowed her eyes, and kept flying.

The memories of the past few days filled her, hazy and thick like dreams in the dawn. For so long there had been pain, water, sky—a flight over the sea, three dusks and dawns, sometimes sleeping in the water, her wings stretched out to help her float, mostly flying, mostly hurting, seeking the northern coast. Then there had been this—snow, cold winds, dark clouds, the hinterlands of the barbarian north, a new world, a world of dragons.

"You're here somewhere, Requiem," Issari whispered. "My sister. My brother. My friends. The dragons of Requiem."

Did they live in peace now, building their kingdom in the north?

"I have to find you. I have to warn you." The shrieks rose again and she shuddered, her scales clattering. "We have to flee them."

Yet how could she find the others? The north was vast and sprawling, far larger than Eteer. And even if she did find the Vir Requis, would she not lead these demons directly to their door?

She looked behind her again, and she saw him there—her father.

From here, several marks away, he was a glint of sunlight on bronze, no larger than a bead of dawn on the sea. But she knew it was him. He led this army, riding upon a great demon as large as a dragon, a human woman broken, stretched, fed the flesh of men, and shaped into an obscene bat. Even from here, Issari felt her father's eyes staring at her, boring into her, cutting her like his whip had cut her flesh.

My father, she thought, and new fire rose in her maw, fleeing between her teeth. *The man who butchered thousands. The man I must kill. The man who tossed me to the demons and will shatter my body if he catches me.*

She roared more flame and flew with every last drop of her strength.

So I won't let him catch me.

The clouds thickened above and a drizzle began to fall. In the north, sheets of rain swayed like curtains, and lightning flashed, spreading across the sky like the roots of a burning tree. A forest spread below Issari, thick with oaks, pines, and many trees she did not recognize, trees that did not exist in her warm, southern kingdom. She dipped in the sky, panting, her chest feeling ready to cave in.

She glanced over her shoulder. The demons were closer.

I can no longer flee them in the sky, she thought. *My scales are too bright, my scent too clear. I'll have to lose them in the forest, a human again, small and sneaky.*

She glided down.

The treetops spread below her, drooping with rain and shaking in the wind. Patches of old snow thumped down like a giant's dandruff. Issari dived lower. Wincing, she turned her head aside, stretched out her claws, and crashed through the canopy.

Branches snapped around her, cracking against her scales. Snow filled her nostrils and mouth. One branch thrust up like a spear, its sharp edge driving under a scale like a splinter under a fingernail, and Issari yowled. She kept falling, shattering more branches, and finally thumped onto the ground.

She lay in the snow, the early spring shower pattering against her. Twigs fell like more rain. Her tail flicked and smoke plumed from her nostrils. When she glanced up, she saw a hole in the canopy, revealing the gray sky. Lightning flashed and thunder rolled, and she heard them in the distance, screeching, laughing, mocking her, flying closer.

A growl sounded ahead.

Issari turned her head slowly.

A bear stood before her, staring at her, a burly animal so small next to her dragon form.

The cries rose from the sky.

"Sniff her out! Find her! Follow her scent."

Issari had spent many hours on her balcony back in Eteer, watching the demons sniff across the city, seeking weredragons.

They'll smell me. They can find me anywhere. I shifted into a dragon; the starlit magic fills me now, forever leaving a trail for them to follow.

The bear growled.

"I'm sorry, friend," Issari whispered. She grimaced, guilt pounding through her, and lashed her claws.

The bear whimpered and fell.

As the demon cries grew closer, Issari worked with narrowed eyes, struggling not to gag. With claws and fangs, she skinned the bear, ripping off a cloak of fur, skin, and blood. The meaty, coppery smell filled her nostrils, mingling with the stench of the approaching demons.

Her work complete, she stared down at the skinned carcass. She grimaced. She had not planned to eat this animal, and the sight disgusted her; back in Eteer, she never ate meat. Yet now her stomach growled, clanking her scales. She blasted out fire, roasting the meat, already imagining the taste.

I need this. I need its energy. I've not eaten for days.

She growled and let her flames die.

No. No! With a dragon-sized stomach full of bear, she wouldn't be able to become a human again, not unless she wanted her stomach to burst. And now she needed to run as a girl, hidden, quiet, disguised.

For the first time since fleeing Eteer, she released her magic.

Her white scales melted like snow under rain. Her wings pulled into her back, her claws and fangs retracted, and her body shrank. She stood in the forest, a woman again, shivering in a white tunic, her black braid hanging across her shoulder.

And still her stomach growled, and still the meat tempted her.

Grimacing, she tore off a chunk of half-cooked, bloody bear meat and stuffed it into her mouth. She chewed, struggling not to gag, and she hated herself, and she cried, and still she savored the sweet meat and hot blood.

"We smell her!" rose cries behind, not a mark away. "We smell the whore. Find her! Break her!"

Panting, still chewing the meat, Issari grabbed her bloodied cloak of bear fur. Bits of flesh still clung to it. Her stomach roiling, she wrapped the dripping coat around her, shielding herself in a cocoon of its wet, hot smell.

With any luck they can't smell me like this.

She ran three steps, heading away from the shattered canopy and into the depths of the shadowy forest.

Blood dripped down her face, her stomach gave a sharp twist, and she couldn't help it. She doubled over and gagged, vomiting up her sparse meal.

"Find her! Rip out her spine!"

She kept running.

She ran between the trees, the canopy hiding her, praying the cloak masked her smell. Tears stung her eyes, her breath shuddered, and her legs shook with weakness, but she wouldn't stop running. The demons streamed above now, spinning, diving, and their drool and rot dripped like the rain, pattering between the trees.

"Her scent is gone!"

"Uproot the forest!"

"Break her!"

Claws shattered a tree ahead. Issari bit down on a yelp, spun, and ran in another direction. Shadows streamed above, and talons uprooted an oak. She turned and kept running.

They can't smell me. I just have to keep running. I have to find the others. She clutched her aching belly, stumbling over roots and stones.

"I'll find you, Requiem," she whispered. "I'll find you and warn you. We will slay them together, or we will flee . . . or I will die as a dragon of Requiem, roaring fire, fighting among my kind."

The demons screamed above, branches slapped her, the meat roiled in her belly, and Princess Issari Seran—a Vir Requis, a child of magic—kept running.

LAIRA

On a beautiful spring morning, flowers blooming and birds singing, Laira woke up to find her brother hanging dead from an oak.

She had woken that morning happy—truly, deeply happy for the first time in many years, the sort of contentment that came from a full belly, a good sleep, and a feeling of love and safety. For so many years, she had suffered—exiled from Eteer across the sea, brutalized as an omega of the Goldtusk tribe, and finally limping wounded through the wilderness, almost dying, seeking a home. A home she had finally found.

Requiem.

Waking that morning, she had gazed around at this new kingdom, this dawn of dragons. King's Column rose above her, a pillar three hundred feet tall, perhaps the tallest structure in the world. The sunlight gleamed against its marble, its dragon capital reared, and even in the morning light, Laira saw the Draco constellation shining above the column, blessing it, blessing her. Birches rustled around the pillar, dwarfed by its majesty, sprouting fresh leaves whose scent filled her nostrils.

"Requiem," she whispered, placing a hand against the pillar. "The beat of my heart. A beacon for my kind. Your light will call all others home." Her eyes stung. "All weary, hunted weredragons will see King's Column, and they will heed its call, and they will gather here. They will become Vir Requis, a people noble and strong."

That light and warmth in her heart, Laira made her way deeper into the forest. After the nobility of her prayer, she needed a moment decidedly less noble, and she sought a private place to relieve her bladder. Leaving the other Vir Requis to sleep—they still lay wrapped in fur blankets around the column, snoring softly—she made her way down a hill.

Past a cluster of birches, a twisting pine with a trunk like a face, and a boulder she had engraved with a dragon rune, she saw him.

Her brother.

Prince Sena Seran.

He hung from the tree, his belt around his neck. His bloated tongue protruded from his mouth, and his eyes stared at her, blank, bulging. A crow was already pecking at his ear.

Laira lost her breath. She couldn't even scream.

A choked whisper finally left her lips.

"Why?"

The crow tore off the earlobe and swallowed, snapping Laira out of her paralysis. She ran forward, tears in her eyes, and she wanted to toss a stone at the crow, but she didn't want to hurt Sena, and the bird wouldn't leave, and she tugged her brother's feet, trying to pull him down, but she couldn't, and finally she simply fell to her knees, hugged his dangling feet, and wailed.

The others must have heard her cry; she heard their feet thumping down the hill, and arms wrapped around her, pulling her back. Tanin was embracing her, stroking her hair, holding her as the others cut down the corpse.

"Why, Tanin?" Laira whispered, held in his arms, trembling. "I thought . . . I thought he was happy here, I . . ."

The brown-haired young man held her close. He said nothing; perhaps he did not know what to say.

Tanin's sister—the gruff, golden-haired Maev—stared down at the body which now lay upon the grass. The wrestler crossed her tattooed arms, spat, and shook her head in disgust.

"Bloody bollocks," Maev said. "I flew halfway across the world to save the damn boy's arse from his prison. And now, when we finally bring the bastard to a safe home, he hangs himself? Stars damn—"

Maev's father—the burly, shaggy Jeid—cuffed the back of her head and glared at her. "Show some respect, Maev." The bearded Vir Requis, the first King of Requiem, turned toward Laira, and his eyes softened. He approached her slowly, knelt, and joined her embrace with Tanin.

"I thought he was happy," Laira whispered, tears streaming down her cheeks. She let the two men—a father and his son—hold her in their arms. "I thought he'd find joy among us."

She lowered her head. Perhaps she had always lied to herself. She had been exiled from Eteer as a toddler, too young to remember much of that realm across the sea. But Sena had grown up among the white towers and golden palaces of that warm, southern kingdom. He had fled into these cold hinterlands as a young man, soft and afraid. On his first day here, Sena had tried to take Jeid captive, to betray his own kind—to do anything to gain acceptance back into his father's court.

My father, the cruel King Raem, hunts Vir Requis, Laira thought. *I've been suffering from this truth all my life, but Sena . . .*

She looked over Jeid's shoulder at the body of her brother.

For Sena it was too much.

She freed herself from the embrace, made her way across the grass, and knelt by his fallen body. She touched her brother's cheek and gazed into his dead eyes. Even in death, he was a handsome boy, his features noble, his hair soft. She pulled his lifeless body into an embrace.

"I'm so sorry, Sena." Her tears dampened his tunic. "Goodbye. I love you."

Before she could say more, a shriek rose above.

Laira raised her head, stared between the trees, and saw it there. For the second time that morning, she lost her breath.

Around her, the others gasped and sneered.

"A demon," Laira whispered.

She had never seen one of these creatures, the unholy things her father had freed from the underworld to hunt dragons. But she had heard the tales, and she recognized it at once. The creature flew down toward them, large as a dragon and shaped as an octopus. Instead of suckers, its tentacles bore many round mouths, each containing a ring of teeth. A central mouth, large as a dragon's maw and full of fangs, opened in the creature's head. It emitted a cry so loud the trees shook, shedding their last patches of snow.

"Stars damn it!" Maev said. "The bastards found their way here."

The gruff wrestler spat, leaped into the air, and shifted. Green scales clattered across her, wings burst out from her back, and Maev soared, a dragon blasting fire. An instant later, the others shifted too. Tanin soared as a red dragon, Jeid as a copper beast. They crashed through the treetops, heading toward the demonic octopus.

Laira hesitated for a moment longer. Her brother needed her. Sweet Sena lay dead at her feet; how could she leave him to the crows?

Above the trees, the demon stretched out three tentacles, wrapping each one around a dragon. Scales cracked and Laira's friends cried out above. Their fire crashed into the octopus, only to slide off its slick, wet body. The blood of dragons spilled.

Today the living need me more.

Laira leaped into the air and shifted.

She beat her wings, her golden scales chinked, and she crashed between the treetops before soaring toward the battle.

The deformed mollusk shrieked ahead, wreathed in flames that did not burn it. Its tentacles were squeezing the three dragons, and the mouths upon them—round and toothy like lamprey jaws—tore into flesh. Maev roared and slammed her tail against the creature, but it was like trying to cut a pile of jelly; the octopus's body kept reforming. Jeid and Tanin were beating their wings uselessly; the demon was flailing them around like a man swinging cats by the tails.

Laira growled and streamed toward the fray.

"Requiem!" she cried. "Our wings will forever find your sky!"

She drove toward the demon, opening her maw wide to bite, to tear into its flesh.

A tentacle snapped toward her.

Laira banked, dodging it, but a second arm slammed into her and wrapped around her neck.

She floundered in the sky, choking. She tried to breathe fire but could not; the tentacle was constricting her throat, blocking both air and flame.

"Stars damn it!" Jeid howled, tossed around by the tail. The burly copper dragon was clawing at the beast, unable to harm it. "Tanin, Maev—you told me these demons are small as horses."

"They were!" Maev shouted back, her green scales chipped. "Most of them."

Laira sputtered, only sparks leaving her maw. She lashed her claws, tearing at the tentacle, but whenever she pierced the boneless digit, it reformed. The grip tightened around her neck, and the small mouths upon it—each as large as a human mouth— tore at her scales, tugging them off her neck. Blackness spread across her.

Do I die here too? she thought. *Do we end up as food for demons and crows?*

Tears stung her eyes; she could barely see. They had founded Requiem, a kingdom for dragons, only this winter; did this dream of a nation now end?

She managed to hiss.

No.

She beat her wings madly.

I did not pass through fire and blood to die above my home.

She gritted her teeth . . . and released her magic.

A human again, slim and small, she squirted out of the octopus's grip and tumbled through the sky.

The beast shrieked, a sound so loud Laira thought her eardrums might shatter. It reached out more tentacles and grabbed her again, but she slipped from its grasp like a minnow from a man's fingers. She flew through the sky, spinning, and reclaimed her magic.

A golden dragon again, she soared with a howl, dodged the tentacles, and crashed into the demon's belly.

Her horns tore through translucent, sticky membranes. The demon's stomach tore open above her, and Laira managed to grin, sure she had killed it.

An instant later, a thousand baby octopi spilled from the slashed belly, raining onto her.

Laira screamed. Each of the spawned creatures was large as a wolf, their tentacles bloody and lined with clattering mouths. They fell upon her, clinging like parasites. Their mouths tugged at her scales, tearing them loose, and her blood showered. Several landed upon her wings, tugging her down toward the forest. She screamed, fell, and slammed against the treetops. She yowled as a branch drove into her thigh. As she crashed through the branches, the demon spawn tore free from her wings, allowing Laira to flap and soar again. The creatures were feeding at her flanks, sucking her blood like leeches. She whipped her tail, knocking them off. When finally she removed the last creature, she saw the spawn—there were hundreds of them—racing through the forest, tearing down trees, and dragging themselves toward King's Column. Their slime covered the holy ground of Requiem.

She beat her wings, rising higher, and returned her eyes to the main battle. The mother octopus still lived, lashing her tentacles; only four of the arms remained. The other three dragons had managed to free themselves, though blood covered them and their scales were chipped.

"Laira!" Maev shouted down to her. Blood and slime filled her mouth and she spat. "You have to bite through the tentacles. Grab them near the body and bite!" With that, the green dragon shot toward the octopus, dodged one tentacle, and grabbed another's base between her jaws. She began to tug like a pup on a rope, tearing off the slimy arm.

The octopus flailed in the sky, spraying black liquid like tar. A stream of the foul ink crashed against Tanin, and the red dragon bellowed and dipped in the sky, wiping off the ooze with his claws. When the octopus spun toward Laira, she banked, dodging most of the attack. The jet of ink sprayed over her head, but some droplets landed against her. They stung like a rain of lava, and she yowled but kept flying.

Hovering before her, the octopus met her gaze. Its mouth opened in a toothy grin. At first, Laira had thought this a mindless beast, but now she saw cunning and recognition in its eyes. A voice emerged from its maw, shrill as trees cracking under ice, as the cries of dead souls, as her innermost nightmares. It licked its chops, tongue long and blue, as words fled between its teeth.

"Laira . . . I recognize you, Laira Seran." It hissed at her, grin widening. "Your father, King Raem Who Lies with Demons, sends his regards."

Laira froze in the sky, terror constricting her.

It knows me. It knows my name.

Its remaining tentacles lashed, holding back the other dragons, as it hovered closer toward her. Its tongue reached out, stretching as long as its arms, blue and dripping saliva. It licked her cheek, then grabbed her horn and tugged her closer. Its mouth opened wider and wider, so large she thought it could swallow her whole. Its uvula swung and its gullet bubbled with acid.

Laira screamed and blew her fire.

Her flames crashed into the creature's mouth, splashed against its palate, and ignited its stomach acid. The creature screamed but would not release her. Its tongue still tugged her horn, dragging her toward the inferno.

She raised her claws, grabbed the tongue, and tore it apart with a shower of blood. Free from its grip, she flew backward a few feet, blew more fire, then drove forward with a scream.

Her horns pierced the creature's eyes with wet *pops*, sank through flesh, then pulled back coated with jiggling globs of brain.

The misshapen mollusk hovered for a moment longer, staring at Laira with empty eye sockets, then crashed down toward the forest.

When it hit the trees, branches and trunks drove through its flesh, tearing the creature apart. Gobbets of flesh, chunks of tentacles, and blood rained, thick with worms.

Wobbling and bleeding, Laira descended, all but crashing through the canopy. She landed in a patch of bloodied snow, yellow grass, and rotted globs of flesh, and her magic left her. She stood shivering in her fur cloak, a human again. The other dragons landed too and resumed human forms: Jeid, a grizzly bear of a man, his beard thick and his hair shaggy; his daughter, Maev, her chin raised in defiance, her tattooed arms crossed, and her yellow hair scraggly; and finally Jeid's son, Tanin, a tall young man with a shock of brown hair.

We are four, Laira thought, staring at the family, perhaps the only other Vir Requis in the world, the only other souls who could become dragons. *Yet once we were five.* Her eyes stung and the hollowness of losing her brother filled her with more pain than her wounds.

"What was that thing?" Laira whispered. She looked at Maev and Tanin; the two had flown to Eteer to save Sena, and they had battled demons there. Their quest felt so meaningless to Laira now; all the blood they had shed to save Sena, all in vain . . .

Maev kicked a fallen chunk of octopus. "A scout. A big one too. This one ate human flesh; it's the only way they can grow this big." She kicked the glob again. "Your father's looking for us, little Laira. But he won't hear any news from our friend here."

Laira closed her eyes and lowered her head, the pain too great to bear. Her chest tightened and her belly felt full of ice.

My mother—burned at the stake. My brother—dead at his own hands. My father—a ruler of the demons that hunt me.

Even standing here among her fellow Vir Requis, Laira felt alone, too hurt to open her eyes again, too broken, too scarred. The grief was a weight she could not carry.

But no, she thought, eyes stinging. *I'm not alone.*

Her memories returned to her last days in Eteer, a child of only three. Those memories were vague, mere hints of pictures and sounds, but among them Laira saw a babe, an innocent girl. A younger sister.

"You're still out there, Issari," she whispered. "My little sister. You're still in Eteer, and I'm so afraid for you." She raised her head, opened her eyes, and looked at the others. She spoke louder. "We must bury Sena. We will bury him with the others— with little Requiem and Eranor. He will rest with them forever. His soul will rise to the Draco stars."

Stepping through puddles of blood, she made her way downhill, moving back toward the place where she'd left Sena's body. When she reached the oak, she froze and sucked in breath. A cluster of the octopus spawn still lived. They were piled together, feasting, guzzling down meat.

Laira shifted into a dragon, roared, and raced toward them. She whipped her tail, knocking the demonic brood aside. They slammed into tree trunks, hissing, blood on their mouths, gobbets of Laira's brother stuck between their teeth. When Laira leaped toward the place where Sena's body had lain, she found it gone. Nothing but blood remained.

She howled. The sound tore through her throat, tore through her soul, a cry of more mourning than she'd felt since her mother had died.

She blew her flames.

She torched the octopus spawn.

They burned, squealing, tumbling over, reaching out their flaming tentacles toward her. They seemed almost to beg.

She could not bury her brother; she would give him a funeral in fire.

By the time the other Vir Requis joined her, the creatures lay as charred clumps, and Laira knelt in the burnt grass, shaking and too hurt to weep.

Goodbye, my brother, she thought. *Fly to our mother and be at peace . . . a peace I've never felt.*

She looked back at the others. They stood together in human forms, watching her, hesitating.

"He will send more demons," Laira said, her voice sounding hollow to her ears. "My father will never stop hunting us. With blood and flame, we forged a kingdom among the birches. Now our war of independence begins."

DORVIN

Dorvin stood above the creature's corpse, spat on it, and kicked the diseased flesh.

"Arse-biting, mammoth-shagging piece of shite." Dorvin gave the beast another kick, his foot sinking into rotted flesh. "What the Abyss is this son of a whore?"

He stared down at the creature, disgust swirling through him. Dorvin was only twenty-two winters old, but he'd fought hundreds of beasts already—mammoths, saber-toothed cats, the cannibals of the east, and even wild rocs. Back in his tribe, the fabled Clan of Stonespear, he'd slaughtered more beasts than even the chieftain. Yet he'd never seen a creature like this.

He brushed flecks of its flesh off his fur tunic. "By the Sky Mother, it's an ugly piss-drinker, it is."

The creature was large as a dragon, and four wings grew from its back, each covered with a rug of human fingers— *thousands* of fingers that grew like grass. Even in death, those fingers twitched as if trying to grasp him. The creature's body was lank and tumors covered its face, some of them leaking. This was no animal. This was an unholy terror from another world.

A soft voice rose behind him. "A demon. A demon from the Abyss."

Dorvin turned to see Alina, his sister, approaching. The young druid—she was only two years older than him—wore lavender robes and moccasins trimmed with fur. Her long auburn hair spilled from under her hood, and her eyes gleamed, large and deep purple. She held a staff formed of a great oak root; at its tip, wooden tendrils clutched a blue crystal. A necklace of beads hung around her neck, and a bracelet of true bronze—a priceless metal—encircled her left wrist.

"A demon?" Dorvin shook his head in amazement, shoved down his spear, and pierced the corpse's flesh. "Bloody mammoth shite."

Alina came to stand beside him, looked at the creature, and closed her eyes. She reached into a leather pouch that hung from her belt, pulled out blue powder, and sprinkled it into the wind. She whispered prayers to the dragon constellation, her goddess.

"Bless us, stars of the Sky Dragon," Alina said, looking up into the sky. Daylight shone and the stars slept, yet Alina claimed that they always listened. "Watch over your children."

Dorvin muttered under his breath. Stars. Goddesses. Demons. What did he know of these things? He was a hunter. He dealt with blood and fire. Let his sister pray to spirits. His task wasn't to follow spiritual leaders but to be a leader himself.

He turned away from the corpse and faced the others, his group of vagabonds. They stood clustered together between patches of melting snow, nineteen souls—elders, children, a pregnant mother, a few young men and women . . . all outcasts. All cursed. All like him. Weredragons.

"What is it, Dorvin?" said Old Nan, seventy winters old, her white hair streaming in the wind. Fear filled her eyes.

"It said it's hunting weredragons!" called out Bryn, a young woman with red hair and blazing brown eyes.

They all began to mutter, glancing around, whispering, weeping, praying. Tears flowed. Panic began to spread. Every one of these souls carried memories of abuse, exile, and fear, and Dorvin had promised to lead them to safety. He would not let this group crumble.

"Silence!" he roared. He sucked up his magic and shifted.

Silver scales rose upon him, his fangs and claws sprouted, and he beat his wings. He rose to hover several feet above the ground, scattering snow, and blasted a jet of flame skyward. His roar shook the forest. All the others froze and stared at him, finally falling silent. Dorvin landed in the snow again, staying in his dragon form. He stared at his people, one by one, smoke pluming from his nostrils.

"By the Sky Mother's swollen teats!" he said. "After all we've been through—fleeing our tribes and villages, trekking through the wilderness all winter, nearly freezing our arses off— are you going to let one little demon frighten you?" He spat a glob of fiery saliva; it burned, digging a hole into the ground. "I am Dorvin, son of Karash, a hunter. I told you I'd lead you to safety, and stars damn it, I will. We will find a new home. We will find this place called Requiem."

Alina stepped up to stand by Dorvin. Still in human form, her purple robes fluttering in the wind, she addressed the crowd. While Dorvin's voice was loud and fast, she spoke in a smooth, slow lilt like the music of flutes.

"Children of Starlight." She pulled back her hood, and her auburn hair billowed. Her eyes shone, deep purple flecked with gold. "Let no fear fill your hearts, for the Sky Dragon constellation shines upon us. The stars of our magic bless us. They will keep us safe. Shift with me, my friends. Become the dragons, take flight, and find the sky."

Smiling softly, Alina shifted and soared, a lavender dragon with white horns. Her scales gleamed in the sunlight, and a stream of fire rose from her mouth, white and blue and spinning as it crackled. Dorvin beat his wings and rose to fly at her side, and they spun together, two dragons, silver and lavender, wreathed in flame.

"Rise, dragons!" Dorvin shouted. "Show me your strength."

The frightened, hungry people—exiled from their homes for their curses—summoned their magic. Nineteen more dragons rose into the sky, their scales of many colors, and their flames rose, many columns of a fiery palace.

"Like this we are strong!" Dorvin roared.

Alina flew above him. "Like this we are blessed."

Dorvin turned in the sky and began flying north, leading the others, leaving the corpse behind. He knew that some among them feared the sky—the sky was full of rocs, pteros, and now demons—but Dorvin would have them conquer fear.

For too many years, we were afraid, he thought. *For too many years we dared not shift. Now the sky is ours.*

Pain welled inside him, and he growled and spewed flames. The damn memories would not leave him. Even here, in the sky, a proud silver dragon, he remembered his old tribe's hunters mocking him, calling him a creature, a reptile, a cursed one. He remembered their Elder Druid, a proud old man with a bald head and stern eyes, striking Alina, spitting upon her, banishing her from their order because of her magic. Everyone who flew behind him had such a story to tell. To the world they were monsters, but Dorvin refused to treat them so.

"We are dragons!" he called out to them now, flying at their lead. "We are proud and strong."

Gliding beside him, Alina smiled. "We are blessed with starlight."

As they flew onward, Dorvin's eyes stung and watered. He told himself it was only the cold wind.

"Do you think it's truly out there?" he said to his sister, his voice too soft for the others to hear. "A kingdom called Requiem, a home for our kind?"

Beads of sunlight glimmered on her lavender scales. "Travelers whisper of Requiem. The demon we slew spoke the name. A place for dragons." She nodded, tears in her eyes. "Requiem exists. We will find her fabled column of marble, and we will find a home."

Dorvin took a shuddering breath, trying to imagine it. An entire kingdom of weredragons! A place where they would be accepted, no longer feared or spat upon. Nobody would call him cursed there. Nobody would strike his sister. In the clouds, Dorvin pretended that he could see this fabled new kingdom, a sanctuary founded only this winter. In his mind, he saw soaring columns of stone, palaces of gold, cobbled streets, statues, and thousands of others like him. Raised in a tribe of hunter-gatherers, Dorvin had never seen a city before, but he had heard tales of cities—they said some existed beyond the sea—and that was how he imagined Requiem. A city of marble, gold, and dragon magic.

They flew onward, crossing plains of grass, rustling forests budding with spring leaves, and chalk mountains whose faces gleamed golden in the sun. Sheets of rain swayed in the east, and the sun gleamed in the west. The shadows of dragons swept across the endless world, crossing rivers, hills, and valleys. Tribes of hunters raced below, smaller than ants from up here, pointing upward at the dragon flock. Mammoths raced through grasslands and wildebeests swept across plains. The world seemed eternal, empty, rising from darkness into a dawn of life.

It's a dawn of dragons, Dorvin thought. *Requiem rises.*

They flew until the sun set and the stars emerged. Millions of these sky spirits gleamed, and among them shone *their* stars—the stars shaped as a dragon, the Draco constellation. Alina called the constellation a goddess, the Sky Dragon who protected their kind, and as she flew, she prayed to those stars. Her voice rose in song.

"Stars of dragons! Forever we fly in your light. Forever you will shine upon us. We are dragons. We are Requiem. Ours are the stars."

The others sang too, twenty dragon voices singing in the night. "Ours are the stars."

They had been flying for many days and nights now, sleeping in the wilderness, crossing the marks, traversing the world, seeking that pillar, that beacon of marble, seeking King's Column—the heart of their legendary home. Sometimes Dorvin wondered if they'd ever find it, if it even existed.

If there is no Requiem, he thought, *and if King's Column is but a fable, we will seek her still. If Requiem does not exist upon the land, she will exist in our hearts, a light that forever guides us.*

Dawn was rising again, gold and blue, when Dorvin saw it ahead, and tears filled his eyes.

At his side, Alina gasped and wept. Behind them the other dragons whispered, cried out in joy, and sang prayers.

"King's Column!" they said. "Requiem! Requiem is real."

Gliding on the wind, Dorvin could barely breathe. He had always thought himself strong, a vicious hunter of beasts, a man with no weakness inside him, yet now tears streamed down his scaly cheeks.

"It's real," he whispered.

The pillar was still distant, ten marks away or more, a mere sliver from here. Yet its light shone across the world. The column rose from a forest, taller than any tree, gleaming white and silver. A sunbeam fell upon its capital, breaking into many rays like the fabled lighthouses said to exist across the sea. Birches spread around the pillar, and blue mountains rose behind.

Requiem. Our home.

All around Dorvin, the dragons sang prayers—singing for their stars, singing for Requiem.

Twenty-one banished, lost, hurt souls, the dragons glided upon the wind, tears in their eyes and songs in their hearts, flying toward their new home.

* * * * *

They spiraled down, twenty-one lost dragons. Dorvin landed first between the birches, and the others landed around him, their claws sinking into the forest floor. Before them it rose—the Pillar of Requiem. King's Column. Even standing in dragon form, Dorvin felt smaller than a mouse. The pillar rose to the height of fifty men, its capital shaped as rearing dragons in the sunlight. A circle of marble tiles spread around its base, and spring grass grew between the tiles. The birches rustled around the column, their leaves fresh. It was a spring for the world and a spring for dragons.

And before the column they stood—more dragons. The children of Requiem.

"Requiem," Alina whispered at his side. The lavender dragon knelt and bowed her head. "A home for dragons."

A silver dragon, Dorvin tilted his head, a sudden tightness in his chest. "Is . . . this it?"

He narrowed his eyes. He had expected cities. He had dreamed of hundreds of dragons—*thousands* of them. And only four stood here before him! Surely they'd come to the wrong place. Surely this couldn't be the kingdom of dragons. Dorvin took a step closer, snorting out fire.

"I am Dorvin! A leader of dragons. We seek the fabled Requiem."

One of the four dragons ahead—a burly, copper beast—stepped forward. He blasted out smoke and bowed his head. "You have found Requiem, my son." The dragon's eyes dampened. "Welcome."

With that, the copper dragon released his magic. He became a hulking bear of a man. His hair was shaggy, his beard bushy, and he wore an old fur cloak. The three other dragons of Requiem took human forms too: a young man with brown hair, a gruff-looking woman with golden hair and tattooed arms, and a runt of a woman—small as a child—with short black hair. They looked as humble, weak, and frightened as the twenty dragons Dorvin himself led.

"Where is Requiem?" Dorvin said, remaining in dragon form. "Stars damn it! What the Abyss is this piss-pot of a camp?" He spat. "I've seen piles of mammoth dung more noble than this. Where are the houses, the towers, the armies of hundreds? Shag-a-sheep! I thought this was a kingdom. With a proper king and all. Not . . . not this."

The bearded man said nothing, but the gruff woman—the one with tattooed arms and blond hair—stepped forth. She raised her chin, bared her teeth, and growled.

"Watch your tongue, boy." She flexed her muscles; they were damn big for a woman. "Requiem is a kingdom—a kingdom in its infancy but a kingdom nonetheless." She gestured at the bearded man. "And you stand before King Aeternum, the Light of Requiem. Your king."

The brown-haired young man stepped forward next; he was a tall one, but Dorvin knew he could take this boy in a fight.

"There are four of us," the young man said. "I'm Tanin, and this is my sister Maev. The fourth is Laira. We are few, but we serve the stars and we're strong." Tanin squared his shoulders. "Join us, friends. Together we will build this kingdom."

Dorvin blinked, scarcely believing it.

Then he burst out laughing—a hoarse, twisted laughter that sounded dangerously close to tears. Finally he released his own magic and stood as a young man again, the wind billowing his black hair and fur tunic. He turned back toward his followers; they were releasing their magic one by one, turning from dragons back into men, women, and children.

"I told you I'd bring you to Requiem!" Dorvin said to them, still laughing, almost sobbing. "Bloody bollocks, here we are. A column and four piss-drinkers whose arses I could kick in my sleep."

Maev leaped forward, sneering, and gave Dorvin a shove so mighty he nearly toppled down. "We'll see whose backside gets kicked."

Dorvin barked a laugh. "I don't normally clobber girls, but today I'll make an exception." He raised his fist. "You lot are a sorry pile of—"

"Dorvin!" The cry rang across the forest. Her lavender robes swaying, Alina—that cursed druid—stepped forth. She grabbed him and tugged him away from Maev, her purple eyes flashing. "You lout! Step back and cool down."

Maev was still growling and trying to lunge at him. Her own companions were holding her back, though their eyes glared at Dorvin; they seemed to detest him no less than Maev did.

Dorvin snickered and mussed Alina's hair. "Hey, sweet sister, I was only joking with them. You know how I like to joke."

The druid shoved him backward and smacked his chest with her staff. "You can have your little pissing contest another time. We stand on holy ground. Go back!" She shoved him another step back toward their followers, then turned toward the four dragons of Requiem. Her eyes softened and she lowered her head. "Please forgive my brother. Dorvin is a child of wildfire, but I was born in starlight. His heart is rash, his mind is small, but he brought us safely to this place." She smiled softly, gazing up at the column. "We've come to join you. To join Requiem." She knelt upon the marble tiles and lowered her head. "We've come to serve you, King Aeternum."

Standing among his followers, Dorvin stared in disbelief. Rage, disappointment, and fear battled inside him. He had thought to find safety here, to find glory, a kingdom he would be proud to join, a king he'd be proud to fight for. Instead he'd found nothing—not even a village. Just four more ragged survivors. And his sister knelt before them? Before this shaggy, bearded brute who called himself a king?

"He's not a king," Dorvin spat out. Several of his people were following Alina's lead; they too were bowing. Dorvin grunted and tugged them up. "On your feet! Stand straight and proud. We do not serve this man." He pointed at Jeid, this so-called King Aeternum. "He's nothing but another outcast. I've led you all winter. I fought for you. I slew monsters for you and brought you here. This is all Requiem is?" Dorvin laughed mirthlessly. "Then so be it. I will lead this kingdom. I will serve as Requiem's king. Requiem will be ours!"

With that, he leaped into the air, shifted into a dragon, and lunged toward Jeid.

I won't kill you, old man, he thought, grinning savagely. *But I will crush you into subservience.*

With a roar, Jeid shifted too and leaped.

As the others cried out, the two dragons slammed together.

Scales cracked, loud as thunder. Fire blasted out and smoke covered the forest.

"Dorvin, stop!" Alina shouted somewhere in the distance.

"Grizzly, kill the boy!" Maev was shouting, shaking her fist.

The two dragons drew apart, and Dorvin grinned again, hissing out smoke. "I'm a leader of dragons." He let the flames grow in his belly. "I lead twenty people; you lead three. Requiem is mine." With that, he blasted out a stream of fire.

Jeid was a larger dragon, wide and cumbersome, a lumbering beast of heavy copper scales. Yet his wings beat mightily, and he soared fast enough to dodge the flames. The jet raced across the earth and slammed into the base of King's Column, blackening the marble. With a roar, Jeid swooped, barreling into Dorvin.

Their horns clattered together like the antlers of battling elks. A silver dragon, Dorvin was smaller than Jeid but also half his age, quicker and more feral. He snapped his teeth, tore a scale off Jeid's shoulder, and spat it out. Blood gushed from the exposed flesh. The tangy taste filled Dorvin's mouth, and he licked his lips.

"Your reign ends now, old man!" He laughed and swiped his claws, aiming at an eye. "I am King Dorvin, Lord of Requi—"

Jeid's tail cracked like a whip, slamming into Dorvin's head.

He fell, seeing stars.

"Kill him, Grizzly!" Maev shouted, hopping up and down.

"Bash his head in!" Tanin cried.

Somewhere, Dorvin heard his own people chanting for him, shouting at him to stand up, to keep fighting. But they sounded so far away; he could barely cling to the voices. Alina was shouting too—something about an end to violence—but Dorvin couldn't hear her either. Grumbling, he shoved himself to his feet. But Jeid struck again. The beast's jaws closed around Dorvin's neck, cracking scales, cutting into flesh.

Dorvin screamed.

He slashed his claws against Jeid, drawing blood. His wings pounded against the earth. He tail whipped, hitting Jeid's back, but the coppery dragon would not release him. The jaws tightened, squeezing Dorvin's neck, constricting his breath. He tried to shove the beast off, to fly, to fight back, but could not.

"Serve me," Jeid grumbled, crushing Dorvin's neck. "Serve me now or I snap your neck. Serve me or die. Choose."

"He chooses death!" Maev said. The young woman ran forward, still in human form, and knelt before Dorvin. She stared into his eyes, smirking. "Say it, boy! Say you choose death. I'll enjoy pissing on your grave."

He tried to burn her, but only a stream of smoke left his jaws, scattering uselessly against the woman.

Dorvin managed to whisper hoarsely. "You dare not kill me, Jeid. You're a coward." He spat out smoke. "I surrender to no one."

"I'm not asking you to surrender." Jeid shook his head wildly, slamming Dorvin's head repeatedly against the earth. "Dragons of Requiem do not surrender. I'm asking you to fight for me. Fight for your king. Fight for Requiem. Do not fight for one you think weak; fight for one who showed you strength."

With that, Jeid tugged his jaws backward, lifting Dorvin's head several feet above the ground. Then Jeid slammed him back down. Dorvin's temple thumped against the earth so powerfully his ears rang, his eyes blackened, and his magic left him. He lay in the dust, a man again, blood trickling from his head. He tried to rise but Jeid stood above him, still a dragon, pinning him down.

"Wormy pig guts," Dorvin said, blinking to bring the world into focus. "You're a tough old bastard, you son of a goat-shagger."

With a grumble, Jeid released his magic and tugged Dorvin to his feet. "Stand up." Disgust filled his voice. "Now kneel before me. Do it now before I clobber you again."

Head spinning and blood trickling, Dorvin looked around him. Everyone was staring at him—his sister, Jeid's people, his own people. They were all silent, waiting for his move. Dorvin cursed inwardly. If he surrendered like a coward, he'd look weak. If he tried to fight again and lost, he'd look even weaker. He had only one thing to do.

Stars damn it.

He burst out laughing, blood in his mouth.

"You bastard!" He grabbed Jeid and squeezed his shoulder. "You're tougher than rocks in a dragon's gullet." He nodded. "I was only testing you, you lump of tarred mammoth shite. Aye. You proved your strength to me. I'll fight for you, old man." He knelt. "There, I'm kneeling all proper like, you grizzled chunk of meat." He rose again, stared at Jeid solemnly, and nodded. "I'll fly for you. For Requiem." He turned toward his people and raised his voice. "We fight for Requiem, for King Aeternum! Ours are the stars!"

They repeated the chant. "Ours are the stars!"

As the others stepped closer, Dorvin thrust out his bottom lip, looking around and nodding. "Well, it's a shite-hole, this place is. But not a bad column you've got here, Grizzly King. This column is a backbone. We'll build a body around it."

His sister smiled and began leading the people in prayer. Dorvin was about to join them, to sing the song of starlight and dragon wings, when the cry rose behind him.

He spun around, narrowed his eyes, and tilted his head.

A young woman came running from the forest, her green eyes wide with fear. A dark braid hung across her shoulder, and she wore an uncured pelt of bear fur. The garment stank of blood and old meat, and flies bustled around it, as if the girl had simply torn it off the animal. Beneath, she wore a bloodstained cotton tunic. Strangest of all was her hand; when she reached forward, she revealed a silver amulet embedded into the flesh of her palm.

"Requiem!" she cried. "Demons attack—an army of demons." She ran a few more steps, then collapsed.

"Issari!" Tanin shouted and ran toward her. He knelt above the girl. "Issari, by the stars, what are you doing here?"

The others all crowded around, gasping and whispering. Dorvin stared down at the strange young woman, confusion welling inside him.

Lying in Tanin's arms, pale and shivering and coated in blood, Issari stared up and whispered through pale lips, "He is coming. Raem. My father. He flies here leading a thousand demons. He flies to destroy Requiem."

With that, her eyes closed, and she said no more.

RAEM

They streamed across the world, festering, screeching, howling for blood, an unholy host, a darkness to crush reptiles. The demon army swarmed.

"You will feast upon dragon flesh!" Raem shouted, standing in his stirrups. "You will drink dragon blood and suck marrow from their bones!"

They howled, cheered, laughed, screeched, hissed, bellowed—a thousand creatures flying around him. Some were balls of fat, their sores oozing. Others were long, scaled strips of festering flesh. Some were feathered, others naked, some encased with the screaming faces of victims like plates of fleshy armor. Drool dripped between their teeth. Their eyes blazed like torches. Their wings churned the clouds and sent waves of stench across the land.

Soon, my daughters. Raem's lips peeled back as he inhaled the sweet miasma of his host. *Soon you will join this army. I will break you. I will reform you. I will turn you into creatures.*

He looked down at the demon he rode, a tortured, weeping thing. Once, they said, she had been a woman, a mere mortal. Her bones had been distended, her skin stretched, her body broken and reshaped so many times her mind had shattered. Today this creature flew as a great bat, mouth smacking, wings thudding.

"An abomination," Raem whispered, disgust flooding him. "And my daughters are sinners. They are abominations too. Soon they will fly as broken creatures. I will ride them."

The north sprawled beneath him, the hinterlands across the sea, barbarous realms of wandering tribes, backwater villages, and that pathetic Requiem the weredragons called a kingdom. He sneered. Eteer, his kingdom in the south, was a land of towers, of high walls, of lush gardens, of civilization. Here was a benighted wilderness. Here was a den of reptiles. Here was a land he must crush.

"Seek their column!" he shouted. "Stare, demon eyes, and scan this world, and find the pillar of marble. They built a beacon to draw in more of their kind, a lighthouse for lizards." He laughed. "It will also summon their doom."

They demons cackled with him. They flew on.

They flew for hours, for days, for nights, never tiring, never resting, seeking Requiem. She would be there, Raem knew. Issari would be among the other filthy weredragons. He caressed his arm where stitches still held his raw wound, the wound Issari had given him when she stabbed him in the cistern. Raem licked his lips as he imagined how she would suffer, how he would cut every part of her. Perhaps he would stitch Issari and Laira together, forming a conjoined twin, a single daughter to torment. He had seen demons perform this art; he would practice it upon the reptiles.

They flew onward, dripping rot, scanning the world. Spring had begun, but their wings darkened the sky, their steam hid the sun, and all wilted beneath their rancid rain.

They flew until they saw the village ahead.

Clay huts clustered together, their roofs topped with straw. It was a place barely worth stopping to piss at. Three reed boats floated in a river, and goats brayed in a pen. A few barbarians stood in the dirt, firing arrows up at the demons; most hid in their huts. Raem wanted to fly onward, but his demons bustled, drooled, begged for flesh.

Raem sighed and stroked the creature he rode.

"Very well." He pointed down at the village and raised his voice. "Land, my friends! Land and feed."

They descended upon the village in a spiral of decay, a dripping tornado of hissing, snapping mouths and raining drool. A few villagers tried to flee, firing arrows into the unholy swarm. Demons descended upon them, ripping off limbs, pulling out entrails, crunching bones in their jaws. Other villagers tried to flee across the fields. A coiling centipede, as long as a fallen oak, wrapped around one fleeing child and squeezed, slicing her to segments. A twitching bundle of arms and mouths, its insect wings buzzing, flew toward one family, regurgitated a net of dripping webs to trap them, and thrust a metal tongue like a tube into the screaming mass. Huts collapsed. Animals screamed and died. Gobbets of meat flew across the village and blood soaked the earth.

Raem's mount, the constructed bat, still hovered above the village. She looked over her shoulder at him, eyes begging, tongue lolling. Sitting in the saddle, Raem stroked her.

"Very well, Anai," he said. He had named her after his dead wife, for this creature had become his new companion. "You may feed."

Not wasting another heartbeat, the beast plunged down, her two spine ridges bulging. She descended upon a screaming, legless man; a second demon was guzzling down the legs a few feet away. The man tried to crawl away, but Anai pounced upon him, thrust down her mouth, and ripped out flesh. The creature wept as she fed, perhaps still remembering her old human soul, but she fed nonetheless.

When they took flight again, the village was gone, its houses toppled, all its life consumed. Piles of bricks, bloodstains, clumps of hair, and steaming demon waste were all that remained.

The host flew on.

"Soon, Anai," Raem said, riding his mount across the sky. He caressed the beast's wispy, pale hair. "Soon you will feed upon the sweet meat of dragons."

Their appetite whet, their bellies still grumbling, the demons flew north, heading across the river . . . heading to Requiem.

LAIRA

Laira knelt above her sister, stroking the girl's hair.

"Issari," she whispered, and her tears fell, splashing against the young woman's cheek. "My sister."

Only eighteen winters old, Issari was younger than Laira, but her limbs were longer, and even bruised and cut and famished, her body seemed stronger. A braid hung across her shoulder, thick and black, and her skin was pale.

"You grew up in a palace," Laira whispered. "You grew up in wealth, a roof always over your head, food always on your plate. And you are beautiful. And I love you."

Having fled Eteer as a toddler, Laira had grown up cold, hungry, neglected, and now—in adulthood—her body still bore testament to those hardships. She stood shy of five feet, her body frail and weak, her limbs stick thin. Her hair, which her chieftain would crop short, was only now growing out, falling across her brow and ears. Her jaw was still crooked, broken years ago, leaving her mouth slanted and her chin thrust to the side—an injury that would never heal. Yet Issari was still pure. Issari was the only pure thing Laira still had from her old home across the sea.

"I lost a brother today," she whispered. "But I found a sister."

Issari mumbled, lying upon a fur rug beneath King's Column. The others stood all around—Jeid, his children, and the newcomers. Some stared at Issari, and others whispered amongst themselves of the demon threat crawling across the land. Grief at Sena's death and joy at finding Issari filled Laira, but fear coiled within her too. War was coming; she smelled it on the wind, a faint stench.

"Wake, Issari." Laira kissed the girl's cheek. "Wake and tell us what you know."

Dorvin paced restlessly beside them, his boots thumping upon the marble tiles. A young man, his black hair falling across his brow, he scowled and clenched his fists. His eyes burned. "She already told us enough." Dorvin hawked and spat. "An army of demons. Flying here. Very well then! We fight. We take flight now. We meet them in battle." He raised his fist. "We blow fire and we—"

Jeid slapped the young man's nape. "Silence, boy. We don't fly to war before hearing more." The king turned toward Alina, the young druid. "Is the drink ready? Issari needs healing. Now."

The druid nodded. She stared up from the shadows of her hood, her lavender eyes glowing in the sunlight. She stepped forth, robes swaying, holding a clay bowl. Within was steaming water thick with healing herbs.

"Help your sister drink," Alina said, offering the mug to Laira. "This will give her strength."

Laira accepted the medicine and tilted the bowl over Issari's lips.

"Drink, sister." Gently, she poured the liquid into Issari's mouth. "Drink a little."

Issari twitched in her sleep, mumbled something unintelligible, and sputtered. With Laira's guidance, the young woman drank a few sips, coughed, and opened her eyes.

At once Issari sprang up to a sitting position, her eyes widening. "Demons!" she cried out. Her voice rang across the camp. "An army of demons. We must flee. Dragons of Requiem! We—"

Her eyes rolled back, and Laira had to catch her to stop her from falling. Gently, she pulled the girl closer to King's Column and propped her up against the pillar. Issari flitted between sleep and wakefulness, mumbling about an unholy host, of her father's cruelty, and of an evil to destroy the world.

Laira sat by her sister, gently letting her sip her medicine, holding her close as she trembled. Finally Issari sat with open eyes, breathing deeply, her hand clutching Laira's. Her cheeks were still pale, and blood still stained her tunic and hair.

When the others stepped closer, Laira waved them back. "Give us room! Let her breathe."

Issari took deep breaths, calming herself. Laira allowed only Jeid to step close. The king knelt before Issari, his eyes somber.

"How far is this demon army?" he said, voice low.

Issari swallowed, squeezed Laira's hand, and spoke softly. "I don't know. I shook them off three days ago in a dark forest. I've been flying since, seeking Requiem. If I found it, they'll find it too. They can pick up any scent; their noses are more powerful than any hound's. I disguised my scent with a bear's pelt, but they'll smell this place." She shivered. "They'll smell us, or they'll see the pillar rising from the forest, and they'll be here soon. Already their scouts scour the land. They will not stop." She trembled. "My father will never stop hunting us. He's fallen to madness."

After a moment of silence, everyone started talking at once.

"We fly and take them head-on!" Dorvin was shouting, a grin splitting his face.

"We should flee and hide!" said Bryn, a young woman with fiery red hair.

One man was trembling. "We're all going to die. Oh stars, we're all going to die."

Voices rose and soon everyone was crying out as one, demanding to flee, fight, or surrender. Jeid was urging calmness, but even the king couldn't silence the voices.

Only Laira and Issari remained silent, sitting under the column. As the others shouted and waved their hands, Laira touched her sister's cheek.

"Do you know who I am, Issari?" whispered. "Do you recognize me?"

Issari stared at her, confused. Her eyes widened and tears streamed down her cheeks. She reached out a shaky finger to touch Laira's hair.

"Are you . . . You're her." Issari gasped and pulled Laira into an embrace. "You're Laira. You're my Laira. You're my sweet sister. Thank Taal."

Even as the others shouted, as fear and rage flowed across their camp, Laira smiled as she cried. She held Issari close and kissed her forehead. "It's me. We're together again."

JEID

For a long time, Jeid stood silently, listening to the others speak, shout, and whisper.

Some demanded to take flight now, to find the demons, to face them head-on. Others cried to flee, to hide in the forests in human forms, to dig holes and tunnels and wait until danger passed. Alina the druid, her eyes gleaming, kept speaking of a fabled settlement of Vir Requis in the west, Vir Requis who would help them. Hearing the commotion, several riders of the Goldtusk tribe joined their council; the fur-clad hunters normally camped farther east in the forest, serving Laira, their new chieftain, but now they too joined the argument, shouting that they could defeat any demonic army crawling across their land.

And Jeid stood, listening to them all.

What do we do? he thought, a chill inside him. *Fight? Flee? Seek others to help us?* He looked at his people: a couple dozen Vir Requis. With them fought only seventy rocs.

Not even a hundred flying beasts, Jeid thought, heart sinking. *Against a thousand demons.* It had taken four dragons to defeat the demonic octopus; how could they face a thousand of those creatures?

He closed his eyes, thinking of all those he had lost. His father. His wife. His daughter. He thought of the others who had died: the young man who had lost his leg, Prince Sena, Laira's mother, and many others across the world.

So many Vir Requis already fallen. Will the last of us die now?

He opened his eyes and looked at his people again. Dorvin was shouting louder, demanding they fly now to battle. Her staff raised, Alina was speaking of finding more Vir Requis in the west. Others were demanding they hide.

Jeid ignored the calls, ignored the hands that grasped at his cloak. He turned back toward Issari. The young woman was sitting down, propped up against the column, wrapped in a cloak.

Stars, she's so young, he thought. *Barely more than a youth, yet she carries the fate of a kingdom on her shoulders.*

"Issari." He knelt before her. "Tell me everything you know of these demons. How did your father summon them? How does he control them? Why do they obey him?"

The southern princess took a deep breath. She clutched her braid like a drowning woman holding on to a rope dangling off a boat. "I read about them in ancient clay tablets. All royal children of Eteer know the tale. Many years ago, the first Eteerian King imprisoned the Queen of Demons, the creature named Angel. She was once a being of great piety and light, a daughter of Taal himself, banished from his realm for her cruelty. In her underground prison, she bred and festered, creating a host of many creatures. She and her minions are bound to the throne of Eteer. Whoever sits upon that throne can command them." Issari took a shuddering breath. "For generations, no king or queen dared free this unholy legion. Until my father." She grimaced. "He hates Vir Requis so much—those he calls weredragons—that he summoned the demons to hunt us. I myself am one of your number."

Shakily, Issari rose to her feet, took a deep breath, and shifted. White scales flowed across her, gleaming like mother of pearl. Snowy horns budded upon her head, and her claws clattered against the marble tiles. She looked at Jeid with deep green eyes. When the dragon spoke, the same high, soft voice emerged from her jaws.

"You see now why I fled Eteer. Why he hunts me and Laira. Why he hunts Sena." Suddenly Issari blinked, looked around, and tilted her head. "Where is Sena? Laira . . . where is our brother?"

Jeid fell silent. Laira—the young woman stood nearby among her fellow Goldtusk hunters—lowered her head, and tears streamed down her cheeks.

The white dragon stared from side to side,. Tears welled in her own eyes and flowed down her scaly cheeks.

"Is Sena . . ." Issari trembled, scales clattering, and lost her magic. She knelt as a human, raised her head, and cried out hoarsely. "Sena!"

Laira rushed toward her sister and embraced her. They whispered soft words to each other, weeping together.

Jeid was about to approach them, to try to speak comforts, when a hand grabbed his arm. He turned to see Alina, the young druid. She stared at him from the shadows of her lavender hood. Her eyes, the same color as her raiment, seemed to shine with inner light.

"My king, I have prayed to the stars, and their light has shone before me, illuminating a secret in the west. More hide there." Alina pulled back her hood, revealing long auburn hair that cascaded around her pale, oval face. Strings of beads hung from her staff, chinking in the wind. "Rumors of dragons in the west travel across the land, not only in the whispers of stars but also the talk of men. We must seek their aid if we are to fight."

Laira approached slowly, still holding her sister. She stared at Jeid, her eyes now dry, and spoke in a voice both hard and brittle like a sliver of granite. "In the north too there is aid for Requiem. The Leatherwing tribe rules there upon Two Skull Mountain. They ride creatures they call pteros—flying beasts with no feathers, their bodies smooth and their snouts long, creatures as large as rocs. For many years, the chieftain of Leatherwing tried to marry his daughter to Chieftain Zerra, to forge an alliance between the two tribes." Laira raised her crooked chin. "I slew Zerra. I am now Chieftain of Goldtusk. I will forge an alliance with Leatherwing and we will fight the southern menace together."

Jeid stared at them all, one by one. His children, Maev and Tanin, who approached with drawn blades. Laira and Issari, grieving sisters. Dorvin and Alina, two newcomers to their kingdom, already as dear to him as the others. A score of others, wanderers come home. They all gathered around, staring, awaiting his words.

I lead them all, Jeid thought. *And I must protect them all. I will not let Requiem perish.*

He addressed the crowd.

"We've tamed the rocs of Goldtusk, but now a new enemy rises, an enemy more powerful than any we've faced, an enemy that threatens to crush Requiem. And we must leave this place." Murmurs rose from his people, and Jeid spoke louder. "We will not abandon King's Column nor our dream of Requiem, but this is not our battlefield. We must seek aid, and we must strike back against this cruel king who sends forth his evil. Three paths now lie before us. We must split into three groups." He paused for a deep breath. "We must seek more Vir Requis in the west. We must forge an alliance with the Leatherwing tribe in the north. And finally . . ." He turned to stare into Issari's eyes. "We must travel south, place Issari upon Eteer's throne, and command the demons back into the Abyss."

MAEV

She crossed her arms and spat. "No. I refuse. It's not going to happen."

Her father grumbled and his beard bristled, making him seem even more like a grizzly bear. "You will do this, Maev. I'm not asking you. I'm commanding you. As your king and father."

Maev snorted and turned away from him, thrusting out her bottom lip in defiance. "I obey nobody. And I refuse." She drew her sword. "I fly north with you. I fly to find the Leatherwing tribe, to fight in a great battle, to—"

Jeid grabbed her and spun her back toward him. Rage twisted his face. "Maev, listen to me. We might not have a battle on our hands, only a slaughter. I need you to fly west with Dorvin and Alina. I need you to help them find the Vir Requis said to live there. If there's any hope for Requiem, it lies in finding others."

She shoved him back, eyes stinging. "So you'll just send me off to safety, a herald of Requiem, rather than let me fight? I'm a fighter. I've fought and slain many rocs, demons, and tribesmen." She growled. "I'm the greatest warrior in Requiem."

"Which is why I need you with Dorvin and Alina," he said. "How can I send only two dragons on this mission? They need your help, Maev. And . . . I need you to watch over them." He lowered his voice. "I don't know that I can trust them. I need my own blood on every path we take."

Maev could scarcely believe his words. Across their camp, men and women were already becoming dragons and rising into the sky. They were heading out to war, yet how could Maev find glory far in the west? If demons could truly pick up the scent of dragons, they would surely follow the largest group north to Two Skull Mountain. That was where battle would rage. That was where Maev had to be. Not some guardian of two pups.

She looked at all the others. "So Tanin and Issari will return to Eteer and claim the throne; their glory will be eternal. So you and Laira will travel north to Two Skull Mountain, forge an alliance, and fight a great battle; forever your song will echo. And me?" She blinked furiously. "I'll be in the west, far from any epic battles, guarding a druid and a blockhead boy."

She watched as the two approached, both still in human form. Dorvin walked with a swagger, a crooked grin on his face, chattering about finding a new group to lead. His sister was more subdued; holding her druid's staff, Alina sang soft prayers. When they drew closer, Dorvin winked at Maev.

"Well, Maev, old beast," he said. "Looks like you and I part ways here." He puffed out his chest. "I'm off to find the others, become a hero, and win the war for us." He shook his head with mock sadness. "You probably won't survive long enough to see Alina and me return, what with all these demons swarming about, but you—"

"I'm going with you." Maev spat in disgust and glared at her father. "Not that I want to."

Dorvin's eyes widened and he raised his hands in indignation. "What?" He reeled toward Jeid too. "I'm not going west with her! I've seen feral mammoths less brutish than Maev. They smelled better too." He pinched his nose. "Don't send your daughter with me, old man, just because you want me to protect her."

Jeid's face reddened and he grabbed the young man's shoulders. "You got it backward, boy. I'm sending her to protect *you*. Maev has slain dozens of demons. You've killed one." He snorted. "Maev will lead you west and back. Try not to slow her down, pup."

Dorvin fumed and began to object, flailing his arms. He strutted a few steps toward Maev, chest thrust out like a rooster, and Maev growled and raised her fists, prepared to pummel some sense into the boy.

If I must travel west with this pup, she thought, *I will tame him now.*

Alina, however, rushed forward and placed herself between the two. The young druid slammed down her staff, and the crystal on its crest blasted out light.

"Enough!" She glared at Maev and Dorvin in turn. "Demons scour the world to slay us. Let us not do their job for them. We've lingered here long enough and we must move. With every breath danger draws nearer." The druid took a few steps back and shifted, becoming a slim dragon, her scales the same lavender as her robes. She beat her wings and took flight. "Dorvin! Maev! Save your strength for the demons. Now come, we fly."

With that, the lavender dragon began flying west, leaving a trail of smoke.

Still standing below, Dorvin gave Maev a wink, a crooked smile, and a nudge from his elbow. "See if you can catch up, Mammoth Arse." He leaped into the air, became a silver dragon, and flew after his sister.

Maev felt like she didn't even have to turn into a dragon to blast out smoke. Mammoth arse! She would shove him up the next mammoth arse they crossed. She made to leap up, shift into a dragon, and chase the damn boy and his starry-eyed sister, but her eyes fell upon her father, and she paused. All day, Jeid had been stern and somber, yet now he seemed . . . Maev tilted her head.

He seems afraid.

She stared at him, her rage leaving her. She had never seen her father look afraid before. She hadn't known he could feel fear. She had seen him in mourning when Mother had died, then when Requiem—little Requiem after whom their kingdom was named—had died too. But not fear. And now she saw it in the stoop of his shoulders, the ghosts in his eyes, the tightness of his lips. Her anger left her, and she hugged him.

"Goodbye, Grizzly. I'll look after the pups."

Her brother approached slowly, hesitating. Maev had spent her life thinking Tanin a soft-headed fool, but now, with the world collapsing around her, she loved him so fully her chest ached. She stepped toward him and pulled him into a crushing hug, then rubbed her knuckles across his head.

"Be strong, Tanin," she said. "Don't be a halfwit. And try not to step on your tongue whenever you look at Issari." She punched his chest. "I won't be there to look after you for a while, so you better not mess things up."

He rubbed his chest, wincing. "I'll miss you too, Maev." He lowered his voice. "I love you, you warthog."

She wanted to say more. She wanted to embrace her father and brother again, to tell them she loved them, but her eyes stung, and her voice caught in her throat, and she dared not show them weakness. She spun around, shifted into a dragon, and took flight.

"Wait up, pups!" she shouted. Dorvin and Alina were flying ahead, silver and lavender, already distant

Dorvin looked over his shoulder at her. "Fly faster, Mammoth Arse!" He blasted flames her way, then turned back forward and kept flying.

"Shut your mouth, Dung Beetle!" Maev beat her wings and flew faster. She looked back only once and saw other dragons taking flight around King's Column. Then she returned her eyes westward, sucked in air, and vowed that if any others existed in this world, she would find them. She would bring them home.

TANIN

The two dragons flew south, red and white, traveling over the ruin of the world.

"A scar rifts the land," Tanin said.

Gliding beside him, the white dragon lowered her head. "The wounds he gave me scar my body." Issari took a shaky breath. "And the wound he gave the world will perhaps forever mar this land."

A line of devastation covered the landscape, coiling from the south like the path of a parasite through a heart. The demon army had flown here, raining its rot, wilting the land. Trees stooped, white and frail as starved corpses. The earth had turned a charcoal color, and globs of red grew upon it like warts. Animals moved along this unholy path, deformed under its curse, twisted beings with many limbs, their eyes bloated and bulging from their sockets, their entrails dragging behind them like clinging lampreys. The creatures wailed up at the flying dragons, hissing, weeping, begging for death. A stench of rot flared, and when Tanin and Issari flew directly over the path, the miasma made them gag. They banked eastward, keeping the living land directly beneath them, but always they gazed upon that cursed line in the west.

"This is what Requiem will look like if my father wins," Issari said. The white dragon stretched her wings wide, gliding on the wind current. "Already Eteer has fallen to this evil." She looked at Tanin, green eyes wide and wet. "We have to stop him, Tanin. We have to take over his throne."

Whimpers sounded below, and Tanin looked back down at the coiling path of the Abyss. Small creatures moved there, raising their hands, pleading. They had the bodies of dogs, but their heads were human heads, bloated and pale like corpses. They yowled wordlessly, but Tanin thought he heard words in the senseless mewling.

"Pleee . . .," they seemed to beg. "Pleee . . . kell . . . kell us . . ."

Tanin shook his head wildly, swallowing down his disgust. He flew on, pity roiling his belly, leaving the creatures behind upon the path. Soon their wails faded, but as he flew, Tanin's heart wouldn't unwind, and his chest felt so tight he could barely breathe. Had those things been demons, animals, or . . . humans?

Please . . . kill us . . .

An image shot through his mind: his family twisted into creatures too, wailing upon a ruined path, begging him for death he would not grant them. In his vision, Issari pleaded among them. She had the same delicate, beautiful face, her skin olive toned, her eyes green, her braid black, but her body was the body of a centipede, thrashing, pattering its feet, and—

No.

He snarled and flew on, banishing those visions. He looked at Issari again, soaking up the beauty of her glimmering scales, small horns, and long claws. She was beautiful and pure—both as a human and dragon. He vowed that he would never let her fall.

"How will we do this, Issari?" he asked. "How will we take over the throne, and how will we summon back the demons?"

Fire flickered between her teeth. "Eteer lies in ruin; its people hold my father no love. When I would walk through the city, saving those I could, I heard nothing but hatred for Raem. As he flies north, I will march into his palace. I will sit upon his throne. If his soldiers too mourn the destruction of their kingdom, they will obey me. And so will Angel."

Tanin shuddered to remember Angel, the Queen of Demons. "Does she fly with this army too, seeking Requiem?"

Eyes dark, Issari shook her head. "The Queen of Devilry remains in Eteer, sitting upon the throne until my father returns. She will serve whoever rules Eteer—my father now, me if I can claim the kingdom. It is her we must dethrone. It is her we must tame."

Belly knotting, Tanin looked down at Issari's front foot. The amulet of Taal was fused with the flesh, a remnant of Issari's battle with the Demon Queen. His own body still bore the scars of his last encounter with the demon.

So we will battle again, Angel. And this time we will tame you.

He had a thousand more questions, and he was about to ask them all, when he saw the village below.

Or at least, what was left of the village. The settlement lay within the dark path, as wilted and ruined as the land around it. Huts lay smashed. Globs of demon drool covered the fields. Bones and gobbets of flesh lay in the village square, the animal pen, and the fields, and demon dung steamed in piles. Tanin wanted to fly away, to keep following the path south to the sea, but when he heard the wail his heart froze.

This was no demon voice. A human was crying out below.

He narrowed his eyes, sucked in breath, and dipped a little lower in the sky.

He heard the voice again, weak and pleading, growing weaker by the word. "Help. Help. Please."

After a glance at each other, the two dragons began to descend toward the ruined village. Tanin wrinkled his snout at the stench; it smelled like rotted meat, blood, and worms. He nearly gagged to see human skeletons litter the place, shreds of meat still clinging to bones. A flock of vultures were pecking at the remains, picking off what the demons had not consumed. A few vultures fled at the sight of the dragons; others were too busy fighting over a ribcage. The huts lay smashed around them, containing more remains, and everywhere spread puddles of demon drool.

"Help . . . please . . ."

The voice came from behind a few ruined huts. Tanin landed, returned to human form, and gestured at Issari. She resumed human form too and raised her palm, shining out the light of her amulet. They walked between skeletons, fallen chunks of clay walls, and toppled fences, following the cry. Tanin drew his dagger, prepared to fight any demon that might approach. A memory of the creatures on the path returned to him, deformed animals pleading for death.

Around a fallen brick wall—perhaps an old smithy—he saw her.

Tanin's heart wrenched and ice flooded his belly. At his side, Issari gasped and clutched his hand.

She was young, no older than ten, a little girl lying in the dust. Her lips trembled as she gasped for breath, her skin was ashen, and blood stained her blue dress and dark hair. Her entrails dangled out from her slashed belly, hanging down to the ground. She clutched the wound as if she could still survive, still stop the trickle of life. She met Tanin's gaze.

"They hurt me," she whispered. "I hid in the cellar. They're gone now. Please. Help. Help me."

Issari raced toward the girl, placed a cloak upon her, and stroked her hair, whispering softly.

She's dead already, Tanin knew, frozen in place, frozen in fear. *It might happen today, maybe tomorrow, but she's dead already.*

When Issari looked back at him, Tanin saw the same knowledge in her eyes.

He thought back again to the miserable creatures on the path. *Kill us,* they had pleaded. *Kill us.* Looking at this girl now, Tanin heard their voices again in his mind.

She's dead already. His knees felt weak. *I have to do it. Painlessly. To stab her head. A quick blow. Maybe to burn her with fire.* The girl began to tremble violently, to weep, and Tanin winced, wanting to do it, to end her suffering. It was the moral choice, he knew. She was dead already. Dead already.

But he could not.

He sat by the girl with Issari, and he held her hand, and he stroked her cheek.

"Sleep, child," he whispered to her.

But she only screamed.

She screamed all that day and into the night, and with every scream Tanin hated himself, knew he was weak, and wanted to do it, to end her pain. But still he could not. And she wept as the dawn rose again.

It was noon when she finally died.

She died in Issari's arms, finally at peace.

"We'll bury her outside the village," Tanin said, voice choked. "Outside this path of disease. In a beautiful place in the shade of trees."

He draped his cloak over the body and carried it through the village. Issari walked at his side, her head lowered, a single tear on her cheek. They moved between the ravaged huts, the bones, the puddles of blood, heading past wilted trees toward the living forest that grew beyond.

There, on the border between life and death, the creature awaited them.

The demon lay against the trees, it legs cut off, bones thrusting out from blue flesh. Arrows pierced its gray, warty skin, and its heart pulsed within an open wound. The creature seemed too weak to rise; it could only hiss at them. Blood stained its maw, and between its teeth lay shreds of blue cotton.

Tanin looked down at the body in his arms. The girl wore a dress of the same blue fabric.

Gently, Tanin placed the little girl's body down, straightened, and drew his dagger. With a hoarse cry, he leaped onto the demon. The creature bucked, snapped its teeth, lashed its claws, trying to resist, but Tanin fought in a fury, stabbing, screaming, tearing into its flesh, driving his blade again and again into its head. Blood splattered him, and the creature fell dead, and still Tanin stabbed, his body shaking.

"Tanin." Issari's soft voice rose behind him, and a hand touched his shoulder. "Tanin, stop."

But he could not. He kept stabbing, the rage overflowing him.

"It's my fault." He trembled. "I flew south to save Sena. I enraged your father. And now this. Now demons are slaying innocents." He stared through tears back at the dead girl. "What did she know of Requiem or Eteer? What did she know of dragons or demons? This is our war. A war for a kingdom my own family founded. And she paid with her life while I live."

Issari pulled him into her arms. "Many innocents die in war. Many pure lives are lost when soldiers fight. Requiem was forged in starlight, but she will be tempered in blood." Eyes dried, she stared at the dead demon. "We will rise from horror. We will overcome darkness. We will find our sky."

They buried the child in the forest, far from the village, in a place of peace and beauty. Anemones grew around her grave, and elm trees rustled in the wind, their leaves like countless dragon scales. The sun shone down and the wind blew from the east, scented of the distant mountains. Tanin placed dandelions upon her grave, and Issari sang softly, songs in the tongue of Eteer. Tanin could not understand the words, but in the music he heard a song of sky, of peace, of memory. A song of farewell.

"Goodnight, child," Tanin whispered. "Sleep well."

They flew on into the south, two dragons, silent. The path stretched below, and the world rolled into the horizon, scarred, a world that could fall, a world they would forever fight for, a sky they would forever find. They flew until the stars emerged above, and the Draco constellation shone upon their scales.

Tanin looked up at their glow. "Illuminate our path, stars of Requiem. We will forever fly in your light."

They descended that night into a forest clearing, shifted back into human forms, and lay upon their fur cloaks. The stars glowed yet Tanin found no comfort, and even when he closed his eyes and tried to sleep, he only saw it again: the creatures begging on the path, the girl with the slashed belly, the demon he'd stabbed again and again, and all those older horrors of war, visions of demon armies, attacking rocs, and everywhere the dead.

A lifetime of pain and death filled his mind like wine overflowing from a goblet.

How do you forget? he thought. *How do you forget so much death, so much terror, and ever find peace in the world again? Even if Requiem rises, if we win this war, will there ever be peace for me?*

He tilted his head, looking at Issari. She lay beside him, but she too was awake. She trembled, her eyes open and damp, staring up at the stars and praying silently. Tanin moved closer to her, pushing their two cloaks together, and touched her shoulder. She looked at him and nestled close, and he held her in his arms. She laid her head upon his chest and slung her arm across him, and he kissed her forehead and stroked her hair.

"I can't sleep," she whispered.

He wrapped his arms around her, looked up at the stars, and felt some of his pain ease. The world crumbled, Requiem struggled for survival, and death sprawled north and south of the sea. But he had Issari. He had somebody pure to protect.

"Have I told you the story of how I used to juggle?"

She shook her head. "No. Tell me."

He smiled. "I was a horrible juggler. One time, I was juggling apples in a village when a seagull flew down, snatched one of my apples from the air, and flew straight off."

"You lie." A soft smile touched her lips.

"I never lie! It flew straight up, then dropped the apple right onto my head. The crowd loved it. Every time I tried to juggle those apples, the damn bird stole them, flew up, and dropped them onto me again. It got ugly once I started juggling torches."

She laughed softly. "You're such a liar."

"Wait until I tell you the story about my dancing routine and the enraged pig. Every time I did a jig, the damn hog would slam right into me, knocking me off the stage."

She closed her eyes, and he kept talking, telling her old tall tales—of fish that tugged him into the river, fairies who taught him to sing, and other stories of sunlight and warmth and better days. He kept talking until she slept against him. He kissed her forehead, and she mumbled but would not wake. Finally he slept too, a fitful sleep, a brittle and fearful sleep, but whenever nightmares woke him she was in his arms, and he held her closer, and they warmed each other until the dawn.

LAIRA

She flew upon Neiva, her dear roc, leading the Goldtusk clan across the sky.

For seventeen years, Laira had lived as the lowliest member of this tribe—beaten, starved, worth less than the dogs. Now she was Chieftain of Goldtusk, Daughter of Ka'altei, leader of a great flock. She no longer wore her old, tattered garment of rat furs, the one Zerra had pissed on and left to stink. Today she wore a resplendent tiger pelt and a golden headdress. Her jaw was still crooked, her body still small, but her hair was growing longer, her limbs stronger, and her spirit soared like the rocs she led. Seventy of the oily vultures flew around her, yellow eyes gleaming, their feathers dank and dripping. The tribe elders, women, and children had always walked upon the earth, too lowly to ride upon the hunters' rocs, but now they rode too, five or six souls upon each bird. Three of the rocs held their totem pole, flying together, and upon the pillar's crest gleamed the gilded ivory tusk the tribe worshiped.

Looking upon her tribe, Laira heaved a deep sigh.

I suffered, bled, and killed for Goldtusk. And now I must give this tribe away. She tightened her lips. *For Requiem.*

She looked to her left. Not a mark away flew the dragons of Requiem, twenty in all. Maev, Dorvin, and Alina had flown west to seek others. Tanin and Issari flew south across the sea.

Here was all that remained, barely a tribe, barely a clan, a humble twenty dragons who would forge a nation.

I wish you were here with us, Sena, Laira thought, the pain still fresh inside her, a raw wound in her breast she did not think would ever heal. *You could have flown with us now.* She lowered her head. *I let you down. We all did. You were strong in your own way, not ours. We failed to see it. I failed. I'm sorry.*

She took a shaky breath and whispered prayers for his soul—a prayer to Ka'altei of the Goldtusk tribe, to Taal the Father God of Eteer, and to the stars of Requiem. She did not know if any of these deities heard her prayers. She did not know if they'd bless her brother who had sinned, who had taken his own life. But it seemed to Laira that as she prayed, she saw those stars above, just a brief glimmer, even in the daylight, and that soothed her. Perhaps Sena was up there now, looking down upon her.

A grunt sounded to her left. She turned to see Jeid leave the other dragons and fly toward the rocs. Largest among the dragons, he flew with a clatter of scales, and smoke streamed from his nostrils and mouth. With his wide wings and bulky frame, he was as large as Neiva, Laira's roc. He glided at her side, the wind fluttering his wings with little thuds.

"How sure are you this will work?" he said, staring at her with one eye. "How well do you know this Chieftain Oritan?"

Riding upon her roc, Laira had to cry out to be heard over the wind. "Better than I knew you when I flew to you for aid!" She gave him a wink and a mirthless smile. "Oritan has been craving an alliance with Goldtusk for years. He practically shoved his daughter at Zerra, demanding a marriage, a joining of the clans. Zerra always refused, but now this is my tribe." She inhaled deeply. "We will forge an alliance. We will fight my father together."

Jeid grumbled something under his breath, and Laira saw the doubt in his eyes.

But I haven't told you all, Jeid, she thought, eyes stinging. *For if you knew, you would try to stop me. But I will do this deed. For Requiem. For our column of marble and our stars above. And for you, Jeid.* Her eyes stung. *For the man I love more than life.*

They had been flying for three days now, barely stopping even for sleep, crossing plains of grass, misty forests, and hills that rolled for many marks. They fed upon herds of deer, flocks of geese, and fish that filled the rivers that snaked below. And always the hint of stench wafted on the breeze, and once a distant shriek—perhaps just the wind—sounded in the distance. Sometimes Laira heard or smelled nothing, but she always felt the presence of pursuit. It was a chill along her spine, an iciness in her belly, a prickling on her nape. Whenever she shut her eyes, she saw it again—the demonic octopus constricting her, speaking her name, and its spawn devouring the body of her brother.

Riding on her roc, she drew her sword and caressed the bronze blade.

"I slew Zerra with this sword." She spoke softly for only her roc to hear. "But now I must face a greater enemy. Now this blade must pierce the heart of the man who hunts me, who unleashed these creatures, who drove my brother to death. Now I must kill my father."

She could not remember King Raem. She had fled him too many years ago. In her nightmares, he was only a shadow, faceless, reaching out arms thrice the usual length, trying to grab her, to tug her into darkness. She took a shuddering breath and clutched her sword. She would not let that figure haunt her. She was done hiding and here, among her people, she made her stand, no longer a frightened girl but a leader of men and beasts.

A mountaintop appeared upon the horizon, a mere bulge from here. Was there the end of their journey? Laira was squinting, struggling to bring the distant crest into focus, when the shriek rose behind her.

Rocs cawed and dragons growled. Laira tugged the reins, spinning her roc around, and her heart sank. It was flying from the south, a single creature.

She cursed. "A demon scout."

The creature buzzed closer, wings moving as fast as a bumblebee's. It looked like a severed human hand the size of an oak. Upon each finger blinked an eye, and a mouth gaped open upon the palm. The creature flew higher, faster than any roc or dragon, then spun to dart away.

"After it!" Laira shouted. "It'll bring news back to Raem!"

She kneed Neiva and the roc beat her wings madly, flying in pursuit. Other rocs flew around her, and the dragons flew at her side. Yet the creature flew twice as fast, shrinking into the distance.

"Shoot it!" Laira shouted. She grabbed her bow and fired. Other hunters fired from their own rocs, and the dragons blew fire. One arrow seemed to pierce the creature. It yowled, dipped in the sky, but kept flying. Within moments, it had disappeared over the southern horizon.

"Stars damn it!" Jeid flew up beside Laira. "We won't catch the bastard."

Laira stared at the horizon. "Perhaps we don't have to." She took a deep breath. "Let Raem know. Let him come here. Two Skull Mountain is near; it will be our battlefield." She caressed her sword again, then tugged Neiva back toward the north. "Fly north, Goldtusk! Keep flying to the mountain."

Leaving the demon scout, they turned. They flew back north, crossing hills and valleys as distant demon shrieks rolled behind them.

Finally, the sun dipping into evening, they saw the mountain ahead.

"Two Skull Mountain," Laira said softly, spine tingling.

She had seen the place once, years ago, from a distance; Zerra had dared not fly closer, for here was the territory of Leatherwing. Two Skull Mountain had chilled her then and it chilled her now. The origin of its name was clear to all who saw it. Caves yawned open upon its crest, forming the rough shapes of eye sockets, nostrils, and mouths like two skulls fused together, melted into each other like conjoined twins joined at the face. The skulls seemed anguished to Laira, screaming silently, begging for a respite from pain. Laira leaned forward in her saddle, narrowed her eyes, and scrutinized the mountain, but she could see no sign of the Leatherwing tribe or its fabled beasts, the pteros. Laira clenched her jaw, remembering the old tales she had heard of this place—tales of flying reptiles tearing into flesh, of hunters who drank blood from human skulls, and of slaves who languished in chains, their limbs food for the tribe.

She tightened her lips. *Zerra feared the escarpment too, but I found my dearest friends there.* She looked at the dragons who flew to her left. *I found Requiem, the anchor of my soul, the light of my heart, the land I will sacrifice everything for.*

She looked behind her at the tribe. Seventy rocs flew there, larger than dragons, dripping the oil they secreted. They stank of old meat, and their yellow eyes always seemed so baleful, and for many years Laira had feared these beasts. For many years they had hunted dragons, slaying many. Yet now this tribe—once her prison, then her enemy, and finally her army—might save the world.

They flew closer, Goldtusk and Requiem, rocs and dragons, until they glided above the foothills. Two Skull Mountain loomed ahead, dwarfing them. Each of the eye sockets, great caverns in the stone, was large enough to house them all. And still Laira did not see Leatherwing. The place seemed too silent; she heard only the squawks of rocs and the thuds of dragon wings. No enemy tribe. No leathery beasts. Had Leatherwing abandoned this place?

Worry gnawed at her, and she was about to call for her rocs to land, to camp upon the mountainside.

Before she could speak, they emerged.

Screams shattered the air. The mountain shook. With battle cries, firing arrows, and the shadows of great wings, Leatherwing Tribe appeared.

They flew from within the skulls—from the eye sockets, the nostrils, the mouths—like bats from a cave. Yet unlike bats, these creatures were as large as rocs, and bloodlust burned in their white eyes. Their wings spread out, formed of translucent skin that stretched from their ankles to the tips of their elongated, clawed fingers. Their long jaws opened to shriek. A single horn grew from each beast's head, crimson like old blood. Upon their backs rode the warriors of Leatherwing. Men and women rode bare-chested, their skin painted white and red. Many rings pierced their lips, noses, and ears. Copper disks filled their earlobes, stretching them to thrice the usual size. Each warrior bore axes, spears, and bows and arrows. They stood in their stirrups, shouting out lilting battle cries.

"Halt!" Laira shouted. "Hear me, Leatherwing. I am Laira, Chieftain of Goldtusk! I fly in peace."

The pteros swooped and arrows flew from their hunters.

Laira cursed. Around her, warriors of Goldtusk nocked their own arrows. Projectiles flew both ways. Laira spun her roc toward her warriors.

"Goldtusk, back! Fly to the foothills. Go!" She turned toward the dragons. "Requiem! To the foothills! Fly now. Fly before blood spills."

The warriors of Goldtusk sneered, tugging back bowstrings. For a few heartbeats, the battle froze, each side watching the other.

"Go!" Laira shouted to her warriors. "This is not a retreat. Wait for me in the valley. Dragons of Requiem! Go with them. I've come here to parley, not shed blood."

Some of her Goldtusk hunters grumbled. A few spat and cursed. They were a proud folk, and they loved bloodshed like they loved drinking ale, bedding women, and feasting on mammoth flesh. But their wives and children flew upon their rocs today, and perhaps the hunters still loved their families more than any glory in war. They obeyed Laira, leaving the mountaintop and heading down to the foothills. The pteros' riders watched their old enemy leave, jeering and waving their spears. They cried out in prayer to Two Skulls, their god of stone.

The dragons of Requiem followed the rocs—all but Jeid. The copper dragon hovered beside Laira and her roc, smoke rising from between his teeth.

"I stay with you," he said.

She nodded, relieved. "Stay."

Laira turned back toward the pteros. The flying reptiles were circling in the sky, cawing and snapping their long mouths. Their wings beat the air, churning clouds. Upon their backs, their riders glared at Laira and Jeid, their arrows still nocked.

What must we look like to them! Laira thought. *A scrawny girl upon a roc and a clanking dragon. I doubt an odder pair ever flew here.*

"Where is Chieftain Oritan!" she shouted. "Let two chieftains meet in parley."

She had seen Oritan once from a distance. Three years ago, the chieftain had visited the Goldtusk tribe after a bitter war that had left many dead on both sides. Clad in bones, he had demanded an alliance, offering to wed his daughter to Chieftain Zerra, to merge both tribes with bonds of family. Laira had been like a shadow that day, darting in and out of the tent where the two leaders spoke; she had served ale and meat, washed sore feet, and mostly listened. Even today, she remembered the moment Chieftain Oritan had looked at her, had met her eyes when taking a mug from her. He had nodded subtly. He had acknowledged her. Whenever Laira would accidentally make eye contact with a warrior of Goldtusk, she would earn a beating. But here a great chieftain, clad in bones and leather, jewelery around his neck, had met her gaze, had nodded to her! Laira had shed tears that night after Zerra had refused the union; he had railed that Goldtusk was strong, that he would not dilute his tribe's worth with scum from the mountain, and Laira had mourned never seeing Oritan again.

Back then I saw a reasonable man, Laira thought. She prayed that reason still filled Oritan.

With a shrill cry and wings that blasted back her hair, a massive ptero emerged from behind the mountain, a beast to dwarf the others. Gold and red paint covered its wings with circles and coiling lines, copper rings encircled its neck, and gilt covered its horn. Upon this lurid beast sat a long-limbed man, his bare chest painted white and red. An ape's skull hid his head—a helmet of bone. Spears hung across his back, and he held a golden bow.

"Chieftain Oritan!" Laira called to him. She lifted her spear; strings of beads dangled from its tip. "I am Laira, new Chieftain of Goldtusk."

His ptero hovered before her, the wind from its wings blowing back her hair and cloak. Through the sockets of his ape-skull helmet, his eyes met hers again—those eyes she remembered from years ago, the eyes that had met hers when no others would.

He spoke in a deep voice like rolling thunder. "Last our tribes met, it was Zerra, son of Thagar, the Burnt Man, who ruled the rocs."

Laira raised her chieftain's old sword. "Now it is Laira, daughter of Raem. I slew Zerra the Burnt and I wield his sword. Three years ago, you came to our tribe to forge an alliance. Zerra turned you down. Now he is dead; now our discussion will resume."

Oritan's eyes flicked toward the copper dragon who flew at Laira's side. "So the tales are true; dragons fly in our skies. Has Goldtusk tamed these scaly beasts?"

When Jeid spoke, the chieftain's eyes narrowed and his mount hissed and bucked.

"No man or woman can tame a dragon, chieftain," said Jeid. "I am Aeternum, King of Requiem—a nation of dragons. Requiem and Goldtusk fly together. We would have you fly with us, for a threat covers this land, drawing nearer, and all who seek to fight darkness must now bind together."

The chieftain's ptero snapped its head from side to side, its mouth clattering open and closed. Its small eyes spun, but Oritan's eyes remained steady, staring at Laira. Finally the chieftain nodded, whirled in the sky, and gestured for Laira and Jeid to follow. He flew toward the mountain, diving to enter one of the eye sockets.

Laira and Jeid glanced at each other, then followed. The two stony skulls upon the mountainside stared back at Laira, craggy and anguished, bitter faces forever fused together. The eye socket gaped open, so large Laira felt like a mere bird flying through a window. Jeid close behind, she flew into the mountain, entering a realm of shadows and light.

A cavern filled the mountain, a hundred times larger than Requiem's old canyon in the escarpment. Dozens of pteros perched upon the walls, clinging to the stone like bats. Torches crackled between them, and fires burned upon the cave floor. Murals of bison, elks, lions, and many other animals covered the ceiling; in the flickering firelight, they seemed almost to race across the stone. Riders of Leatherwing filled the cave, drinking from clay bowls, praying to stone idols carved as obese women, and sharpening spears. All turned to stare and hiss at the roc and dragon entering their domain.

A massive stalagmite, a hundred feet tall, rose like a tower in the cave's center. Upon its flattened crest perched a seat carved of granite inlaid with golden runes. Oritan led his ptero there. The lanky reptile clutched the stone pillar, allowing Oritan to dismount and claim his seat; then the ptero flew off to cling to the ceiling high above. Jeid too flew to the pillar, released his magic, and landed before the throne in human form. Laira led her own mount to this seat of power. Neiva clutched the stalagmite, and Laira dismounted and stood upon the stone tower before Oritan and his throne.

"Wait for me outside, Neiva," Laira said softly, stroking the roc, who still clung to the pillar. "Join the others. I'll return to you soon."

Neiva tilted her head and nuzzled Laira with her massive beak, a beak the size of Laira's entire body. Then the roc turned and left, wings scattering droplets of oil, and exited the mountain.

"Speak, Laira, daughter of Raem." Oritan leaned back in his throne of stone and gold. "Speak of this alliance which your tribe once spurned. And speak too of this enemy you claim draws near. And finally, speak to me of these dragons, of this so-called king who comes into my hall."

Laira tried to quell her dizziness. This pillar of stone was narrow, barely large enough to support the throne, her, and Jeid. The cave walls seemed to spin around her, alight with torches and clattering with pteros. The animal murals seemed to race above her in a great hunt, and the murmur of many tribesmen rose from the cave floor far below. She took a deep breath, steeling herself.

"Demons!" she said. "A host of a thousand demons flies across the world. They fly from Eteer across the sea. My own father, king of that southern realm, leads them in conquest." She pulled from her pack the coiled, severed arm of one of the octopus spawn. She held it forth. "Here is a single arm from a single demon; a great swarm of the creatures flies north. All free tribes and kingdoms of the north must band together now. We must defeat them."

Within the sockets of his helm, Oritan's eyes narrowed. He leaned forward in his throne, took the severed demon arm, and examined it. The arm still twitched, the mouths upon it opening and closing, snapping their teeth. Disgust mingled with fascination filled Oritan's eyes as he held the wriggling tentacle.

"That arm came from a demon babe." Laira's heart twinged to remember these creatures feasting upon her brother's body; this very arm had fed upon Sena. "The adults are as large as rocs. And they're spreading across the land."

Oritan draped the tentacle across the arm of his seat. He returned his eyes to her. "Your father leads these demons, you say? A king of Eteer?" He leaned closer. "Who are you, Laira of Goldtusk? A chieftain? A princess? A friend to dragons?"

"I am all those things," she said. "And you know me. Three years ago, Chieftain Oritan, you came to Goldtusk, and you spoke to me, though you do not remember me. As you spoke to Chieftain Zerra, I served you wine and I washed your feet. Zerra offered me to you, telling you I could warm your bed, but you refused the gift of my body. You met my eyes once." Her heart beat faster to remember that moment. "You saw only a servant."

Oritan inhaled sharply, stared in silence for a moment, then removed his ape-skull helmet. His face was hard but not unpleasant. His nose was straight, his lips thin, his jaw square. Dark hair fell across his brow. He seemed no older than forty winters, and a small scar marred his left cheek.

"Yes." His voice was soft, contemplative. "I remember you, child. I pitied you then. I felt rage at your chieftain for mistreating you. Your hair was shorter then, your frame more frail, but I remember your eyes, the large green eyes of those who dwell across the sea. I indeed looked into them. I thought about them for long after returning home."

My mother's eyes, Laira thought. *They've always been my only beauty.* His words filled her with a hint of warmth, like a fire just beginning to rise on a winter day.

Standing at her side, Jeid cleared his throat and spoke for the first time since entering the cavern. "Will you fight with us, Oritan? Will you send your beasts to battle alongside ours?"

Oritan turned his eyes toward the grizzled king, and now those eyes hardened, losing what warmth they had given Laira. "Why should Leatherwing fight the wars of others? These demons do not hunt us." He gestured at the severed tentacle. "Laira's father leads them, she said. This is a war between father and daughter, between demons and rocs. It does not concern my tribe." He sighed and shook his head. "Perhaps you are both honorable leaders and strong. But I will not help you. Leatherwing

Tribe is safe within our mountain; what dangers lurk outside are not our concern. Leave this place. That is my decision."

Jeid grumbled and clenched his fists. "So you will hide here in your mountain, chieftain, as the world burns? Where is your pride, a warrior's honor?"

The chieftain snorted. "Goad me and you'll see, weredragon. I would gladly slay you."

Jeid growled and raised his fists, and Oritan reached for a spear. Laira stepped between the two before they could come to blows. She pushed Jeid back and stared up at Oritan, her chin raised.

"You will fight because you want my rocs," she said. "You remember my eyes, and I remember your words. You all but begged Zerra to wed your daughter, a pretty thing with long black locks. You spoke of a noble marriage, a merging of two tribes. No doubt you planned to slay Zerra—perhaps a knife in the back, perhaps poison in the cup—and become ruler of both pteros and rocs, a single chieftain with a great horde. Zerra saw through your trickery." She took a step closer to the throne and placed her hand on Oritan's knee. "I offer you a better deal. You will have your marriage, and you will become chieftain of two tribes." She took a deep breath, steeling herself. "I will marry you."

Jeid gave a strangled sound halfway between choking and snarling. Laira placed a hand against his chest, holding him back, and did not remove her eyes from the chieftain upon his throne.

Oritan stared back at her, his eyes hard, betraying nothing. But she knew what he was thinking. She could see it in the tension of his body, the twitch of his lips.

He pities me but he craves me. And he craves my rocs even more.

"Laira, this isn't the way," Jeid began. "I—"

She hushed him with a finger to his lips, then turned back toward Oritan. "Speak, chieftain! If I join my tribe to yours, will you fight with us against the demon host?"

Slowly, Oritan leaned back in his seat. He spoke in a low voice. "In Leatherwing Tribe, a chieftain must only marry the greatest female warriors. After my first wife died in battle, I sought others to wed, but they all failed the test." He stared at her, eyes narrowed and blazing. "If you pass the test, Laira of Goldtusk, we will wed. And we will fight together."

Cold sweat trickled down Laira's back, and she gulped down a lump. "A test?"

The chieftain rose to his feet. He stepped to the edge of the pillar, stared down into the cavern, and shouted. His voice echoed through the chasm.

"A bride will be tested!" He raised his fist. "Open the pit! Release the Beast of Bride's Blood."

Tribesmen cheered below, and the chamber swam around Laira. She glanced at Jeid, winced, and clutched the hilt of her sword.

TANIN

Two dragons flew over the sea, landed on the dark beach under the stars, and beheld the ruined city of Eteer.

His claws in the sand, Tanin turned to look at Issari. She stood before him, her alabaster scales gleaming in the moonlight, and firelight glowed between her teeth. The white dragon's eyes shone damply as they gazed upon the walls of her city. They had landed a mark away, too far for any guards on the walls to see them.

"Home," Issari whispered and lowered her head. "A place of ruin, of darkness, of evil."

Tanin folded his wings around him. Smoke wafted from his nostrils. "A place we will rededicate."

She looked at him, eyes moist. He could see the sea reflected in those orbs, the waves crested with moonlit foam. "But not tonight. Not in the darkness, for fear of that city's new queen still chills me. In the light I will feel brave again. Will you stay with me here, Tanin, on the beach outside my home? For one last night—you and me in the darkness, safe from the horrors of the world?"

He nodded and nuzzled her with his snout. "Of course."

They released their magic and sat in the sand, humans again, facing the sea. A path of moonlight spread into the horizon, and the waves whispered, their crests silver. The stars shone above and the city festered to their east; tonight Tanin pushed that city out of his mind, staring only at the waves.

Issari wriggled closer to him, place a hand on his thigh, and leaned against him. He slung his arm around her.

"I used to come here sometimes as a child." She stared ahead into the water. "With Sena. I miss him so badly. I miss those days—before the war, before all this happened. I wish I could go back, to be a girl again."

The breeze blew, warm and salty. Tanin placed his hand upon hers. "You know what I wish for?"

She looked at him, the stars reflected in her eyes. "What?"

"A nice, big, roasted slab of ham." He smacked his lips. "And some hot bread rolls and butter. I haven't had bread in many days; damn hard to find in the north."

She smiled hesitantly. "Bread and ham? Not me. I miss roasted pine nuts mixed with leeks and wild mushrooms. I miss the fine wines of southern vineyards. I miss honey cakes thick with almonds and pistachios." She placed a hand on her belly. "I miss that feeling of being full, lounging by a fireplace, and dreaming."

He raised his eyebrows. "Well, look at the fancy princess. Your tastes are far too fine. How could you tolerate a lowly barbarian like me?"

Her smile widened, and she kissed his stubbly cheek. "Part of the terrors of war, I suppose."

He rummaged in his pack and produced a wineskin—their last one. He uncorked it, took a sip, and handed it to her. "It's not fine wine like you're used to. Simple grapes from some riverside farmer, but it'll soothe us tonight. One last night."

She drank and they passed the skin back and forth. Tomorrow they would have nothing more to drink. Tomorrow they might die. Tomorrow the fate of the world would be sealed. Tonight they simply sat, drinking, watching the waves, scared in the dark. Tanin ran his fingers slowly over hers, again and again, and looked at her in the night. She was still facing the sea, and he admired her moonlit cheek, the dark braid that hung across her shoulder, and the strength he saw in her, a quiet strength like a slender oak sapling rising from the ash of a burnt forest.

He found himself thinking back to Ciana, the woman he had loved in his youth, so many years ago in the village of Oldforge. He had kissed Ciana in the fields, vowed to forever love her. And once she had learned his secret, learned that he was Vir Requis, she had screamed. Called for her father to kill him. Became a huntress of dragons herself. For so many years, the pain of that day had clawed at Tanin—the day he'd been banished, the day Ciana had shattered his soul, the day Zerra had murdered his mother.

But now I've found something new to live for, he thought, holding Issari's hand. *For Requiem . . . and for you, Issari.*

She saw him staring, turned toward him, and looked at him. Her lips parted slightly, and he caressed her cheek, marveling at how soft it was, at how pure she seemed, a doll in a world of demons. He kissed that cheek, and she smiled softly. Her lashes tickled his face. He held her hand, and he kissed her ear, a little peck, and she placed her arms around him. His lips brushed across her neck, moving upward, hesitating, and though he had fought armies of demons and rocs, now Tanin was afraid, nervous, awkward. She turned her head slightly toward his, trembling in his arms, and his lips brushed the corner of her mouth. She met his gaze, and her green eyes were so large, and he leaned forward and kissed her lips. Fast as the waves washing over the shore, she melted into his kiss, their mouths open, their tongues moving together.

The waves whispered, and they kissed for a long time, and their hands grasped at each other, desperate, exploring, and all the pain Tanin had lived through these past few years—all the hopes and dreams and nightmares—emerged now, needing relief, needing her, Issari, a woman he loved. Her hands slid under his shirt, and he helped her, pulling it over his head, and she pressed herself back up against him, kissing him. He reached under her tunic, feeling the soft skin beneath, and she helped him remove her garment and tossed it aside. She gazed at him with those huge eyes, and he pulled her onto his lap, and she buried her hands in his hair, her head tossed back. He kissed the declivity below her neck, moving his lips downward, kissing her chest, then back up again to her lips.

I love you, Issari, he thought. *I've loved you since the moment I saw you. I will love you forever.*

They spread their cloaks upon the sand, then lay down upon them, pulling off their last items of clothing. Her body was slim and silver in the moonlight. Tanin had bedded women before, villagers he had met on his wanderings—quick, cold encounters that had left him feeling more lonely than ever. With Issari it felt warm, real, and so pure he never wanted it to end. She moaned beneath him, eyes closed, mouth open, and their naked bodies moved together. She cried out and dug her fingers into his back, and he let himself flow into her until he lay still. He kissed the tip of her nose, then lay beside her. She nestled in his arms, nuzzling his cheek.

He looked up at the stars. They shone down, not just the Draco constellation but millions of others. The music of the waves played, and from where he lay, he couldn't see the city of demons. He could see only beauty, feel only warmth.

I don't know if I'll die tomorrow or if I'll live another fifty years. But I know this: Whatever happens, this is the best moment of my life. This is the best moment of life I can have. I'm happier than I've ever been, perhaps more than I'll ever be. This is magic—no less than becoming a dragon—and I will cling to this memory forever, even if all the world burns and all our kingdoms fall to ruin.

She fell asleep in his arms, her head on his chest. He lay awake for a long time, stroking her hair and watching the stars.

DORVIN

"Bloody bull bullocks!" Dorvin blasted out flame and whipped his tail. "You two are duller than my grandmother's cold dead corpse. Why aren't you singing with me?"

Flying across the sky with his sister and that mammoth's bottom Maev, he tossed back his head, cleared his throat, and launched back into his song. The lyrics—telling the tale of a hearty lass whose father tossed her into the river, only for her ample bosom to keep her afloat—did not seem to amuse his companions. His sister, a lavender dragon, glared at him. Maev, a green beast, banked toward him and thumped her tail against his cheek.

"Be silent!" said the flying mammoth posterior, eyes flashing. "I'll cut out your tongue next time. Your song's disgusting, and demons could hear you for marks."

He growled and blasted sparks of fire her way. "Good! I like rude songs; keeps things interesting. And I like when demons can hear me. I'd prefer a straight fight to this dull flight with two lumps of airborne shite."

Maev flicked her tail again, slamming it against his flank. "Be silent or the only thing you'll be fighting is worms in your grave."

Dorvin watched the green beast fly off, wincing at the pain of her blows. Damn creature. He grumbled under his breath. He had to admit Maev wasn't bad-looking, at least not in human form. Her hair was long and golden, her body was fit, and her face was pretty enough—at least when she wasn't thrusting out her bottom lip, haughtily raising her chin, and glaring at everything that moved. If you removed the tattoos on her arms, cleaned the mud off her, and maybe removed that old buffalo hide she always wore, she could be a fetching woman.

"It's too bad she's got the personality of rhinoceros snot," he muttered.

They kept flying westward. The sky was blue. The land was green. A few distant hills rose in the north. The same thing mark after mark. His two fellow dragons flew silently. Dorvin couldn't take it anymore. They had been flying like this for days now, and he was bored senseless. Why had he ever agreed to this mission? He could have gone north with Jeid! Surely the north had some demons in it. He could have gone south with Issari and Tanin; Eteer was the land of demons, surely full of many interesting creatures to vanquish. Instead he had agreed to fly here, seeking more dragons, a decision he was quickly regretting. Even if he did find other Vir Requis, they'd probably be just as stiff as Alina and Maev.

"Oi, girls!" He flew closer to them. "All right, no singing. How about some jokes instead? What do you call a woman who's got a small head and a big arse? Huh? Anyone?" He winked. "Maev, you'd know wouldn't you?"

Alina only rolled her eyes, but Maev fumed. Showering flame, the green dragon roared and shot toward him, claws lashing. Dorvin braced for impact, and the two dragons crashed together. Scales cracked and their horns locked. Maev's fire flowed over him, and Dorvin shut his eyes against the heat. His scales expanded and one cracked with a blast of pain. He growled, shoved Maev off, and barreled into her, snapping at her, trying to bite through her scales. The two dragons spun in the sky, wings beating madly.

"Good!" Dorvin laughed. "Now this flight's a little more interesting."

Growling, she grabbed his horns and began tugging him down. They tumbled through the sky, the ground spinning beneath them.

"I warned you!" she shouted. "I'll cut your tongue out now."

He laughed. "You can have my tongue if you just give me a kiss."

She twisted his neck, drove her weight against him, and they plunged downward. Dorvin winced and beat his wings, struggling to slow his fall. He managed to free himself from under Maev, soar a few feet, and avoid the ground, only for her to grab his tail and tug him back down. They slammed onto a hilltop, shattering a fallen log and digging ruts into the earth. Dorvin groaned, and when he struggled to rise, Maev clobbered him so hard with her tail she knocked out his magic. He fell onto the hill, a human again, groaning.

The green dragon placed a foot against his chest, pinning him down. She panted, her tongue lolling, and blasted smoke down onto him. He reached up, grabbed that lolling tongue in his hand, and tugged it down hard.

"Looks like it's your tongue that's about to get lost!"

Maev yowled and released her magic. She slammed into him in human form, growling, and pinned him down. "Stupid boy. I used to wrestle men twice your side for a living. Now I'll show you the meaning of pain."

Her tattoos coiled across her arms. She raised her fist, prepared to slam it into his face.

"Maev, no!"

Lavender wings fluttered, and Alina landed upon the hill. She resumed human form and grabbed Maev's wrist, holding her fist back.

"Let go of me, Alina," Maev said softly, staring down at Dorvin. "The boy needs to learn a lesson."

Lying beneath her, Dorvin managed to grin. "Teach me. Let's see how hard you cry once I—"

Growls sounded to their side.

They froze.

Dorvin bit his lip. "Maev, is that your stomach growling?"

She leaped off him, drew her sword, and stared down the hill. Standing beside her, Alina gasped and took a step back. Dorvin struggled to his feet, rubbed his sore shoulders, and stared downhill with them. He raised his eyebrows.

"Well, bloody stars." He cracked his neck. "Some entertainment at last."

A pack of hairless wolves crept up the hill, foaming at the mouth. Each was large as a bear, and warty, spiked tails hung between their legs, dragging along the ground. Human limbs grew from their backs like fins, twitching like antennae. Dorvin counted six of them.

"Bet I can kill them without becoming a dragon," he said to Maev and hefted his spear.

She spat and raised her short, leaf-shaped sword. "Bet I can kill all six."

Face pale, Alina took a step back and raised her staff. "Stars of Requiem, protect your children, shine your light upon—"

Dorvin did not wait to hear the rest of her prayer. He flashed Maev a grin and burst into a run, racing downhill toward the wolves. They howled and ran up toward him, kicking up dust. Dorvin leaped onto a boulder, vaulted off its top, and tossed his spear from midair. The projectile flew and sank into a wolf's neck. The creature yowled and fell, and Dorvin unstrapped his second spear off his back.

"That's one, Maev!"

She was still running downhill, her hair streaming in the wind. Two wolves reached her, snapping their teeth. Maev dropped to slide downhill on her backside, moving between a wolf's legs. She thrust up her blade, driving the sword through its jaw and into its head. The second animal pounced. Maev leaped onto the corpse of the wolf she had killed, hurtled herself into the air, and slammed into the second demon. Her blade drove into naked, warty flesh, and the creature snapped its teeth, whimpered, and fell dead too.

"Two, Dorvin!" she shouted back. "With no dragon magic."

"Get shagged!" he cried toward her. He was about to hurtle more insults when two more wolves slammed into him, knocking him down. He grunted as claws slashed his tunic. His blood dripped. He swung his spear, slamming its shaft against one wolf's head. He leaped to his feet and thrust the weapon, but a wolf grabbed the spear between its jaws and yanked it free. The two demons circled him, hissing. The human arms growing from their backs twitched, their hands opening and closing. Foam filled the beasts' mouths, oozing down to the ground. Weaponless, Dorvin reached down, grabbed a stone, and tossed it. The rock hit one wolf's head, only enraging the creature. It pounced, and Dorvin winced but refused to summon his magic, to let Maev win.

He roared and leaped toward the wolf, fists flying.

Before the two could slam together, the demonic canine yowled. Dragon teeth drove into its flanks, tugged it up, and tossed it aside. A spiked tail slammed down, crushing the second demon.

"Stars damn it, Alina!" Dorvin shouted. "I had them."

The lavender dragon hissed at the two wounded demons. Both creatures tried to drag themselves forward, to attack again. Alina torched them with a blast of flame. She turned back toward Dorvin and glared.

"You were going to die just to prove some point to Maev." She released her magic and slapped him. "Oaf of a brother!"

Dorvin rubbed his sore cheek, glaring at the druid. "I could have had them."

Laughter sounded behind. Dorvin spun around to see Maev trudging uphill, a mocking smile on her lips and blood on her hands. She pointed behind her where lay the corpses of three demon wolves.

"Well, well," she said. "Looks like I killed three demons, Alina killed two, and you, Dorvin?" She pretended to count on her fingers. "Oh my. Only one kill for you."

Both of Dorvin's cheeks burned now. He grabbed one of his fallen spears and thrust it into a corpse. "Both of Alina's were mine! I wounded the damn things before she torched them."

Maev nodded and patted his cheek. "Wounded, not killed." She mussed his hair. "Better luck next time, Dung Beetle."

"Go to the Abyss, Mammoth Arse."

She raised her eyebrows. "I could kill more demons than you there too."

He spat, shifted back into a dragon, and took flight. "Come on, girls!" He blasted smoke down onto them. "Enough dallying. We've got to fly west and find more Vir Requis, and hopefully not dull ones like you two."

He beat his wings, flying again, until he caught an air current and glided. The girls flew alongside, and Dorvin ignored them, not singing or joking for once. For the rest of the day, his thoughts kept returning to the battle—to Maev wrestling him, patting his cheek, mussing his hair. He knew he should hate her. He *did* hate her. So why in the Abyss's name did he keep looking her way, keep thinking of how her body had pressed against his?

"Damn rhinoceros snot," he muttered.

They flew on, moving farther west than Dorvin had ever flown, crossing mountains and heading into lush woods of secrets and shadows and hidden hope.

ISSARI

They walked through the gates, entering a ruined city, and Issari shed tears for her home.

"Eteer," she whispered, pressing a hand against a stone column. "Poets have sung of your towers and gardens. Soldiers have wept at the sight of your banners and walls. You were a city of light and now you lie in darkness. I am Issari. I am your daughter. I have returned home."

At that moment, staring upon Eteer, she was more a child of this kingdom than of Requiem across the sea.

Tanin took her hand in his. "We will rebuild. We will bring back the light."

They walked down the street, hand in hand, moving slowly and silently, solemn as if walking through a graveyard. And much like a graveyard Eteer was. Skeletons of animals and humans lay discarded in street corners, the bones shattered. Windows and doors were boarded up on some houses; other houses had fallen into heaps of bricks. No more peddlers, priests, and buskers lined the streets. No markets bustled with shoppers. Eyes peered through cracks in boarded windows, and the only living creature to cross their path was a scrawny, feral cat. Aerhein Tower, once the tallest structure in the city, stood no more. The palace still rose upon the hill, its columns blue and crested with gold, but no more gardens grew atop its balcony and roof; they had burned in the great battle when Issari had fought Angel, when the amulet had fused with her flesh.

She raised her hand and gazed at her palm. The amulet of Taal, her mother's amulet, gleamed there.

"This was the amulet of a queen." She caressed it. "Now I will be Queen of Eteer. King Raem's throne must be mine."

She thought words she would not speak. *You died in the north, Mother. You have fallen, Sena, my dear brother. But you still look down upon me from Requiem's stars. I will make you proud. I will save both our kingdoms—the kingdom of our birth and the kingdom of our constellation.*

"All the demons have flown north." Tanin walked with a drawn dagger. He glanced around nervously. "We can take this city easily if the generals accept your leadership."

She nodded. "All have left but Angel. She still lurks in the palace, warming the throne as my father is away. And she frightens me more than an army of demons."

Tanin shuddered and said no more. They kept moving through the city, climbing over a fallen column, skirting a shattered statue, and walking down a boulevard where blood still stained the flagstones. Banners hung from roofs. Some showed the god Taal, a slender man with open palms, while others showed the god Kur-Paz, a winged bull. Other banners were more lurid; some were mere sheets stained with blood, and others showed crude images of broken men, of red eyes surrounded with teeth, and of a winged woman of fire. Demon banners.

"My father perhaps is still king by name," Issari said. "But it seems that Angel governs here now."

They were walking by the canal when they saw the first pregnant woman.

She sat on the docks, leaning against a lantern pole, her face ashen. She gazed at Issari with sunken, vacant eyes—the eyes of a soldier who had seen too much, of the sole survivor of a slain family, of one so ill that only the grave could offer comfort. Her belly was grossly distended—twice the size of any pregnant belly Issari had ever seen. It bulged out from her tunic, the skin so stretched it looks ready to tear, and strange figures moved behind that skin, kicking, scratching, tracing the symbols of demons. A rustle rose from within the woman like the buzz of cockroaches, and Issari knew: *She is gravid with a demon child.*

As they kept walking, they saw more of these poor souls, their bellies large, their eyes glassy, their lips whispering prayers. Dozens seemed to fill the city, maybe hundreds—lying on streets, too weak to rise, demon spawn scuttling inside them, shoving at the skin, begging to emerge. Issari whispered prayers to all she passed, knowing she had no way to heal them, knowing all she could do was claim the throne and banish the horror back into the Abyss.

"Taal looks over you, my children," Issari said as she passed, holding up the amulet embedded into her palm. "His light shines upon you. I am Issari Seran and I am home. I will look after you."

They couldn't reply, only stare with anguished eyes, the creatures kicking within their bellies. Tears in her eyes, knowing there was no more she could do, Issari walked on. Tanin walked at her side, eyes dry but haunted, his blade raised.

The noon sun was blazing overhead when they rounded a charred garden, its palm trees blackened and its cobblestones cracked, and saw the city fortress ahead. The complex rose upon a hill, watching over Eteer. Walls snaked around the hill in a ring, topped with battlements and turrets. Beyond, upon the hilltop, rose several buildings: a columned temple to Sharash, the god of war; squat armories, silos, and smithies; and a towering round barracks, nearly the size of the city palace, holding the city garrison. Once cypress trees had grown beneath the walls, and once a gilded statue of Sharash had stood upon the hill. The trees were now burnt, and demons had severed the statue's head, replacing it with a metal mockery, a demon head with a lurid tongue and hollow eyes. But soldiers still guarded this place; Issari could see them on the ramparts, spears in their hands, helmets on their heads. Eteer's army still stood.

Issari walked uphill, moving along a pebbly path between burnt trees. Tanin walked close behind. The wind stung Issari's face, hot and scented of ash. A skeleton lay on the hillside to her left, bite marks in the bones, the skull stuffed into the ribcage. A single banner thudded above from the citadel's wall, the only movement she saw. The soldiers stared down, still as statues.

When she reached the gates, she looked up and called out, "I am Issari Seran, Daughter of Raem, Heiress to Eteer!" She was only the youngest princess, but with Laira outcast and Sena fallen, she supposed that left her the heiress. "I've come to shine the light of Taal and cleanse this city of darkness." She raised her palm, and the amulet blazed with light. "Allow me entrance and I will speak with your lord."

She stared at the doors, thick oak banded with copper. The marks of demon claws marred them, and black blood stained the path below her feet. Slowly, creaking on their hinges, the doors opened.

Issari glanced at Tanin. He gave her a slight nod. They entered together.

They found themselves in a cobbled courtyard surrounded with columns. The statue of Sharash rose ahead upon a pedestal, fifty feet tall, its new demon head leering down at them. Stairs rose between charred cypress trees, leading to the barracks.

Several soldiers stood in the complex, their bronze breastplates and shields dulled with ash. Still no sound rose, only the single banner that rose and fell with thuds, hiding and revealing the sigil of the city, a winged bull. Issari and Tanin climbed the staircase, stepped between columns and onto a portico, and finally walked through an archway into the city barracks.

They found a vaulted hall, larger even than the palace throne room. Statues of Sharash—a soldier with a raised spear and a beard of serpents—stood between columns that lined the chamber. Many living soldiers stood here too, clad in bronze and holding true spears. All eyes turned toward Issari and Tanin, a princess and her companion from the north.

How must we look to them? Issari thought. She no longer wore her fine cotton tunic hemmed with gold, and her old headdress of lapis lazuli had been lost in the war. She wore the fur and leather of the north now, and gone was the innocent softness of her old life; she knew her cheeks were gaunter now, her eyes harder. At her side, Tanin looked out of place, like a dragonfly among bees—a tall young man, his brown hair mussed and dusty, his cloak made of rich fur, a northerner that must seem like a barbarian to these southern soldiers.

"Hear me!" Issari stepped forward and raised her amulet. "I am Issari Seran. I have come to rededicate Eteer, to reclaim our kingdom and banish the demons who infect it. My father, Raem Seran, is a killer of kings; he slew his own father, the wise Nir-Ur. My father, Raem Seran, lies with demons. He must fall! I claim dominion of Eteer." The light blasted out from her amulet. "Follow me, soldiers of Taal! March with me to the palace. We will banish Angel from the throne, and I will be your queen. We will banish these demons back into the Abyss."

She stood, panting, waiting for a reaction.

The soldiers only stared.

From the shadowy back of the room rose mirthless laughter. Issari stiffened and her lip curled up. At her side, Tanin raised his dagger. The shadows stirred and a soldier stepped forth, his smile cruel and his eyes hard.

"General Gateris," Issari said, her voice cold.

He walked toward her, a hint of swagger to his step. A grin split his face, revealing a wide space between his front teeth. Wrinkles crinkled the corners of his eyes, and lines marred his forehead, but he still stood tall and strong, and his hair was still jet-black. A bronze breastplate covered his chest, and a khopesh—the traditional sword of Eteer, shaped as a sickle—hung at his side. Issari had always feared this man. Once, as a child, she had run into the barracks while chasing a butterfly. Gateris had grabbed her, twisted her arm, and sent her fleeing with a slap—but not before grabbing the butterfly in his hand, crushing it, and wiping the mess against her shirt. Since then she had cowered whenever she encountered him, trying to ignore the lustful looks he gave her growing body.

But today I will not fear him. Today I will be his queen.

"General Gateris!" She stared at him, the amulet thrumming on her palm. "Follow me with your troops to the palace. We have a demon to tame."

His grin widened, cruel and taunting. The same malicious mirth filled his eyes. "And so, the wayward pup returns home. Or should I say . . . the wayward weredragon?" He drew his sword, pointed the blade at her, and raised his voice to a shout. "I have seen this wretch shift into a dragon! I watched her fly across the city. I will have no reptile ruling over me." He spat at her feet. "Raem Seran is my king. Raem Seran is—"

"A weredragon himself!" Issari said. She turned toward the soldiers. "I've seen my father shift in the city cistern. He himself carries this magic; all in our family do. My siblings, Laira and Sena. My late mother, Queen Anai. And my father. Dragon magic is not a curse; it's a blessing of starlight. This city *is* cursed—with a demon infestation, with a cruel king who aligned himself with the Abyss. I've come to purify Eteer—with Lord Gateris or without him."

The soldiers stood still, but she saw their eyes darting from one to another. She saw the doubt in them. Tanin stepped up closer to her, dagger raised, as if his small blade could do these armored swordsmen any harm.

"March with me to the palace, soldiers of Eteer!" she said. "Accept me as your queen, and we will—"

Laughing and shaking his head, Gateris swung his sword at her.

Issari hissed and leaped back. The sickle-shaped blade sliced the air.

"You want control of this army?" Gateris said, grin wide. "Fight me for it." He grabbed a sword from one of his soldiers and tossed her the blade, hilt first. She caught it. "Fight me, Princess of Dragons." He brandished his blade, spinning the khopesh with skill more elaborate than the greatest juggler. "Slay me and this host will be yours to comma—"

Issari shifted into a dragon, blew her fire, and roasted the man.

Gateris fell, burning and screaming. A white dragon, Issari stomped upon him, driving her claws through his armor and into his flesh. He lay still.

She released her magic, stood above the burning corpse, and stared at the soldiers around her. A few had drawn their blades, but they froze under her glare. She spun around slowly, staring at them man by man. Her amulet buzzed on her palm, its light blazing.

"Soldiers of Eteer!" She raised her chin. "Follow me to the palace. Follow me to dethrone the Demon Queen. We will reclaim Eteer!"

For a moment, the men were silent. Issari wondered if they too would attack her. She could not defeat so many, not even as a dragon; dozens stood in this hall, and hundreds more filled the citadel. She took deep breaths, refusing to lower her gaze.

Finally one soldier, a young man with green eyes, raised his spear high. "For Issari!" he cried. "For a new queen!"

The floodgates broke. Dozens of spears rose, and dozens of voices shouted out, echoing in the hall. "For Issari! For a new queen!"

She took a shaky breath and her eyes stung. She spoke softly. "For Eteer."

At her side, Tanin blew out his breath. "Bloody stars, I was almost worried there for a moment."

Issari turned and marched out of the hall, stepping into the sunlight. Behind her, the soldiers streamed out in a sea of bronze. From buildings across this hilltop citadel, more soldiers emerged into the sunlight, and their voices rang. "For Issari! For a new queen!"

RAEM

After scouring the barbarous hinterlands for days, Raem finally saw the Weredragon Column rising ahead from the forest. Flying upon Anai, his deformed bat of the underworld, Raem spat sideways and snickered.

"So here is their kingdom!" he cried for his thousand demons to hear. "Here is the fabled Requiem, the land of dragons—a single bone rising from the wilderness."

He laughed and his demons laughed with him. Their chortles filled the sky. Raem twisted in his saddle, looked over his shoulder, and admired them. They were beautiful. They were the most beautiful things in the world. Great balls of fat dripped ooze, their tongues thrusting out between folds of skin. Cadaverous creatures beat insect wings, leering, their teeth longer than human arms. Twisted clusters of limbs and torsos rolled in the sky, stitched together, flapping wings of skin stretched over bones. Naked moles the size of dragons. Naked men with beards of snakes and wings of bats. Creatures of fire, of stone, of rot. All flew here, seeking the meals they craved, the meat of dragons.

"Where are you, my children?" Raem whispered. "Where are you, Jeid the so-called King of Dragons?"

They flew closer. Soon Raem could see details on the column; it rose taller than the tallest tree, even taller than his palace back in Eteer. Its capital was shaped as rearing dragons. No other structures seemed to stand here, just a single pillar. He tugged the reins and his mount descended, the wind shrieking around them. A circle of marble tiles lay around the pillar, and Raem landed upon them, his demon's claws clattering against the stone. The rest of his demons circled above, screeching and sniffing. Raem could see none of the weredragons he sought. His demon's nose twitched.

"Do you smell them, Anai?" He stroked her wispy hair. "Where are they?

He dismounted. A few of his demons landed too, and they scuttled around on clawed feet, slithered and left trails of slime, and clattered on centipede legs. Most of the creatures still flew above, sniffing, snorting, seeking their enemy. Raem frowned, gazing at the place.

"This is no kingdom," he said softly. "This is nothing but a dream I will crush."

All of Requiem, it seemed, was this pillar of stone, these marble tiles, and a wooden hut between the birches. The footprints of dragons covered the forest floor beyond the tiles, but he could see none of the beasts; if any were here, the cowards hid. Holding his khopesh, he walked between the birches, leaving the column and approaching the hut. He kicked the door open to reveal an empty room. Inside he found five piles of straw topped with fur blankets, a brazier full of cold embers, a few bowls, and a clay tablet bearing the cuneiform writing of Eteer. When Raem lifted and examined the tablet, he recognized the words—it was a tale of the god Sharash and his journeys, a tale Sena used to enjoy.

"Did you engrave these words, Sena, after fleeing me as a coward?" Raem tossed down the tablet; it shattered on the floor.

Snorts sounded from the doorway, and he turned to see Anai gazing into the room. The demon's bloated, vaguely human head sniffed, and her distended body rose behind her, too large to enter.

"The weredragons lived here," Raem said to her. "They fled."

He was walking back toward the door when his boot hit something. He knelt and lifted a wooden doll. Upon it appeared more Eteerian letters, markings that would be meaningless to anyone born in the north. "Mustardseed." It was the doll's name, perhaps.

"Laira's old doll." He caressed its wooden cheek, then snapped off its head. He tossed the broken toy aside and stepped back outside.

He stood before the column, tilted back his head, and coned his palm around his mouth. He shouted for all his demons to hear. "Crush the column! Tear it down."

The creatures descended like insects upon a fallen morsel. They bit at the marble. They clawed. They kicked it, drove horns against it, gnashed their teeth, rubbed hooks and jagged scales.

Not a scratch appeared upon the marble.

"Pathetic weaklings!" Raem shouted. "Topple it!"

The demons howled. They slammed against the column again and again, ten at a time, storming around it, shoving, scratching and biting, yet still it stood. Light fell upon the creatures, and when the clouds parted, Raem saw it above. Even in the blue sky of day, it shone—the Draco constellation, the stars the dragons claimed blessed them.

The demons mewled, covered their eyes, and cowered between the trees.

Raem spat in disgust, walked toward the column, and swung his khopesh.

The blade shattered against the marble. A shard scratched along his hand, and Raem spat and cursed.

"The gods of the dragons protect their column." Clutching his wound, he stared up at the stars and shouted hoarsely. "You will watch, weredragon of the heavens! You will watch as I slaughter all your children."

The stars gleamed down upon him, their light soft, comforting, and he imagined that he could hear a soothing voice inside him, a voice of starlight. *You are one of them, child. You are blessed with our magic. You too are a child of Requiem.*

Raem covered his ears, ignoring the words, ignoring the need inside him, the urge to shift into a dragon. He had shifted many times in the city cistern, chastising himself every time. *No. No! I am not cursed. I am not a reptile. I am a pure son of Taal.*

A high whimper—not the cry of a demon—rose above from the stars. Raem looked back up and sucked in breath with a hiss.

Dragons! Two dragons flew above, descending from the starlight!

The demons roared and squealed and bustled.

"Do not feed yet!" Raem shouted. "Bring the dragons to me alive."

He licked his lips, his body crackling with energy. He felt more alive than he had since slaughtering weredragons back in Eteer. Finally—to kill again! Killing was the greatest joy there was, greater even than shifting.

The demon army swarmed, and the two dragons cried out and tried to flee. They were too slow. The demon horde rose from the forest like flies from a disturbed carcass, grabbed the two dragons, and tugged them down. The demons slammed the scaly creatures against the marble tiles at the column's base.

Raem stared down, eyes wide. "Children," he said in wonder. "They're no larger than horses. Mere children."

The two dragons, both green, whimpered and flicked their tails, and their wings beat weakly against the tiles. They were trying to take flight again, but demon legs pinned them down. The creatures hulked over the two, licking their maws, their drool dripping onto the dragons. The demons panted, begging to eat.

"Not yet!" Raem said. "Now is not the time to feed."

He stepped closer and placed a hand against one of the dragons. It stared at him, pleading, teary.

"Please," the dragon spoke. "Don't hurt us. We're looking for Requiem. We've heard tales."

The other dragon, even smaller, spoke too. Her voice was the voice of a little girl. "My brother said there are other dragons in Requiem! We came here from the east." Tears rolled down her scaly cheeks. "Please, master, don't hurt us. We only came to find the others."

Raem walked back to his mount. Several weapons— spears, bows and arrows, clubs, and two more khopeshes—hung from the saddle. Raem chose a bronze-tipped spear and approached the two dragons again.

He drove the weapon down. Its bronze head crashed through the female dragon's soft scales. In death, her magic left her. She returned to human form—a young girl, no older than six or seven, a spear in her chest. Blood puddled around her, and Raem pulled back his spear.

The second dragon—her brother—roared in grief. He thrashed madly, wings beating, tail flicking, unable to free himself from the demons pinning him down. Raem approached the creature, his dripping spear raised.

"Be thankful," he told the beast. "I'm showing you a mercy. I'm killing you *before* the demons feed." He smirked. "My own children will not be as fortunate."

He thrust his spear.

The green dragon died upon it, returning to human form—a small butchered boy.

Raem pulled the spear out and smiled. He raised his hand to the sky. "Well, my friends? Enjoy!"

The demons plunged down with the urgency of starving dogs upon a piece of meat. Blood and gobbets of flesh flew. Within instants, the children were gone, leaving only a single heart upon the marble tiles; it lay where the little girl had died. A demon raced toward the morsel, but Raem waved it aside. He knelt, lifted the heart in his hand, and stared at the little organ—soft, pure, hot. He kissed the heart and licked his lips, savoring the blood. He stepped toward the column, slapped the heart against it, and drew a picture in blood—the sigil of Taal.

He spoke softly. "A message for any of you who return."

Demons gathered around him, panting, begging for the treat. Raem tossed the heart toward them.

Before the dripping organ would reach the demons, an arrow sailed through the air, pierced the heart, and pinned it against a birch.

The demons squealed. Raem stiffened, raised his spear, and stared into the forest whence the arrow had flown. A figure emerged from between the trees, holding a bow.

"Hello, mighty King Raem! The whole north is speaking of you and your demon horde. I see you've arrived at fabled Requiem a little too late."

It was a woman, young by the sound of her voice. Raem could not see her face; a bronze mask hid it, shaped as a blank face with only small holes for the eyes, nostrils, and mouth. She wore a leather tunic, long gloves that rose to her elbows, and a fur cloak. A copper dagger and a quiver of arrows hung across her hips.

"We will find the creatures," Raem said. "Our scouts scour the land for them. Who are you?"

She stepped closer. "A huntress. A warrior. One who will slay dragons. I wounded their king once with many arrows; now I seek to finish the job."

He narrowed his eyes, not lowering his spear. "Who are you?" he asked again.

"A daughter of Oldforge, a village in the shadow of the escarpment where dragons once flew." She snickered. "As a child, I even loved one, a boy named Tanin. Of course I didn't know he was a diseased reptile then." Her voice dropped. "One day, I managed to trap Tanin's father, a beast named Jeid Blacksmith, the King of Weredragons. I brought him to our village. I fired arrows into his flesh. He escaped half-dead . . . but not before blowing his fire."

Slowly, as gingerly as one lifting a newborn babe, the woman removed her bronze mask.

Raem's lip twitched.

The woman's face was gone, burned away with dragonfire. She hadn't much of a mouth left, but Raem thought that she was smiling. She placed the mask back on.

"I am Ciana," she said. "I've hunted weredragons for many years. Now I will hunt with you."

LAIRA

Laira stood upon the stalagmite, her fingers tingling. All around her, the tribesmen of Leatherwing chanted, their voices echoing in the craggy, torchlit innards of Two Skull Mountain.

"Release the Beast of Bride's Blood! Release the hydragrif!"

Laira gazed around. The vast chamber seemed to spin around her, the torches all whirring into blurred lines. Hundreds of tribesmen stood below, raising their spears, their voices thudding against her eardrums. Standing by the throne of Chieftain Oritan, she swallowed the lump in her throat.

"A beast? I have to fight to wed you?"

Oritan placed the ape-skull helmet back over his head, hiding his face. He stared at her through the eye sockets. "It is the custom of Leatherwing. Chieftains of our tribe may only marry the strongest women, those who can defeat a hydragrif in battle. Summon your roc, Laira Seran of Goldtusk. You will ride upon her in battle here in this cavern."

Laira stared down from the pillar of stone she stood on. Upon the cavern floor—a hundred feet below her—men were tugging on ropes, turning winches, and opening a massive trapdoor built of the natural stone floor. The opening began to widen like a woman in labor, and in the shadowy womb below, white eyes stared, claws scratched at stone, and grunts echoed. A beast hid within that underground cavern—it seemed larger than a dragon—though she could see only its eyes and tufts of white fur.

She stared back at Oritan. "This is wrong. This is barbaric!"

"This is the way of our people, Laira Seran." He leaned back in his throne. "Do you want my help fighting a demon army? Prove that you yourself are a warrior."

The creature's grunts below grew into squeals. The entrance opened wider, and claws ringed with white fur emerged into the chamber, scratching at stone. The tribesmen cheered. Laira's heart thudded, and she spun toward Jeid, hoping he'd have something to say, a way to stop this madness.

The shaggy, bearded King of Requiem grumbled. "Let us leave, Laira. We'll return to Requiem and defend it as best we can. With our rocs. With our dragons." He shook his head. "This is not the way."

Laira narrowed her eyes, tilted her head, and stared at him, and she saw something in his eyes—something more than fear. What was it? Jealousy? Did Jeid object to her fighting a beast, or did he object to her marrying this chieftain?

She took a deep breath. She looked down. The opening was wider now, and a head emerged from below. It was shaped like a great, albino eagle, but a mane of white fur—like that of a lion—encircled its neck. It stared at her with white, baleful eyes and shrieked, the sound deafening. The creature's body still lurked below. Across the cavern, a hundred pteros clung to the walls, mouths clattering open and shut, screeching down at the beast in the pit.

I need these pteros, Laira thought. *I need the hunters who ride upon them.* She thought back to the demon she had slain, to the thousand others said to be flying north in search of dragons. *I will not turn away this chance for victory.*

She stepped closer to Jeid, placed a hand upon his shoulder, and kissed his cheek. "I will fight for Requiem," she said. "And I will marry this man. And we will fly with this tribe to victory."

She saw the pain those words gave him. He held her hand. "There are other ways."

She shook her head. "Not for me. Not for the kingdom we are building." She turned back toward Oritan. "I will fight. But not upon Neiva. I will risk my life, not that of my roc. I will fight as a dragon."

With that, she leaped into the air and shifted. Her wings burst out from her back. Flames roared from her mouth and crashed against the ceiling. Across the chamber, tribesmen stared and roared. Their voices echoed.

"Release the Beast of Bride's Blood!"

Finally the stone doors fully opened below, a craggy cervix birthing a beast. Laira flew above, hissing out smoke. She had never seen a hydragrif before, and the creature shot bolts of fear through her. It emerged shrieking into the cavern, lashing its claws, a massive beast twice her size. Its body was that of a dragon, covered in white scales. Tufts of white fur rose across it like patches of crabgrass, and its tail whipped, spiked and cruel. Its wings were not leathery but instead covered with white feathers, and they ended with claws longer than swords. Strangest of all, three necks grew from the creature's body, each supporting the head of a pale eagle. The three beaks opened wide, and cries emerged from them, and six eyes blazed as they stared at her.

The creature soared through the cavern, beaks clattering.

Laira roared down her flames.

The fire streamed over the creature. Its tufts of white fur ignited, but the fire flowed harmlessly across its scales. It kept soaring, reached her, and snapped its beaks. Laira yowled as one beak closed around her shoulder, cracking scales, trying to reach her flesh. Another beak closed around her tail.

"Fight it, Laira!" Jeid's voice rose from below.

Her blood dripped. Her wings beat against the ceiling. Pain fueled her, and she thrust her claws into the head that bit her shoulder. The claws drove through flesh, and the beak opened, releasing her.

I defeated Zerra. I can defeat this creature.

She grabbed a neck between her jaws, bit and twisted, and tore off the eagle head. It tumbled down to the sound of cheers, leaving a severed stalk.

The other two heads still bit at her scales, struggling to reach the flesh. One beak grabbed her tail, and the other clutched her leg. The creature's wings beat madly, holding it aloft, pinning Laira to the chamber ceiling. Far below on the cavern floor, the tribesmen waved their spears and roared. Laira blasted more fire, baking the hydragrif. It released her tail, and she swung that tail, driving the spikes into the beast's neck. With another bite, she tore off a second head. Spurting blood, the head tumbled down.

Only one head remained, gnawing on Laira's foot. Its bite worked through her scales, and her blood dripped. She thrust her claws, tore through its muscles and tendons, and ripped off the last head. She tossed it down.

The creature hovered below her, wings beating. It flew in circles, headless.

Laira breathed out in relief.

"I beat it!" she cried out. "I defeated the hydragrif! I—"

She bit down on her words. She stared in horror.

Three new heads sprouted from the severed necks.

Healed, the hydragrif flew back toward her, its three new beaks clattering.

"Oh bloody mammoth shite," Laira cursed, shocked at her words; she must have picked up a thing or two from Dorvin. She winced, beat her wings, and skittered across the ceiling. The hydragrif slammed into the stone, cracking a mural of racing bison. Bits of painted stone fell into the pit.

Laira flew toward one of the cavern walls, spun around, and reared in the air. When the hydragrif charged toward her, she bathed the beast with fire. The flames raced over it harmlessly. All around the pteros shrieked, clinging to the walls like bats, and below hundreds of voices rang out.

The creature passed through the flames, its three beaks snapping, and barreled into Laira. Hydragrif and dragon flew backward. Pteros shrieked and scattered, and Laira slammed into the wall. Torches blazed against her back. She yowled, beating her wings, flailing her tail. The creature's beak drove into her chest, blood spurted, and she screamed. The pain knocked the magic out of her. She returned to human form.

A fraction of her previous size, she tumbled down the wall, momentarily free from the hydragrif's grip. The cavern floor rushed up to meet her. She glimpsed the pillar of stone rising ahead; both Jeid and Oritan still stood upon it, shouting. Tribesmen scattered below, awaiting her crash. The hydragrif swooped from above, beaks opening wide.

An instant before Laira could slam into the floor, she summoned her magic again.

She flew, roaring fire, and skimmed along the cavern floor. Tribesmen fled from her, and she soared higher, rising along the pillar of stone. She shot past Jeid and Oritan on its crest, spun around, and charged toward the hydragrif.

Her tail lashed. Her claws slashed. Her jaws bit.

A hydragrif head tumbled down.

Burn it! screamed a voice inside her. *Burn it like you burned the octopus!*

She spun back toward the creature, wings churning smoke. It reared before her, its two remaining heads shrieking. The stalk of its left neck was red and dripping. Already a nub was sprouting; soon it would turn into a new head.

Bleeding, so weak she could barely cling to her magic, Laira blasted out her flames. The fire crashed into the creature, cauterizing the stump of its neck. The creature bucked, scratched the air, and wailed in pain.

I hurt it, Laira thought, panting. *It can be hurt.*

The head would not grow back, and Laira charged, new vigor filling her, and slammed into the creature. They tumbled through the air, dipped, and crashed into the stone pillar. Cracks raced across it. The hydragrif shrieked in pain, trying to bite, to scratch, to knock her off. Laira wouldn't release it. She grabbed another neck, tugged the animal down, and slammed it against the cavern floor.

The chamber shook. The hydragrif whimpered. Blasting smoke through her nostrils, Laira grabbed the creature's foot and dragged the beast across the floor. Tribesmen fled. When she reached the pit whence the hydragrif had emerged, she gave a mighty tug, tossing the creature down into the shadows. It tumbled into the chasm, slammed against a shadowy floor far below, and let out a miserable wail. When it tried to rise again, Laira blasted flames into the pit, and it twisted and fell back down.

A deep voice rose from above. "Slay it! Slay the beast!"

Still in dragon form, Laira raised her eyes. She saw Chieftain Oritan still standing upon his tower, staring down at her.

She shook her head. "I defeated it! I tamed the creature. I will not slay it."

A hundred feet above her, Oritan placed his fingers in his mouth and gave a short, loud whistle. His ptero—the great beast with the painted horn—detached from a wall and flew toward the chieftain. Oritan leaped into the saddle, and man and ptero swooped. They landed on the cave floor before Laira. The ptero stretched its wings wide and hissed, tongue extended. The chieftain stared down from the confines of his ape helm.

"Prove yourself strong," the chieftain said. "Kill it now, and you'll prove yourself worthy to be my bride."

Again Laira shook her head, scattering smoke. "Strength is not measured by killing an enemy but by showing that enemy mercy." She released her magic and stood at the edge of the pit, a human again. "I proved this strength to you here. Now honor your word. Join our tribes together." She took a step closer to him. "Fight with us."

The chieftain dismounted his ptero, approached her, and stared at her with hard eyes, judging, scrutinizing. He towered above her; her head didn't even reach his shoulders. Armor of bones, copper plates, and clay covered his chest, and the bronze tips of his weapons gleamed in the torchlight. With gruff fingers, he touched her cheek.

"You are strong, Laira of Goldtusk, Laira of Eteer . . . Laira of Requiem." To her surprise, he knelt before her and clasped her hand in his. "We will be wed. Our tribes will unite. And then, Laira . . ." Fire burned in his eyes. "Then we will slay demons together."

She took a deep, shuddering breath, and for the first time in many days, hope kindled inside her. A shadow stirred ahead, and she looked over Oritan's shoulder. Jeid stood there, staring at her, and no hope filled his eyes, only cold, haunting hardness.

MAEV

"So where the Abyss is this place, Alina?" Gliding on an air current, Maev spat out flame. "We've been flying for days now, and I see no damn dragons. Are you leading us on a wild mammoth hunt?"

The lavender dragon flew beside her. A drizzle fell, and drops shone upon her scales. The druid stared ahead into the misty distance. Forests rolled under the rain into a green haze, and the blue-and-gray sky roiled above like a sea. "The stars are veiled but their whispers still guide my way. Other Vir Requis live in the west. We will find them."

Maev twisted her jaw, not as sure. They had seen no signs of humans, dragons, or any other intelligent life for days now. Past the mountains, which they had crossed two days ago, rolled a forest that seemed endless, lusher than the woods back in Requiem. The canopy was so thick Maev couldn't see through it, and only a silver stream broke the green carpet, coiling across the land like a great dragon's tail. Birds flew below and distant thunder rolled. No villages. No wandering tribes that Maev could see. And certainly no dragons.

"If you ask me, those stars are nothing but pretty lights." Maev grunted. "Gods that can guide us? I'm guided by my heart. That's it. Not pretty sky lights."

With a twist to that heart, she thought of her grandfather, the wise druid Eranor. The kindly old man, fallen to the rocs, had believed in the power of the stars. He had prayed to the Draco constellation, had tried to get Maev to pray too. She never would.

How did those stars help you? she thought, and her eyes stung. *They couldn't save you from the rocs. You fell while I linger on, no beacon to guide me.*

The pain clutched her like claws. She had not shared her grandfather's faith, but she missed him so much that breathing hurt, and her throat felt full of coals.

The blast of wings sounded from behind, and Dorvin flew up toward them. He held a goose in his mouth, which he chomped and swallowed, spitting out the beak. "And I follow my belly, and these geese are delicious." He coughed feathers right onto Maev. "I think the flying mammoth arse here is guided mainly by her loins, which burn for me." He whistled. "Hotter than dragonfire, they are."

She showed him her dragonfire, blasting him with a jet. He winced and swerved, dodging the brunt of the attack, though not before she had charred several of his scales.

"You're certainly not guided by your mind, Dorvin." Maev growled at the boy. "You don't got one."

He rolled his eyes. "That's your insult today? You're as witty as you are beautiful, Maev, old beast."

When she tried to roast him again, he darted off with a smile to hunt more geese. Maev grumbled. The journey could have been pleasant if not for that damn boy. Alina was too quiet, too mysterious, too pious, but at least she mostly kept to herself. Dorvin was a constant thorn in Maev's side; he couldn't last a moment without taunting her, singing bawdy songs, telling rude jokes, or nipping at her tail. Sometimes Maev wanted to stab him in his sleep.

"Let go!" she shouted when he grabbed her tail between his jaws, tugging at her just to hear her yelp. She freed herself and slapped her tail across his face, but he only grinned and flew off again.

Maev couldn't take it anymore. She just wanted to turn back, to fly home to the others. Even her brother, Tanin—a silly oaf of a thing—would have been preferable company.

Maev sighed. *Where are you now, Tanin? Have you reached Eteer with Issari? Are you safe, and are you thinking of me too?*

The unspeakable seemed to be happening. Maev was missing her family. She wished she could fly with Tanin again, even if they'd taunt each other and often come to blows. She wished Jeid were here, her gruff grizzly of a father, even if he'd spend the journey scolding how she spat, cursed, and rushed headstrong into fights. She even missed Laira; she hadn't known the young woman for long, but over the winter, Laira had become a dear friend. The Eteerian was perhaps more quiet, more reserved than Maev, but there was strength in her, a strength Maev saw and respected.

Where are you now, Father? Laira? Have the demons found you yet? I pray we meet again.

Maev took a deep breath and nodded. Despite Dorvin, and despite the ache in her wings, she had to keep flying. She had to find others, more dragons to blow fire and lash claws, to fight Raem and his demon host. She would not abandon this quest.

The three dragons kept flying: the green daughter of a king, a lavender druid with gleaming eyes, and a damn silver pest who wouldn't stop singing. The lands rolled endlessly below, mist floated, clouds roiled, and beams of light fell through the drizzle, gleaming with rainbows that appeared and vanished as quickly as winks. It was an empty land, an eternal wilderness, and Maev began to wonder if Jeid had sent her here not to find others but to protect her, to send her far from the demon threat.

They slept that night in the forest between the trees, maintaining their dragon forms, as animals scurried around them and distant wolves howled. When dawn rose, casting rays of light between the trees, they flew again.

The clouds were parting, and the noon sun shone, when Maev saw the city ahead and lost her breath.

She considered herself a gruff warrior, a woman with a heart of metal, but flying here, seeing the wonder ahead, tears filled her eyes.

"It's beautiful," she whispered.

At her side, Alina wept as she flew. "The fabled kingdom of Bar Luan. The jewel of the west."

Dorvin puffed out smoke and flicked his tail about. "Not bad. Sure beats that shite-hole called Requiem." He only winked when Maev glared at him.

She returned her eyes to the city ahead, inhaled deeply, and let her eyes drink it all in. With every flap of her wings, she drew closer and more details appeared. Great triangular buildings rose from the trees; they reminded Maev of Laira's stories about pyramids that rose in the deserts south of Eteer. These structures seemed as tall as King's Column, maybe taller, and large enough to house thousands of people. Staircases rose along their facades, leading to archways flanked by statues of lions. Among the pyramids snaked lofty walls, and upon their facades stared stone faces the size of houses. Cobbled roads coiled between the trees, leading to courtyards where rose statues of robed, bearded men with their palms pressed together. Towers rose here too, some ten tiers tall like boxes stacked together. As Maev drew closer, she saw people too. They bustled along the streets, seeming as small as insects by the grand structures. Everything was built of the same rough bricks, a painting in green and gray, a marvel of architecture, sculpture, and civilization in the wilderness.

"They're here," Alina said, her voice barely more than a whisper, as if she spoke to a spirit rather than her companions. "More Vir Requis. I sense their light in this city."

Maev began to descend. "Land among the trees. We'll walk the rest of the distance. Safer."

Dorvin spat an ember. "The Abyss we will! I'm not walking. We fly in like the mighty dragons we are. We roar, blow fire, and—"

Maev grabbed his snout, stifling his words, and tugged him down toward the forest. He struggled but couldn't free himself. The three dragons descended, crashed through the treetops, and thumped down onto the forest floor.

"I'm not releasing you until you take human form," Maev said, still clutching the silver dragon's snout.

Smoke puffed out from his nostrils, and he gave her a deathly glare, but he obeyed. Back in human form, he crossed his arms, and his glare did not wane. Maev looked at him and sighed. The damn kid looked harmless enough—a shock of black hair, a bit of stubble on his face, sharp eyebrows, and a face tanned bronze. Maev might—might!—have even thought him handsome, had she not known how insufferable he was.

He slapped her scaly snout. "Well, Mammoth Arse, shift too! Back into a human with you."

She groaned but she too resumed human form. "Slap my snout again, and I'm going to knock your teeth so far down your throat, they'll bite your bullocks."

He groaned. "Lovely as always, you are. Be thankful I didn't slap your backside." He began to trudge through the forest, heading west. "Well, come on you two! While we're young."

Alina shifted too, returning to her human form—a woman with lavender eyes, clad in flowing druid robes, her auburn hair cascading from the shadows of her hood. She looked around the forest, closed her eyes, and clutched her wooden staff. "This place is dangerous." The druid touched her amulet, a silver circle inlaid with gemstones in the shape of the Draco constellation. "There is fear here. It is everywhere."

Maev narrowed her eyes, and her belly turned cold. She had never seen Alina look so frightened; the druid's face was even paler than usual, and her hand shook around her staff. "Demons?" Maev drew her sword. "I don't smell any."

"No." Alina shook her head. "A colder evil. Demons are hot and red and always moving. This fear is like blue ice, frozen, still, and very old." The druid shuddered. "Maybe even older than the Abyss. I don't know its source, but it permeates these trees. And it comes from the west. From Bar Luan."

The druid was trembling. Maev placed her hand on the woman's shoulder. "Whatever evil lurks here, we'll defeat it. I've fought many demons before; I slew dozens in Eteer. I fought Angel herself and lived. I'm not afraid of whatever creature might be here."

"Yet I am." Alina opened her eyes and stared at Maev; those eyes were deeper than starry skies, blue and purple flecked with gold. "We must be careful here. Our greatest challenge awaits us."

Maev shuddered. She didn't fear men or demons; those were things she could fight. But what was a blue, icy, frozen fear? How could she fight something she didn't understand? She was about to ask more questions when Dorvin shouted from the forest ahead.

"Bloody stars! Are you two following?" He peered from around a tree. "Come on! By the gods of hairy feet."

After sharing a glance, Maev and Alina followed. The forest rustled around them, and for once, Dorvin was silent. As they walked, Maev reached into her boot, drew her hidden copper dagger, and handed it to Alina. "Keep this."

The druid shook her head. "My faith in the stars protects me, as does my staff. They are all the weapons I need. And I have a feeling weapons will be of no use here." She shook her head, auburn hair swaying. "We will need more than metal in Bar Luan."

Maev didn't know what that meant, but she kept her sword drawn. This blade—she had forged it herself in Grizzly's old smithy—had served her for years. Whatever enemy waited here, she swore that she could slay it—with metal if not dragonfire.

They walked through the forest. The trees were different here than back home; she did not recognize them. Their trunks were pale and coiling, soaring far taller than any trees Maev had ever seen. Their roots twisted like serpents, wrapping around boulders and smaller trees. Mist floated and dark birds flitted between the branches. The air was thick and soupy, rich with the smell of age. Everything seemed old here, ancient beyond knowing, and the trees seemed to stare into Maev, disapproving of strangers disturbing their old guard upon the land.

After a mark or so, the trees finally parted, letting in cool air. The city of Bar Luan lay before the three Vir Requis.

A cobbled road stretched ahead, lined with brick buildings that stood several stories tall, each level smaller than the one beneath it. Stone reliefs of animals, druids, and warriors rose upon the walls, gazing upon the sunlit boulevard. Two great statues, each larger than three dragons, flanked the road, shaped as robed men with the heads of apes. When the companions stepped down the road, entering the city, Maev gaped. The pyramids rose ahead, even taller than the great King's Column back in Requiem. Staircases ran up their sides, lined with many statues. Towers, walls, and silos rose everywhere, some topped with gardens, their walls sporting embossed faces larger than men.

Just as much as the architecture, the people of Bar Luan amazed Maev. They were a small, slender folk, no larger than her friend Laira. They wore flowing white robes, and elaborate copper plates hung upon their chests, the metal inlaid with gemstones. Maev half expected guards to rush forth and attack, but she saw nobody carrying weapons. The people walked with bowed heads, rushing from home to home. Their faces were pale, their lips trembling. Only a few raised their eyes and seemed to notice Maev and her companions; they quickly looked away and shuffled off, a tremble to their knees.

Alina tightened her robes around her. "I sense great fear here."

Dorvin rolled his eyes. "You don't say. What wonderful, magical powers of insight will you reveal next?" He spat. "These Bar Luanites are more timid than sheep. Bloody stars." He turned to look at Maev. "Psst, Mammoth Arse. You see any Vir Requis around here?"

Maev was about to grumble and slap the damn boy, but suddenly she froze and sucked in her breath. Her heart leaped and cold sweat washed over her.

"Mammoth Arse, what the Abyss?" Dorvin tilted his head. "You look like you saw a damn ghost's dangling naughty bits."

She blinked. "I . . ." She blew out her breath slowly, her fingers shaking. "It's nothing."

But she *had* seen something. For an instant—just a heartbeat—Dorvin had been . . . Oh stars, but he hadn't looked like Dorvin at all. No skin had covered his face, leaving only red, raw flesh and terribly white, bulging eyes. But it had lasted just that instant. He stood before her now with the same mocking, tanned face.

"I know I'm devilishly handsome, Mammoth Arse, but you have to stop staring." He patted her cheek. "Now come on. If the druid here says there are Vir Requis in this pile of rocks, we'll find them." He began walking deeper into the city. "The locals won't bother us; they scatter as soon as I walk near." To demonstrate, he jogged forward a few steps, then laughed as the Bar Luanites fled.

Maev was going to follow when Alina grabbed her arm and held her close. The druid narrowed her eyes, scrutinizing Maev. "What did you see? You're afraid."

The vision filled her mind again: Dorvin with flayed skin, a living corpse. Maev licked her dry lips. "I . . . I don't know exactly. A quick vision of Dorvin hurt." She took a deep breath, trying to steel herself. "I'm simply tired and he's been fraying my nerves. Let's keep going."

The young druid kept staring at Maev, head tilted, her purple eyes intense as if trying to peer into Maev's mind. Finally Alina nodded, tugged her hood lower over her face, and began to walk forward. The two women followed Dorvin through the city of stone.

They walked along the boardwalk, moving between the towering gray buildings of craggy stone. The pyramids soared ahead, their tips shrouded in clouds. Statues lined their way, each taller than dragons, shaped as stoic priests in flowing robes. Trees rose along the roadside and between the buildings, their pale trunks coiling, their roots rising between the cobblestones like sea serpents breaching from a stony sea. The place was deathly silent. It was a city large enough to house thousands, but Maev saw barely a hundred people, all hurrying about as if the air itself hurt them. One woman, her long pale hair gathered into a bun, ran across the street, tears in her eyes, swatting at invisible insects.

"They're all bloody mad," Dorvin said, turning toward Maev and Alina. "Look at that one." He pointed at an old man who sat in the corner, hugging his knees and rocking, begging in a strange tongue.

Maev knelt by the old man. She tried to soothe him with soft words, but he kept rocking and shaking, not acknowledging her. Sweat beaded on his brow, and his eyes stared into the distance. Tears rolled down his cheeks.

"Dragons!" Dorvin said, forming a little dragon with his hands, the fingers flapping as wings. "Have you seen dragons?"

The man's mouth opened and closed wordlessly, and he covered his eyes. Even Alina, singing softly, could not soothe him. They tried approaching a few other people, and Dorvin again performed his little dragon show, but everyone here had the same reaction. They stared at the empty air, whimpered, and fled.

As Maev walked through the city, seeking anyone who could help, she frowned. Something felt wrong in her mouth. When she tapped her tongue against her front tooth, she winced. The tooth was loose. Maev grumbled. Too many damn fights. Too many punches to the face. It was a wonder she had any teeth at all. As she kept walking, her tongue kept seeking that tooth, wiggling it. It felt ready to fall out, and the more she played with it, the looser it became, yet she couldn't stop. Trying to ignore it, she pointed at a great pyramid that rose ahead, taller than the others.

"If there's a king in this place, he lives there." Gilt covered an archway high upon the pyramid, gleaming as a beacon. "If anyone here would know about Vir Requis, he will."

They kept walking, heading toward the pyramid. The massive structure seemed close, but as Maev kept walking, it seemed to keep getting farther away. She turned around a bend in the road, walked between buildings, and found herself heading in the wrong direction, leaving the pyramid behind her.

"Stars damn you, Mammoth Arse." Dorvin grabbed her arm and tugged her. "This way."

They turned around a corner, and the street became narrow and steep. The houses alongside seemed to close in around Maev, silent and craggy as prison cell walls. The road kept twisting, growing more and more narrow. Maev cursed and ran, having to escape, to find the pyramid again; she couldn't even see it now, only the stone walls around her. A great sense of urgency filled her. She knew she had to find the pyramid soon, to save whatever dragons she could. If she was late, they would die. She would fail. Requiem would fall, and her father and brother would die in fire. She kept running, lost now, and she realized this was no mere city; it was a labyrinth, and she was trapped within it.

"Dorvin!" she cried. "Alina!"

They did not answer. She looked around but couldn't see them, and she panted, and cold sweat soaked her. She tried to shift into a dragon, to soar and find them, but she couldn't grasp the magic. Whenever she felt the tendrils of starlight within her, they fled her grasp. She cursed again. She forced herself to stand still, to focus, to grab the magic. But it was no use; she was too nervous, too scared, and the power evaded her, leaving her in human form. She ran again.

"Dorvin and Alina!" she shouted, running through the maze. "Stars damn it, where are you?"

She did not focus on finding the pyramid anymore, just to leave this maze, to return to the boulevard, to feel oriented again. As she ran, shadows darted behind her. At first she thought them her friends, but no. Red eyes blazed in doorways and alleys, and black wolves bristled, baring their fangs. With growls, the beasts burst into a run, chasing Maev. She ran, fleeing them, pawing for her sword but not finding it. Damn it! Where was the blade? The sun dipped behind the buildings, shrouding the labyrinth in darkness, and the wolves were gaining on her, and—

"Mammoth Arse!" Dorvin grabbed her shoulders. "Bloody stars, you almost ran over me. What are you running from?"

She blinked. "I . . ." The sunlight was shining again. She stood on a cobbled street, and the pyramid rose ahead behind trees and homes. She shook her head wildly. "There were wolves. Did you see them? More wolves like the demon ones we saw."

His eyebrows rose so high they almost touched his hairline. "Wolves? You're out of your gourd. There are no wolves here." He dropped his voice to a whisper. "But say, have you seen any outhouses? I've really got to piss bad. Thought I found a few places—a few trees to water, if you will—but everywhere people are looking at me, and I can't piss with anyone looking at me." He winced and danced around. "Damn it, I got to go, or I swear I'll explode. I—" He reached down to his crotch, then froze. "It's . . . Oh, stars." He paled, trembled, and reached into his pants.

"Dorvin!" Maev groaned. "That's disgusting, even for you."

"Mammoth Arse, be serious!" He rummaged inside his trousers. "It's gone. My manhood. It's been cut off." Tears filled his eyes.

"You had a manhood?" she asked.

He fell to his knees, trembling, pawing at himself and blubbering. Before Maev would say more, Alina raced toward them from an alleyway. Her arms were crossed over her chest, and she panted, knelt, and trembled.

"Maev, a cloak!" she said. "Please. My clothes just vanished. They can all see me naked." The druid looked up with entreating eyes. "They can all see me."

A chill washed over Maev's belly. Alina was still wearing her flowing, lavender robes. What was the woman talking about?

Maev understood.

"Dreams." She growled and clutched her head. "We're asleep. We're dreaming!"

Before Maev could say more, the loose tooth in her mouth fell out. She reached up to touch her gums, and more teeth fell, crumbling to the touch. No. It wasn't real. It couldn't be real.

"Maev, help me!" Dorvin begged, reaching toward her. "Help me find it. Help me sew it back on."

Alina trembled. "Please, Maev, a cloak."

"Listen to me!" Maev said. "We're just dreaming now—all of us. We're having a nightmare. Maybe we're asleep or maybe . . . maybe something in this city has us dreaming when we're awake." She grabbed the siblings by their collars and yanked them up. "Hurry up. We must find the Vir Requis who live here, then leave this place. Follow me and remember: Whatever terrors you see are not real."

As they kept walking through Bar Luan, Maev forced herself to ignore the nightmares: the growling wolves, her falling teeth, her arms dwindling to rubbery strands, and the visions—more terrible than any other—of her family burning, dying, begging for her. Tanin crawled along the cobblestones, cut off below the ribs, his entrails dragging through the dust. He reached out to her, pleading for death. Her father hung from a tree, his neck stretched, his tongue hanging loose, his eyes staring at her with condemnation, blaming her for his death. Her little sister, fallen Requiem, was still alive here, still only a toddler, racing toward Maev only for arrows to pierce her flesh.

Just dreams, Maev kept telling herself. *Just waking nightmares.*

They kept walking, soon reaching a wide, cobbled courtyard larger than the entire village of Oldforge. A single tree grew from the center, taller than any tree Maev had ever seen; it must have stood three hundred feet tall. Its trunk and branches were black, and its leaves were deep blue. Golden pollen glided from the tree like countless fireflies. Many Bar Luanites—at least a thousand—moved in circles around the tree, all clad in white robes, all praying. They reached out to touch the black trunk, and they breathed deeply, inhaling the pollen, chanting out a word again and again: "Shenhavan. Shenhavan."

The three Vir Requis walked slowly into the courtyard. The crowd swept them up, tugging them into the circular movement. The chants rose, and the people wept as they prayed to the tree.

"I think it's their god," Dorvin said.

Alina smiled wryly. "You yourself have some magical powers of insight."

One Bar Luanite turned toward them. He was an old man, his face oval, his eyes wide, so short he barely reached Maev's shoulder. He wore white robes and a silver necklace. Or was he old? No wrinkles marred his face, and Maev wondered if he was even older than her; like most Bar Luanites, he seemed ageless.

"Pray," he said; Maev was surprised to hear him speak her tongue. "Pray to Shenhavan. Shenhavan always listens. Pray in your mind."

With that, the man vanished into the crowd as quickly as a drop of water into a maelstrom. Maev moved her tongue in her mouth, feeling more teeth crumble. She looked up at the tree, and the tree seemed to stare back. Every one of its blue leaves seemed like an eye. The soul of the tree thrummed through her, ancient and all knowing, invading her like cold wind cuts through flesh, like icy water sends chills through bones. She saw the tree and it saw her.

Please, Shenhavan, she prayed. *Let this be a dream. Let my teeth grow back.*

She had never believed in prayer. Her grandfather had prayed to the stars; he had fallen in the escarpment. Alina prayed every day and Maev had yet to see a miracle. Yet today she prayed, for today she was afraid, far from home, and caught in a waking nightmare. The tree seemed to grow larger, towering over Bar Luan, consuming her life. The crowd, the city, the world itself seemed as meaningless as insects beneath this god of wood and leaf.

Please, Shenhavan. Let this just be a dream.

She reached into her mouth and found her teeth restored. She shook with relief. The old Bar Luanite's voice echoed in her ears: *Shenhavan always listens.*

She looked at her side. Dorvin and Alina were praying to the tree too, eyes closed, palms pressed together. When they opened their eyes, they breathed out in relief. Their prayers seemed to have been answered. Dorvin patted his groin and whispered feverish thank-yous to the tree, while Alina gratefully stroked her robes.

Maev took the two by the hands. "Come, friends. To the pyramid."

They stepped out from the swirling crowd, walked down a road, and approached the towering structure. Statues shaped as men with reptilian heads rose from grass, flanking the way to a staircase that ran up the pyramid. The stairs led to a gilded archway hundreds of feet above. Maev began to climb, leading the way. Dorvin and Alina walked close behind. As they climbed, leaving the city below, the air grew cooler, easier to breathe. After a hundred steps, Maev found the fog in her mind lifting; clarity filled her as after a good, long sleep. She indeed felt as if she were waking up from sleep, leaving stifling blankets and the strange whispers of her mind. When she looked back down at the city, she still found a place of wonder—of many streets, towers, and walls—but it had become again a physical place, untouched by the surreal edges she had seen while walking through it. There was no labyrinth below, only simple streets. There were no wolves, only birds that fluttered between the trees. The great god Shenhavan no longer towered over the world but grew no taller than any other tree; its leaves were still blue but no longer invaded her like staring eyes.

She looked back up toward the archway upon the pyramid's crest. As she drew closer, she saw two guards stand there. They wore tortoise-shell breastplates, and tiger pelts hung across their shoulders. They held long clubs, the round heads spiked. When the three Vir Requis reached the archway, winded after the long climb, the guards stepped closer together, blocking the entrance.

Maev did not speak their language, but she thumped her chest and said, "Maev! Maev of Requiem." The guards remained stone-faced, and she took a step closer. "Let me through. I've come to see your leader. I've come seeking dragons."

At that last word, the guards' eyes widened. They spoke in urgent tones. "Draco! Draco!"

Maev nodded. "Yes, dracos." She raised her chin. "I myself am one among them. Let me through."

The guards sucked in breath and turned toward Alina. They stared at the druid with wide eyes. One reached out, lifted her amulet, and stared at the jewels shaped as the dragon constellation. The man dropped the talisman as if it burned him. The guards raced around the Vir Requis, blocking their descent, and unstrapped copper-tipped spears from their backs. They goaded the Vir Requis toward the archway.

"Hey, watch where you point that!" Dorvin said, shoving a spear aside. The young Vir Requis reached for his own spear. "My spear is longer than yours, and I'm going to stick it so far up your arse, it'll clean the guck between your teeth."

"Dung Beetle!" Maev shoved his spear down. "Stop that. Walk. Into the pyramid. Let's find who's in charge."

The guards prodded them with their spearheads, and the companions stepped through the archway and into the pyramid. A vast triangular chamber awaited them. It was easily the largest chamber Maev had ever seen; which, she supposed, wasn't saying much, as she had spent most of her life in a cave. Still, the place made her lose her breath. Statues lined the walls, depicting robed priests, their eyes closed, their palms pressed together. Murals of beasts covered the walls, and live beasts stood chained to columns. Maev had never seen such animals; they looked like dogs but were large as horses, and their necks were longer than their bodies, coiling toward the ceiling. At the back of the room rose a throne of granite, gold, and jewels, and upon it sat a man as strange as the animals. Clad in robes of blue and gold, he sported a white beard that flowed down to his feet. His fingernails were as long as his arms, coiling inward, and his eyebrows thrust out several inches, white as snow. Rings circled his neck, stretching it to thrice the usual length.

The guards goaded the Vir Requis down the hall toward the old king. They spoke harshly in their tongue; Maev only recognized the word "draco."

When she stood before the king, Maev raised her chin defiantly, crossed her arms, and spoke so loudly her voice echoed in the hall. "I am Maev of Requiem! We seek dragons. Do you understand my words?"

The old king leaned forward in his throne, staring down at her. His eyes narrowed, and a mirthless smile split his face. He spoke with a thick accent. "We have captured the Reptilian Ones. Their dark magic brought nightmares to our waking life." His grin widened, showing many sharp teeth. "The Reptilian Ones now languish in our dungeon, clutched among the roots of wise Shenhavan. They have cursed the glorious land of Bar Luan; they will never see daylight again." He stared at Alina. "The druid wears the Draco amulet. You three bear the black magic. You will join your brethren in darkness."

Maev growled and Dorvin raised his spear. The king snapped his fingers. Warriors emerged from shadows and unleashed the strange, gray dogs with the coiling necks. With howls, the creatures stormed forward.

JEID

He sat on the mountainside, looking south toward the hills, swaying grasslands, and misty mountains. The sun was setting, shadows and light spread across the land, and distant sheets of rain fell like curtains of gossamer. Somewhere over that southern horizon, the demon army was advancing, sniffing them out. Raem's scout had seen them; the full wrath of his host would soon swarm over Two Skull Mountain. Yet despite the fear of that southern, shadowy wilderness, Jeid preferred gazing at it than at the mountainside around him. Upon the stony slopes, the tribes of Goldtusk and Leatherwing were preparing for a wedding—a celebration that to Jeid felt more like a funeral.

He sighed and spared the wedding preparations one more glance. To his left side, the Goldtusk tribe had raised a tent upon the mountainside. Warriors guarded it, clad in the bronze breastplates Raem had given them under Zerra's rule. Laira was inside that tent now with the tribe's elder women; they would be painting her face, combing her hair, cladding her in finery, and preparing her body for her wedding night. Behind the tent rose the tribe totem pole, the gilded ivory tusk gleaming upon its crest—the god Ka'altei forever overlooking his people. The rocs of Goldtusk perched upon boulders and aeries across the mountain, staring south, and upon them sat the tribe hunters, weapons in their hands. It was a wedding, and it was a preparation for war—Jeid didn't know which coming event he feared the most.

He turned toward his right side. Here the Leatherwing tribe too prepared for both wedding and war. Chieftain Oritan stood among his people, dressed in a tiger pelt. One by one, his people approached to draw a line in white paint across his chest— a show of respect and servitude. A golden vessel lay at Oritan's feet, and every tribesman placed a gift within it—a seashell from far in the south, a metal bracelet, or simply a piece of fruit. Behind, high upon the mountain, perched the great pteros of the tribe, beasts as large as rocs, waiting for the demons to arrive.

A voice spoke behind him, high and soft. "Do not worry about her. Laira is strong. She does what she thinks is right for Requiem."

Jeid turned around. Behind him upon the mountainside sat his own people, the Vir Requis. All of Requiem, this so-called kingdom he had forged, was smaller than either tribe. Only twenty people followed him—a handful of elders, children, and young men and women. Barely a tribe, yet they were his people, and looking upon them soothed Jeid's heart and filled him with pride.

It was Bryn who had spoken, one of those Dorvin had led to Requiem. A young woman of fiery orange hair, she gazed upon him with brown eyes. Freckles covered her face, as plentiful as dandelions upon a spring field. She wore deerskin breeches, a gray-blue tunic, and a leather belt.

"Laira is the strongest woman I know," Jeid replied. "And for that I worry. She deserves more than to be a chieftain's wife."

Bryn sat down beside him. They stared south together at the misty landscape. Bryn pulled her knees to her chest and laid her chin upon them. "I lived in a village somewhere beyond the horizon, I did. Tended to sheep and all. Lived in a little hut with a leaky roof. Sometimes I gathered berries in the forest, walking barefoot like a beast. But Laira is a great leader of a great tribe;

she will now become a queen of two tribes." Bryn smiled softly. "A queen of two tribes! What could be greater in the world?"

"To be a queen of *Requiem*," Jeid said firmly.

Bryn looked at him. She raised an eyebrow and smiled crookedly. "You are Requiem's king; would you have her be your wife instead?"

"That's not what I meant," Jeid said. "I mean that Laira is one of us—a Vir Requis. The first one to have joined my family. She suffered, fought, and rose to power, and now . . . now Requiem loses her."

The wind ruffled Bryn's curly red hair. "I had a boy I loved once. Foolish thing, he was. Wandered aimlessly about the village most days, charming girls when he should have been tending to crops. I chased him for years until he married another." She sighed and tsked her tongue. "Sometimes they get away."

"That's not what I meant!" Jeid repeated, feeling his cheeks flush. Of course he didn't want Laira to be his own wife. It was preposterous. First of all, Laira was far too young for him, only half his age. Secondly, Jeid only loved one woman—his late wife, the beautiful and wise Keyla, her hair golden, her eyes kind. He loved Laira as a friend, as a great light of Requiem, and he wanted more for her. He wanted her to fly at his side, a leader of dragons. Not to surrender herself to Oritan, to sacrifice her joy for her kingdom. That was all . . . wasn't it?

He closed his eyes. He thought back to the first night Laira had come to him—starving, wounded, half-dead and half-naked, a waif covered in cuts and burns. He had healed her. He had slept with her in his arms. He had loved her from the first moment she had stumbled into the escarpment. He had watched her grow from that broken, dying girl into a strong woman, a leader, a great warrior for Requiem.

And now she will be his wife. Now she will belong to a stranger.

His throat constricted.

I love you, Laira, he thought. *And I can't bear to lose you to him.*

Bryn was looking at him, her eyes soft, and Jeid had the strange feeling that she could read every thought in his mind. She wiggled closer and placed her hand on his knee.

"You are our king," she said, her brown eyes earnest, her hair like a pyre of flame in the sunset. "And you will lead us to victory. I do not know if Dorvin and the others will return. I do not know if Issari will claim the throne of Eteer. I do not know if Laira's heart will lie among the stars of Requiem or the might of her tribes. But I know this: I will fight for you, King Aeternum. I will forever fly by your side." She raised her chin. "Requiem! May our wings forever find your sky."

Jeid repeated the prayer, but it felt hollow to him. Tonight he wanted to be strong, proud, a great leader for Bryn and the others to follow. But he felt afraid. When he looked into the southern horizon, he wanted to think of King's Column rising there, of the glory and light of Requiem. But he only thought of the demon menace, of the host of many terrors flying here, of King Raem whom he would face in battle. For all her proud words, would Bryn die in this battle? Would he lose her and the others like he'd lost so many—his wife, his daughter, his father? Jeid's heart sank and he could barely breathe, and even the sight of Bryn's earnest eyes could not soothe him.

ISSARI

She marched toward the palace, leading an army of a thousand men, prepared to tame a demon.

The city of Eteer lay in ruin around her, eerily silent. Only a few cypress trees still grew upon the once-lush hills; most lay charred. Once hundreds of ships had sailed in the canal that flowed below the western hills; now only a few military vessels patrolled the water, all the merchants gone. Once many city folk had bustled on this very boulevard where Issari walked; now the people hid in their brick homes, the doors and windows barred. Even the great temple of Taal—she could see its columns a mark away upon the Hill of Vines—had lost its glory. The claws of demons had scarred its columns, and soot darkened its walls.

Tanin walked at her side, his eyes dark. He held his dagger before him. "Whatever happens, I will fight for you, Issari—with blade and with fire."

She looked at the young northerner. The sight of him— tall, a little awkward, clad in fur, his hair in disarray and his face so earnest—soothed her. Evil darkened the world, but Tanin was good. Tanin was loyal. Tanin was perhaps the brightest beacon of her heart.

"When we face Angel, I don't think bronze or dragonfire can help us." She opened her palm, revealing the amulet embedded into the flesh. "If there is any power to tame her, it lies with Taal."

Yet she heard the doubt in her voice. If Taal was truly the Father of All Gods, a great deity who loved Eteer, how had he let this evil befall them? Was Taal himself aligned with these demons? After all, some old books of lore claimed that Angel was Taal's daughter. Raem too worshiped the silver god, and he commanded an unholy host. How could Issari stake the future of her kingdom on a god whose love she doubted?

She took a deep breath. *Perhaps you are testing me, Taal. Your light has helped me before, and your power has joined with my very body. I am your priestess, your warrior, your servant. Be with me today.* She raised her eyes. The sky was blue and bright, the sun beating down, but Issari prayed to other gods too. *If you look down upon me, stars of Requiem, and if you see me as your daughter, help me too. Help me defeat the demon host that would kill your children.*

They kept walking, heading closer to the palace. It rose ahead upon a hill—her old home. Blue bricks formed its base, inlaid with golden reliefs of winged bulls, roaring lions, and chariots full of soldiers. Indigo columns lined the palace's higher floors, capped with gold. Balconies thrust out like mushrooms upon a tree. Once lush gardens had draped off these balconies and the palace roof; they had burned in the war. Once a waterfall had cascaded down the palace wall into a pool in the gardens; it had run dry. Once this had been a home to Issari; today a creature of flame and stone lurked within.

She turned to look at the soldiers who followed her. Each man wore a bronze breastplate and helmet, and they held round shields and khopeshes. Spears hung across their backs. She had a thousand men; she had to fight only one demon. Issari suspected this might be like a thousand butterflies attacking a bear. She caressed her amulet. *Just so long as there's one bee in the bunch.*

She raised her head, squared her shoulders, and marched on, climbing the hill toward the palace gates.

No guards stood here; none were necessary, for nobody sane would enter this place with the creature that lurked within. The bronze doors seemed to glower at her, their knobs shaped as great phalli, symbols of fertility. She grabbed the handles, took a deep breath, and shoved the doors open.

A dark hall awaited her, lined with columns. Once a mosaic had covered the floor; it lay smashed and stained with demon drool, blood, and seed. Once statues of erstwhile kings had stood between the pillars; their heads had been removed, replaced with demon sculptures of stinking flesh stitched together into mocking faces. Once the throne had risen here in a beam of light, and great kings had sat upon it. Now, coiling around this chair, slumbered the Queen of the Abyss.

When first risen into the world, Angel had been no larger than Issari, a woman of stone and fire and bat wings. After feeding on human flesh, she had grown to an obscene size. The Demon Queen was now as large as a dragon, too large to stand upright within this hall. She lay on the ground, wrapped around the throne like a girl holding a doll. Cracks appeared on her stony body, seeping smoke and lava. Her chest rose and fell, and her eyes were narrowed to orange slits. Her wings stretched out like sails, and her claws rose taller than swords. With every deep breath, she exhaled smoke and sulfuric fumes. A small scar still marred the demon's cheek—the mark Issari's amulet had given her.

I hurt her, Issari thought, hiding the amulet within her fist. *I can hurt her again.*

She stepped deeper into the hall. Tanin walked at her side, his jaw clenched, his brow damp, his dagger raised. Behind, the first of Issari's soldiers entered too, their helmets hiding their faces. Still the Demon Queen slept—the deep slumber of one so powerful she knows none can hurt her.

Issari took several more steps until she stood in the center of the hall. To her right rose a statue of her father, the only one still with its original head. Issari took a deep breath and spoke so loudly her voice echoed.

"Arise, Queen of Devilry, and heed me! I am Issari Seran. I am henceforth Queen of Eteer. Release my throne and obey me!"

For a long moment, Angel still lay with closed eyes, though her breath grew more rapid, and her claws trailed along the floor. One red eye opened, blazing with the light of a sun. The demon snorted.

"You are Queen of the Whores. You're not worthy of a latrine for a throne. Return to your banishment or wait here until your father returns to slay you."

Issari smiled thinly. "Last time we met, Angel of the Abyss, you screamed, leaped upon me, tried to crush and deform me. Now you tell me to leave? I see the mark on your face. Do you fear me, Angel?"

The demon queen hissed, her tongue flicking. Slowly she rose to a crouch, body creaking like moving stones, her wings spreading wide. She moved like smoke unfurling from burning forests. Both eyes opened now, smelters of molten rock, and lava dripped between dagger-like fangs. She slammed her claws down, clutching the throne.

"Take one more step, reptile, and you will not die. Not for thousands of years." Angel licked her lips, her tongue as thick as a human arm, dripping sizzling saliva. "But you will beg me for death. As I sew more heads onto your body, you will beg. As I drink your blood, only to pump you full of more hot liquid, you will weep and beg harder. As all the creatures of the Abyss consume you—and thousands still lurk below—you will scream for death. But I will not grant it. Not until you are the basest of my demons, the most monstrous among them. Only one part of you I will leave unbroken." Angel grinned. "Your mind. Your sanity, your consciousness, your memory, your sense of self—all those will remain. Forever will you feel the pain, the horror, the ripping agony over what you've become. That will be your lot." She rose higher, and fire blazed within the cracks along her body. "So step closer, Queen of Filth, and we will begin."

Issari took a deep breath, and her eyes stung. *For Eteer. For Requiem. For Tanin.*

She raised her fist and uncurled her fingers, revealing her amulet. "By the light of Taal, I tame you!"

Her palm thrummed and light blazed out in a beam.

Angel screamed.

The light crashed against the demon's chest, cracking stone. Lava spilled and smoke blasted out. The demon's wings beat madly, and she tried to lunge forward, but the light slammed her back against the wall. Stones cracked. A chunk of the ceiling fell. Issari took a step closer, hand held before her, drenching the towering demon with her god's light.

"Kneel before me, Angel!" Issari shouted. "Kneel and accept me as your queen, or die in my light."

Angel hissed, cursed, retched out embers. She spat a glob of dark drool, trying to block the light. Issari, expecting the attack, dodged the projectile. She took another step forward. Her talisman's light spun, howling like a storm. The palace trembled. Angel thrashed against the wall, tail whipping about, wings churning smoke.

"Kneel, Queen of Demons! Kneel and serve me. I am Queen of Eteer and you will accept my reign."

The Demon Queen began to laugh.

It was a horrible laugh, a sound of anguish, of pure hatred forged in the depths. Even in the light drenching her, her chest rose and fell, and her eyes burned, two mocking forge fires. The queen rose taller, her head brushing the ceiling, and opened her arms wide, her claws sprouting flame.

"It will take more than the light of a sunlit god to burn me." Angel flexed her claws. "Taal is my father, but he too will beg me for death. I will crush him like I will crush you. The silver god will be my slave. You two will rut in the mud before me."

Keeping her light upon the queen, Issari looked over her shoulder at her army. The soldiers stood in the hall, swords and shields raised. Issari spoke only two soft words.

"Kill her."

With howls, Tanin at their lead, the soldiers rushed forth.

Angel's laughter echoed in the hall.

The soldiers roared for their god and kingdom. Khopeshes swung. Spears flew.

Blades shattered against the demon's stone skin. Spears splintered. Angel swiped her claws, tossing men aside like plates knocked off a table. Soldiers clattered down. Arrows fired, snapping against the demon. She laughed, swung her claws again, and tossed men against the walls. They thudded and crashed down, and angel stomped her feet, crushing their armor and bones. Tanin slammed his dagger into the queen's leg, thrusting the blade into a crack in the stone. The queen shrieked, a sound like shattering glass. A column cracked. Angel kicked, and Tanin flew through the air and thudded against the floor.

"Tanin!"

Issari's eyes stung. She wanted to run to him, but she couldn't. She forced herself to step closer to the Demon Queen, shining her light upon her. Angel still had her back to the wall, battling the soldiers; the men seemed as small as wolves trying to take down a mammoth. But Issari was hurting her; she could see scars upon the demon's chest where the light shone. She raised her palm higher, bringing the light to blaze against Angel's eyes.

The Demon Queen screeched. This time there was no mirth in her voice, no cruelty—only pain.

"Men, chain her up!" Issari said.

Soldiers rushed forth, tossing grapples connected to thick chains. The bonds swung across Angel and men tugged back, tightening the chains. One grapple drove into a crack in Angel's belly, and she screamed again.

"The sweet spawn!" Tears of blood poured from her blinded eyes. "The child of a king! The babe in my womb!"

Issari froze, fear gripping her. The child of a king? Did . . . No. No, it was impossible.

"Tug her down!" Issari shouted.

Angel flailed, struggling to toss off the chains. The grapple dug deeper into her belly. "You are slaying your brother, princess!" cried the demon. "Your father's son festers within my womb. You are killing him."

Issari could barely breathe. Tears flooded her eyes and bile filled her throat. "You lie!"

The demon shrieked, wings beating, legs kicking back soldiers. "Cut me open and see him if you like. Your own flesh and blood."

My father has lain with her. His child is within. Issari trembled. *Oh, Taal . . . don't let this be true.*

She trembled so violently she lowered her beam of light.

The instant Angel was free from the ray, she screamed hoarsely, and her fire blasted out in rings. Men fell, burning. The Demon Queen kicked, overturning the throne. The heavy seat of stone slammed into Issari, knocking her down. She lay pinned beneath it.

Her eyes rolled back. Darkness spread across her. She struggled for consciousness. She blinked feebly, and through smoke and flame, she saw Angel battling soldiers, tossing them aside, cracking their bodies, tearing off their limbs and guzzling them down. Issari tried to raise her hand, to shine the light, but she was too weak, and the glow of her amulet dimmed. In the darkness, Angel's fire grew, licking the ceiling, blazing over men.

"You have failed, Issari!" Angel's voice rose from the battle. "Eteer is mine. Requiem will fall. Your long night begins. Your—"

Angel screamed.

She stumbled back.

Tanin stood before her, no taller than her waist, driving his dagger into a crack along her belly—the same place where the grapple had cut.

"If light will not tame you, metal will." Tanin twisted the blade and tugged it back; it came free covered in ooze. The demon crashed down, wailing, clutching her belly. At once soldiers leaped around her, tossing chains.

My brother. The thought rose through the fog enveloping Issari's mind. *My brother is in her belly. He's hurt.*

As Angel writhed on the floor, chains wrapping around her, Tanin ran toward the fallen throne. He gripped the seat, strained, and pulled it back upright. He knelt above Issari, concern softening his eyes. A bloody gash dripped upon his forehead, and he touched her cheek. His voice seemed to come from far away.

"Issari! Issari, oh stars. Can you hear me?"

She nodded and, with his help, rose to her feet. She stared at the corner where Angel was screaming. Chains engulfed her, the grapples digging into her innards. Her tongue flailed, and soldiers slammed shields against her head, knocking it against the floor. But Issari knew that mere mortals could not keep Angel down for long; the Queen of the Abyss had reigned in the underworld for millennia, and already her wounds were healing, the cracks on her stony body closing up. Already fresh fire blazed in the demon's eyes.

Issari looked back toward the throne.

The throne of Eteer. The throne that will give me power over her.

She walked toward it, each step feeling like a journey of many marks. With a deep breath, her fingers trembling, she sat upon the throne.

Angel screamed.

The demon convulsed, her tail cracking the wall. Bricks fell. The floor cracked open. Fire leaked and lava flowed along the floor. The demon's eyes blazed as Angel struggled to rise.

"You will scream, harlot! You will be eating your own hands with hunger! You will tear apart your own body to end your pain but live on! You—"

"I am your queen!" Issari stared down from the throne, palm raised. "I sit upon the throne. The army of Eteer obeys my command. You are bound to this throne, Angel, and you will serve your rightful ruler."

Tanin raised his dagger and shouted, "Queen Issari!"

Across the hall, the soldiers picked up his chant. "Queen Issari! Queen Issari! Blessed be Issari, Queen of Eteer!"

Issari rose to her feet, left the throne, and walked toward the palace doors. She stepped through them and gazed down upon the city of Eteer, heart of the Eteerian civilization: thousands of houses, the canal with its ships, the city walls, the sea beyond. Her soldiers stood at her sides.

One soldier, a young captain, blew a silver horn. People emerged from their homes below, climbed onto roofs, and stared at the palace. Issari gazed down upon her people.

"Queen Issari Seran reigns!" shouted a soldier. "Behold Blessed Queen Issari!"

And she knew: The kingdom was hers. The people accepted her; so would Angel.

When she returned to the throne room, she found the chained demon shaking, lying on the floor, bloody tears leaking from her eyes. Her wounds dripped, and her wings lay limp.

"Do you accept my dominion?" Issari asked. "Answer, Creature of the Abyss! Do you accept me as your ruler, the rightful Queen of Eteer?"

Angel fixed her with a narrow, pained stare. She hissed, smoke seeping between her teeth. "By the ancient laws binding me to servitude, I accept, Queen Issari. Your father no longer rules. The throne is yours . . . as is my allegiance."

Issari took a shuddering breath. Tanin approached her and she clasped his hand, relief spreading across her.

"Then I command you to call your demon soldiers home," said Issari. "Withdraw them from the northern lands. Return with them into the Abyss, and never more emerge."

But Angel seemed not to hear. She writhed on the floor, her teeth clenched, and she let out a howl. Her claws dug into the floor. Her belly bulged and contracted. Her legs spread open.

"What is she doing?" Tanin whispered, face pale.

Issari took a step back. Terror flooded her. She could not speak.

"I serve you, Queen Issari," said the demon, voice dripping with pain. Blood beaded upon her brow. "But our children, Issari . . . our children are only half-demons. No laws of servitude bind them." She tossed back her head and screamed. "Welcome, children of darkness! Welcome, sons and daughters of mortals! My rein ends; the age of the nephilim begins."

A cackle rose.

A creature emerged.

Issari screamed.

RAEM

The scout flew upon the wind, heading toward the demon host.

"Ah, our dear friend returns," Raem said. "The dragons have been found."

He rode upon Anai, his bat-like demon, leading his host of a thousand. The sky was clear and blue, though the smoke of demons darkened the land. Below them the forests wilted, the rivers turned gray, and the grass burned. The trail of death spread behind them across the land, all the way to the southern coast. Ahead still stretched the wilderness, the untamed land that he would bring under his dominion. With the power of his demon army, he would not only crush the fledgling nation of Requiem; he would conquer the open north, turning Eteer into an empire.

"What is it?" Ciana asked, disgust filling her voice.

The young woman sat in the saddle before Raem, her back pressed to his body. Her weapons hung from her belt, and the wind ruffled her fur tunic. She wore the bronze mask that hid the ruin of her face, but Raem could see the scars of dragonfire peeking from beneath. She had only taken off her mask once, but the memory still pounded through Raem—a faceless woman, ravaged, deformed, an abomination unto Taal and his vision of purity. The dragons had done that to her. The dragons would suffer tenfold.

He stroked her hair. "Do not fear my scout, Ciana, my dear. It is a disgusting creature, an unholy insult to Taal, but a useful servant. It will deliver the dragons to us."

The creature that flew toward them looked like a severed hand the size of a tree. An eye blinked upon each shriveled finger, and a mouth opened upon its palm, lined with many teeth. When it reached the demon army, it fluttered toward Raem and panted, tongue dripping. It spoke in a high-pitched voice, the voice of a child.

"King Raem! Weredragons in the north. Four hands of them. Rocs too. Flying north! To a mountain like two skulls. I see them. I lead you there."

Raem smiled thinly. Four hands—only twenty weredragons. He laughed. Was that all this King Aeternum could muster—twenty lizards? Raem looked behind him at the sprawling host. Twenty dragons wouldn't even feed these creatures.

"This is no war," he said. "This is stomping on an insect."

Ciana twisted around in her saddle. She stared at him through her mask holes. "King Aeternum—Jeid Blacksmith was once his name—is crueler than any other weredragon you've ever seen. He burned me. He took my face. He is not an insect but a terror." She sneered and clutched her bow. "And we will slay him. We will slay them all. The king, his son, and all the rest of them."

They flew on, the land wilting below them, until they reached a gushing river that split the land. Upon its bank nestled villages, benighted human settlements barely better than the dens of animals. Ciana pointed down at one of the backwaters.

"Oldforge," she said. "My village. The weredragon family lived there once. That is where Tanin loved me." She clenched her fists. "That is where Jeid burned me."

Raem stared down at the village, sneering. As they flew closer, details emerged. He saw only a few scattered clay huts, their roofs thatched with straw. Only a single brick building rose here, perhaps a smithy, smaller than even a humble Eteerian home. Reed boats swayed at the docks.

Raem laughed. "The fabled King of Requiem—not a son of nobility or light after all. A simple barbarian. He may style himself a royal leader, but—"

He bit down on his words and frowned. Seated in the saddle before him, Ciana was trembling. When Raem leaned around her, he saw tears pouring from beneath her mask. He felt something he had not felt in a long time, not since before his children had betrayed him. He felt pity. He felt . . . love. He stroked the young woman's hair.

"Sweetness, why do you tremble? Why do your tears fall?"

She stared down at the village. Her voice shook. "I can still feel it. His fire flowing over me. I can still hear it. My own screams. Even now it burns." She touched her bronze mask. "I now have a face of metal. I now have a mind of memories. They did this to me here. This village is the scar that will forever mark my body and twist inside me."

Raem held her close to him, and his rage flared. His voice hissed through his clenched jaw. "Then this is the village where you will be reborn. Here you were hurt. Here I will heal you." He dug his spurs into his demonic bat and he roared for his army to hear. "To the village! Land in Oldforge."

As they descended, he sucked in strained breaths. His fingers trembled and Ciana was warm against him. He had seen it done before. He had seen the masterwork of these demons, their hooks and needles creating artwork from flesh and bone and blood. They had used their art to torture; now they would use it to heal.

He kissed the back of Ciana's head. "You are a true warrior of Taal, a great huntress of dragons. I will heal you."

Villagers fled as the demon army landed in the village. They locked themselves in homes, only for demons the break down the doors and drag them out. Some fled into the fields, only for more creatures to pounce and grab them. A few villagers tried to fight with arrows and spears; demon acid, claws, and fangs tore them apart.

"Do not yet feed!" Raem shouted. He dismounted his bat and walked among the huts. "Bring all the women to me. Line them up."

His creatures bustled through the village, dragging women out of homes. They all seemed crude compared to the beauties of Eteer; these northern women were taller and wider, their hair lighter, their garments made of fur, leather, and homespun. Yet he would find a suitable one among them. A few were screaming, others weeping; all tried to flee, but the demons held them fast with constricting tongues and coiling claws. A few of their menfolk tried to save the women, staging some heroic assault; they fell fast, their blood feeding the soil. Finally a score of young women stood in a line, clutched in the grip of the demons.

"Come, Ciana!" Raem said. "Come see them. Is there one you favor?"

Ciana stepped forward hesitantly. "Raem, what . . . I know these women. I know them all by name." She tilted her head. "What will you do to them?"

He turned toward her, smiling. Her bronze mask was beautiful, but behind it her face was gone, and that was an insult to his god, an insult he must erase. "Who among them is prettiest, do you think? Which face do you like?"

Her hand crept toward the hilt of her dagger. "Raem, what—"

"I like this one," he said, interrupting her. He pointed at a tall, lovely woman with full red lips, pale cheeks, and long eyelashes. "She will suit our purpose. Stitchmark!" He coned his palm around his mouth. "Stitchmark, to me!"

Rancid wings buzzed. A demon landed and clattered toward him on many hooked feet. Stitchmark looked like a great gray beetle, its shell spiked. Long arms grew from its body, and each hand sprouted metal tools as fingers. There were needles, scalpels, spools of thread, bone saws, and more. A series of glass lenses on hinges covered its eyes. When the demon reached Raem, one lens left its eye, replaced with another. The demon bowed.

"Stitchmark, I like this young woman's face." He pointed at the villager; she was weeping and screaming, trying to escape the creature that held her, looking lovelier than ever. "Give Ciana her face."

The woman wept.

Ciana took a step back, gasping.

Stitchmark leaped forth and began to work.

"Hush, Ciana," Raem said as the young huntress trembled. "Here, lay down in the grass. Close your eyes. Let Stitchmark do his work and soon it will all be over."

Blood flowed across the village. The demons crowded around, licking their chops, admiring the work in progress. Raem stood among them, a smile stretching across his lips. Scalpels cut and spools turned and needles raced.

When Ciana rose to her feet, blood trickling down her neck and forehead, Raem approached her. He touched her pale cheek, and he kissed her full red lips. The demons feasted behind them.

"You are beautiful, my Ciana, my sweet killer of dragons."

They left the village full of blood, bones, and a discarded bronze mask.

LAIRA

She stood in her tent, remembering the day her mother had died.

She had stood waiting in a tent then too. She had spent days in that tent, the sounds of her mother's trial—screaming, shouting, cursing—rising outside. That day eleven years ago, she had emerged into the daylight to see her mother burned at the stake, to see life change into a fever dream of hunger, abuse, and hope for dragons. Now she waited in a tent again, and again when she emerged, her life would change, and the Laira she had known would be gone, replaced with somebody new.

She lifted the bronze handheld mirror and examined her reflection. So many times, Chieftain Zerra would force her to look at her reflection, to see the creature he had turned her into—a waif with a crooked chin, slanted mouth, sheared hair, and cheeks gaunt with hunger and neglect. Her chin was still crooked, her mouth still slanted, but she no longer saw a starving wretch. Her cheeks were fuller, her hair longer, her green eyes brighter. A headdress of silver and topaz adorned her, and she wore a fine cloak of wool woven with golden threads. Beneath it, her tribe's women had painted totem charms upon her body—paw prints upon her belly, rivers that coiled around her breasts, and golden tusks upon her thighs. The symbols would make her fertile, the women had said, and they would make Chieftain Oritan desire her. Today she would be his.

She closed her eyes, shuddering to remember the only other man who had lain with her. She had given herself to Chieftain Zerra in return for a roc to ride, and the memory still made her wince. Would Oritan too take her roughly, hurting her innards, drooling upon her, digging his fingernails down her back? Or would he be gentle like some women whispered their husbands could be? Laira did not know, but whatever happened, she swore to bear it. For her people. For Requiem.

The tent flap opened. Lokania, a gatherer of berries of the Goldtusk tribe, stood at the entrance. She held a jeweled bowl of ram's blood, signifying the purity of matrimony. The young woman had long golden hair and blue eyes. Fifteen years old, she was slim of body and quick of fingers; she had woven Laira's garment herself. Since Laira had become chieftain, Lokania had served her—preparing her meals, tending to her hair and garments, and running her errands in the tribe. Today Lokania's eyes were bright, her mouth solemn.

"It is time, my chieftain. He awaits."

Laira took a deep breath. She laid down her mirror and stepped closer to Lokania. The girl kissed her fingertips, then placed them against Laira's neck, an old blessing.

"You will please him in his bed, my chieftain." The young woman lowered her eyes and blushed. "He is very strong."

Laira touched the girl's hair. "Walk with me, Lokania. Walk with me to the tusks."

They left the tent together. Upon the mountainside stood the two tribes. The Goldtusks stood to Laira's left, lower upon the slope, clad in fur, bones, and beads, their beards long, their bronze armor bright. To Laira's right, higher up on the mountain, stood the Leatherwing tribe; they had no bronze, but they wore armor of bone and boiled leather, and apes' skulls hid their faces.

In a small cluster ahead stood the Vir Requis, twenty in all—
haggard, wearing only tattered wool and fur. As she walked
forward, Laira did not know who her people were, who she was.
Was she a princess of Eteer, seeking a new home? Was she a
daughter of Goldtusk? Was she a new bride of Leatherwing?

She raised her eyes and found Jeid staring at her across the
mountain path. His eyes were hurt, but she saw the love in them,
and she remembered the first time she had met him, how he had
healed her, how she had slept in his arms, how he had made her
dream of dragons come true. And Laira knew: *My home is Requiem.
I may wear the clothes of Goldtusk, and I may be a bride of Leatherwing,
and I may be an exiled princess of Eteer . . . but I am only one thing. A Vir
Requis. What I do today I do for Requiem.* She looked into her king's
eyes. *Even if I hurt you, Jeid.*

Two scrimshawed mammoth tusks rose ahead, forming an
arch. Strings of beads, dried animal hearts, and raven skulls hung
from them, swaying in the wind, symbols of fertility and fortune.
Laira approached the ivory archway, walking slowly, all eyes upon
her. Lokania walked ahead of her, holding her jeweled bowl,
sprinkling droplets of ram's blood with every step. The blood
stained Laira's bare feet as she walked, blessing her path toward
her new lord. The ram who had given this gift burned in a fire pit
upon the mountain, its smoke rising to curl around Goldtusk's
totem pole, a sacrifice to Ka'altei. A second fire burned higher up
near the mountaintop, its smoke thicker and darker—a young
woman of Leatherwing, given alive to the flame, a sacrifice to the
cloud-gods of Two Skull Mountain.

Thus do I buy hope for Requiem, Laira thought, eyes stinging
from the smoke or perhaps from her grief. *With the life of a ram and
the life of a girl.*

She reached the mammoth tusks. Chieftain Oritan stood
under the arch, clad in his armor of bones—an ape's rib cage

around his chest, its skull over his head. His blades hung from his belt, and a necklace of scalps hung around his neck, trophies from his enemies. As Laira looked at him, she saw a leader, a warrior, a killer, and she thought of Jeid's kind eyes, and she steeled her heart. If Oritan hurt her, she would bear it. If she suffered, well— she had already suffered much in her life, and her heart was hardened. Her father flew toward this mountain, perhaps only moments away. Laira needed this chieftain's warriors, and she would sell herself to him, and she would endure any pain for her kingdom.

Let the stars above know, she thought, *and let future poets sing, and let all generations of dragons whisper of Laira, a daughter of Requiem— and the sacrifice she made for the light of King and Column.*

"For King and Column," she whispered and stepped under the archway.

She stood before the chieftain, so small by his towering form. Lokania stood at her side, holding her bowl, her eyes lowered. At Oritan's side stood one of his servants, a young woman clad only in a loincloth, her body painted white and red, a headdress of bones and beads upon her dark hair. Lokania dipped her finger into her bowl, then pressed the blood on to Laira's lips; it tasted coppery and was still warm. Oritan's servant reached into a box of ashes—taken from the burnt woman upon the mountaintop—and scattered them on Oritan's chest, a blessing from the dead. A shaman of Leatherwing stepped forth, an ancient man with a long white beard, three ape skulls stacked together above his head. He chanted, scattered green powder from a bowl, and prayed to the gods. And with that they were joined. And with that Goldtusk and Leatherwing were one. With that Laira was his.

The tribesmen cheered. Songs erupted across the mountainsides, even with an enemy approaching, even with the darkness inside her. Men drank spirits from copper-banded horns and skulls, and bison and deer cooked in pits. An entire mammoth, hunted on the plains below, roasted atop a great fire, the centerpiece of the feast. Men played drums and lutes, and people danced, and the smoke and firelight stung Laira's eyes. She wanted to return to her people, to the Vir Requis, to stand among them, but perhaps they were no longer her people—only in her heart. Today she had given herself fully to both tribes, and so she sat upon the mountainside with Oritan, accepting the gifts the people brought forth—pelts, beads, pottery, weapons, statuettes, jewels. Food and spirits were brought to them, though she ate and drank little; her belly was already full with fear.

And thus the beaten, half-starved girl has become a great leader, she thought. She looked over the crowd, seeking Jeid. *Yet I would gladly become a wretch again if I could be by his side instead.*

The crowd cheered with renewed vigor as Oritan rose to his feet, motioning for Laira to stand too. Tribesmen roared and raised their weapons as he led her away. They stepped into a cave—the skull's mouth—entering a cavern whose walls were lined with holes, each hole a home. The crowd raced around them, sweeping them into a torrent, taking them deeper into the cave, up a path, and toward one of the alcoves. A curtain of bones hid the entrance, and a song rose as Oritan led her into the chamber, leaving the crowd outside.

Laira took a shaky breath. *For Requiem.*

She found herself in a round room, its walls painted with scenes of running bison, saber-toothed cats, and herds of mammoths. Many trophies filled the chamber: chalices of silver, shields of bronze, gilded skulls, and many blades and bows. A bed of furs lay at the back, and to there Oritan led her. The crowd still sang outside, but the sound was muffled.

He stood before her, clad in his armor of bones. His helmet still hid his head. He stared at her silently. She stood before him and met his gaze.

"By the custom of my people," she said, "take my blade, and cut my garment from me."

She handed him her bronze sword. He accepted the short, leaf-shaped weapon, stepped closer to her, and slid the blade under her embroidered bridal garment. With a single, swift movement, he tugged the sword backward, slicing the fabric. The garment split open, revealing her small, painted breasts. He cut again, and the tatters fell to her feet, revealing her full nakedness and the totems painted upon her. She was not wide of hips or heavy of breasts as most other women of her tribe; she was small and slim, for she had spent so many years as a servant, and many scars adorned her body. She expected to see disgust in his eyes, but she saw only softness.

He dropped her sword, and Laira winced, expecting him to shove her down, to thrust into her, to claim her as Zerra had. She braced herself for the pain, and she inhaled sharply when he drew nearer. But he only touched her cheek and caressed her hair.

"Laira," he whispered. He removed his helmet, leaned down, and kissed her forehead.

She trembled as he took her into his bed of fur. For a long time, he simply caressed her hair, stroked her body, and let his lips flutter over her, tickling her with his breath. Even when he doffed his clothes, he was not rough but held her delicately, exploring her as if marveling at her body.

"You are strong but fragile," he whispered into her ear, holding her close. "You are brave but timid. And I promise you, Laira, that I will always praise your name, and I will always make you proud to be my wife."

She closed her eyes, her fear easing, and she smiled softly as his fingers trailed down her belly and reached between her thighs. And he did not hurt her, but he loved her, and she buried her hands in his hair, and for the first time in her life, Laira found pleasure in the love of a man, and she began to understand those secrets the women of her tribe would whisper in the nights. Here in their bed, he was no warrior, no slayer of enemies; he was her husband, and it was good and warm and safe. A demon army flew toward her, and the world burned, but this night she slept naked in her husband's arms and she did not dream.

ALINA

The guards shoved them into the dungeon, and the stone door slammed shut behind them, scattering dust.

Alina fell, banging her knees against the dirt floor. She coughed, her robes tangling around her, the ropes chafing her wrists and ankles. At her side, Dorvin and Maev thumped down into the dirt, their limbs tied with thick ropes. The chamber was dark; only a small hole in the ceiling let in a beam of dusty light. For long moments, Alina struggled to reclaim her breath, to focus her eyes, to make sense of her surroundings. She could see only shadows, but she sensed a presence here, something very old, very strong. A power filled this chamber, a great darkness, an ancient wisdom crushed under fear. It was so thick it spun Alina's head; she had not felt such power in the air since witnessing the magic of King's Column.

"Let us out!" Dorvin was shouting, struggling to rise, only to fall again.

"Open that door and face us like men!" Maev cried, mouth full of dust, and spat. "Cowards!"

Yet the stone door remained closed. The guards had manhandled them here across Bar Luan, taken them into a tunnel that led to this chamber beneath their holy tree, and entombed them in the shadows.

"This is all your fault, Alina." Dorvin glared at her. He managed to rise to his knees, and his eyes blazed. "Mammoth Arse and I wanted to burn the bastards. Why did you stop us?"

She glared back at him, her eyes still adjusting to the darkness. "We've not flown here to slay men. We're Vir Requis, not monsters."

"Well, now we're imprisoned Vir Requis." Dorvin huffed and tugged at his bonds. "I hope you're happy."

Maev too grumbled. "I can't believe I'm saying this, but I agree with the dung beetle. We should have burned them. This is war. You shouldn't have stopped us, Alina, and we shouldn't have listened to you."

Alina's eyes stung in the flying dust, and her wrists blazed; the rope was digging into them. She took a deep breath and stared at her companions—her oaf of a brother and the brute Maev.

"War?" She shook her head, hair flouncing. "We're at war with the demons of Eteer. Not Bar Luan. The people of Bar Luan are scared. They've been suffering nightmares for too long; we all suffered the same waking dreams. So they blamed the Vir Requis, us among them. Out of fear."

Maev gnashed her teeth. "Fear always leads to hatred. It does not excuse one's crimes." She grimaced, struggling to shift. Scales began to flow across her, and horns began to bud from her head. But when her body began to grow, the ropes dug into her wrists and ankles, shoving her back into human form. "Damn useless."

Dorvin hopped toward the wrestler. "I can try to bite the ropes off."

"Bite my backside, Dung Beetle."

"I'd love to. Meatier than a mammoth steak."

The two began to bang into each other, cussing and trying to bite. Alina sighed and looked away from the pair, examining the rest of the chamber. Her eyes slowly adjusted to the darkness, and she gasped.

Stars above!

For the first time, she noticed that others were imprisoned here—all staring at her silently. She knelt, staring back, eyes wide. Thirty or forty other prisoners were here, huddled in the shadows—men, women, children. All were tied with ropes. All were thin, pale, haggard. All were Bar Luanites, short and slim, their hair pale, their faces oval and their eyes large. Yet there was something different about them. When Alina took a deep breath, she saw it around them, limning their forms, the auras she knew no others could see. Starlight. The glow filled her eyes and warmed her heart.

"Vir Requis," she whispered.

Her brother's voice rose louder behind her. "Stars damn it, Mammoth Arse, stop biting my heels!"

Maev's voice rose in answer. "I'm trying to bite the ropes off, you puddle of piss. Stop moving! By the gods, your feet stink worse than a bloated dead marmot."

The other prisoners stared with wide eyes. Alina spoke softly. "Dorvin? Maev? We're not alone."

"Damn right we're not alone," Maev said. "The stench of your brother's feet is its own entity. Damn smell's more powerful than any totem pole. I—" She bit down on her words, finally noticing the other prisoners. "Oh soggy witch's teats."

Dorvin too finally saw the others. He spat and his eyebrows rose. "Well, bugger me. Are these the other Vir Requis?" He groaned. "Not an impressive lot, these ones. Why is it Vir Requis are never the ones in charge, always the ones hunted, killed, or tied up in a dungeon?"

Because we have no kingdom of our own, Alina thought, gazing at the others, and her eyes dampened. *Because we are scattered, misunderstood, feared, hated. But Requiem will rise. A dawn of dragons will light the world. We will unite and we will stand, and we will escape the darkness.*

"Hello, friends." She raised her amulet, and the jewels upon it glowed, forming the shape of the Draco constellation. "Hello, children of Draco, my people."

One among them stepped forth. He was a slim man, his cheeks gaunt, his eyes and hair black. He seemed taller than the others, darker, his face longer. He spoke in a heavy accent. "Hello."

Alina smiled softly. "You speak our tongue."

The man nodded. "My father is from the lands across the mountains; he was a fisherman upon the River Ranin. I know your tongue. I am Auben." He hobbled closer; his ankles and wrists were tied like all the others. "Are you too a draconian?"

"I am." Alina bowed her head. "Though we call ourselves Vir Requis—people of Requiem. A kingdom of us rises in the east, blessed in the light of our stars—a kingdom called Requiem. We've come here to find you, friends, and to bring you home."

The others whispered behind Auben, and he spent a moment translating Alina's words. Voices rose higher. One man spoke in anger, and one woman barked out what sounded like curses. Auben looked back at Alina, his eyes dark. "They say they are proud Bar Luanites, that this is their home. They scoff at a kingdom for our kind." He shook his head sadly. "For many generations, we lived in Bar Luan. Our ancestors built many of the pyramids above. Three generations ago, some among us fell ill. We could become dragons, take flight, roar fire. And for three generations, the people of Bar Luan blessed us, worshiped us as gods. And then a few years ago . . . it began. The *tanari kar*."

The people behind shuddered at the word. Some pressed their hands together in prayer.

Dorvin hobbled forward, frowning. "The tanner-what?"

Auben lowered his head. "The *tanari kar*. It means the dream curse in your tongue." He hugged himself with thin arms. "At first, the nightmares only filled our sleep, but then we began to dream in waking hours. The leaves on Shenhavan grew blue with mourning. Bar Luan fell into disrepair. The people hid in their homes. The king refused to leave his pyramid. The gardens are not tended, the forests are not hunted, the gods are not worshiped. The people of Bar Luan needed somebody to blame, and they blamed us, the draconians, those who can become the great beasts. We turned from gods in their eyes to demons. They imprisoned us here."

Maev scoffed. "That's ridiculous. The people of Bar Luan still suffer from waking nightmares. We had them ourselves up there. How can they still blame you?"

"They believe that other draconians still live aboveground, hiding their curse. Our king believes that once we are all imprisoned here, amid the roots of Great Shenhavan, the nightmares will end."

Alina looked around her, and her eyes widened. She had not seen it at first, but now she moved around the chamber, gazing with awe. The roots of a great tree grew all around them, framing the chamber like the bars of a cage. Of course—the roots of Shenhavan. The great tree itself imprisoned them here. She recognized the source of the power she had first felt when entering this place; it had not flowed from the prisoners but from the roots of the old tree. Only it was not a tree at all, at least not like any other tree in the world. This was a being far older than trees, a being of many planes of awareness, seeing from many eyes, its tendrils of thought digging deep. Its roots were like eyes, like thoughts themselves, always digging, seeing, hearing, sensing. Even now they sensed her, and Alina approached one root and placed her ear against it.

She winced and cried out in pain. A shock like a bolt of lightning shook her body. She yelped and fell.

"Alina!" Dorvin rushed forward and knelt beside her. "Alina, what in the Abyss?"

She shook, eyes wide, tongue dry. Her legs convulsed. The pain! The fear! Tears filled her eyes. "It's hurting, Dorvin. It's sensing too much. Too much. Its nerves are exposed, raw, wounded, feeling everything. Everything." Her tears streamed. "All its filters are removed, all the stimulus is overwhelming, overflowing, eyes that cannot be closed, thoughts that never end." Her voice faded into a hoarse whisper. "It's feeling us now, feeding upon us, and it wants to stop. It cannot. They dug too deep."

Dorvin held her and shook her. "Alina! What in the name of all gods are you talking about?"

"She's having a nightmare," Maev said. "It's hitting her even here."

Alina shook her head. No. No, this was no nightmare. This was too real, too raw. "Let me speak to him." She struggled to rise, still shaking. "Let me speak to Shenhavan."

She approached one of the roots, wincing at the pain emanating from it. She braced herself and placed her forehead against it. She gasped as its presence flowed into her. She whispered into it, not whispering with her mouth but letting her thoughts flow into the root.

Hello, Old One.

It replied with many voices. *It hurts us. We are exposed.*

I know, Old One. You hear too much.

We hear it all! They dug too deep. They opened our nerves. The diggers. They removed our soil, our flesh. They were afraid. We heard them.

Alina placed her hand upon a root. *You dreamed of them.*

The root thrummed. *No. We heard their dreams. We could no longer feed on soil. We fed on their nightmares. On the diggers. On the prisoners who followed. Their dreams became our nourishment, flowing through our trunk, turning it black, entering our leaves, turning them blue, flying in our pollen upon the wind.*

Alina gasped. Her chest constricted. The pollen. Of course. *You took the nightmares of prisoners into you. You could not stop it.*

The tree seemed to weep. *We could not stop it.*

Tears streamed down Alina's cheeks. *The nightmares rose through you, and you expelled them into the air. You infected the others.*

We are sorry. We are sorry. Please make it end.

Alina could no longer bear it. She pulled back from the root, and she fell onto the ground, weeping. Dorvin and Maev leaned over her, speaking to her, but she could barely hear. She whispered, her lips wet with tears. "The Vir Requis do cause the nightmares."

Auben's eyes widened and his cheeks flushed. "That is a lie! We do not—"

"By no fault of your own!" Alina said, lying in her brother's arms. "The roots of the tree. The soil was removed to create this dungeon. The roots were exposed. Lacking soil to feed upon, they fed on your dreams. Do you have nightmares in this place?"

Auben froze. He nodded slowly.

Alina smiled wryly. "In the shadows of a dungeon, most prisoners have nightmares. So did the first prisoners here— thieves and murderers imprisoned before you. The tree fed, and the nightmares spread through its pollen. The king blamed you. He imprisoned you here. But he only gave the roots new nightmares to drink." She rose to her feet. "We must leave this place. We must reveal the truth. We must end this tree's suffering."

Dorvin cleared his throat. "And free everyone. That too. That's also a little important, Alina."

She returned to the roots that enveloped the chamber, placed her forehead against one of the ropey strands, and closed her eyes. She whispered, head lowered, "You can answer prayers. You are good in your core. Free us, Shenhavan. Free us from our bonds and we will refill this cavern with soil."

For a long moment, nothing happened. Alina tugged at her bonds, but the ropes would not loosen. Alina's belly curdled. For many years, she had been able to speak to the stars, to sense warmth and guidance from them. Was her power, the insight of a druid, limited to the stars?

"Please, Shenhavan." Her eyes stung. "Free us."

Silence filled the cavern. Alina lowered her head.

I have failed.

Her eyes stung, and she thought of Requiem and her people—of Jeid, of Laira, of all the others waiting for them. The demon army would reach them, and she would perish underground, bringing no aid to her people. She—

She frowned.

She gasped.

The walls of the chamber were shaking around them.

I have no power over matter, child of starlight, spoke a voice in her head. *Only thought. Only dreams. And not only the minds of men.*

Soil fell from the walls, and rustling rose all around. A hundred holes broke open in the dirt walls between the roots. Noses and whiskers twitched. A hundred mice scurried into the chamber.

Dorvin squealed like a little girl. "Stars damn it! Get them away from me!" He began to hop around, sweat on his brow, as the mice raced around his feet. "Get them away, get them away!"

Maev rolled her eyes and snorted. "Bloody bollocks, Dung Beetle. Is the brave warrior scared of mice?"

The dark-haired young man grimaced and hopped around. "They're climbing me! Mammoth Arse, bite them off!"

The mice were not climbing only Dorvin; the rodents were scurrying up everyone's legs. Alina laughed as their fur tickled her, and she smiled because she knew that there were greater powers in this world, powers large and small that looked after her even in the darkness. Little teeth worked at the ropes binding her. All across the chamber, the mice chewed, and the bonds fell to the ground.

"Thank you, Shenhavan," she whispered, touching the roots of the tree, and she felt the warmth against her palm. She turned toward the other prisoners, their limbs free. "Stand back, friends. Stand against the wall. Make room."

The prisoners obeyed. Maev had to guide Dorvin backward; he was still slapping at his clothes, shuddering, and muttering about still feeling whiskers against him. Once they were all pressed against the opposite wall, Alina summoned her magic. Her body grew, unencumbered by the ropes. Her scales clanked. Fire filled her mouth. A lavender dragon, she raised her claws and began to dig.

She carved a tunnel, reaching far into the soil, digging through the earth, and the prisoners followed behind her.

She dug for a long time, letting the starlight inside her guide her, until she rose and emerged into a dark forest. Cold air flowed into her lungs, and the moon shone above between the branches. When Alina climbed out of the tunnel, she could see Bar Luan behind her; she had dug their way out of the city, and its pyramids and walls rose silver beyond the dark trees. She released her magic, returning to human form, and the others emerged into the night and stood around her. Alina raised her staff, and the starlight shone into its crystal and grew, a beacon for the others to circle, a light to guide her flock.

She climbed onto a fallen log and gazed upon her people. She spoke softly in the night.

"I am Alina, a daughter of Requiem, a priestess of the Draco constellation. I do not deign to lead you, for you are now free souls. But I would offer to guide you. As I've guided you to freedom, I would guide you to a revival of starlight. Requiem lies in the east beyond the rivers and mountains, and she is a kingdom of dragons, of our kind. Three generations ago, the holy stars bequeathed a blessing unto the world, gifting their magic to only a few scattered souls. For three generations, we were hunted, imprisoned, feared—here in Bar Luan, in the eastern forests, even south in the seafaring realm of Eteer. For a hundred years, we thought we are alone, but we have found one another, and we rise." Tears filled her eyes. "Join me, my friends. Follow my light, the staff that glows with starlight. Follow me to a land of scales, wings, and fire—a land of dragons. Follow me to King's Column and to King Aeternum, and Requiem will shine with our all lights. You were born in Bar Luan, a land that imprisoned you; follow me across the wilderness to Requiem and find your pride and freedom."

The Vir Requis of Bar Luan conferred amongst themselves. Alina could not understand their words, but she could guess at their meaning. She had spoken the same words to Dorvin when they had left their tribe. All those who had made it to Requiem had left their homes with heartbreak and fear, but they had all chosen the path of the stars. So did these people. Auben detached himself from the others, approached Alina, and nodded.

"We fly with you."

Alina smiled. "We will fly. But not before we heal a friend."

She returned to Bar Luan then, holding her lit staff before her, and the others followed, her light guiding them. In the city they found the people in a daze, whispering, rubbing their eyes, finally woken from the nightmares that had plagued them for so long.

"There is no more fear underground," Alina said when the King of Bar Luan approached her, riding upon a palanquin. "The roots of Shenhavan no longer feed upon the nightmares of prisoners, no longer spread those nightmares in the pollen. We will fill the dungeon with soil, and we will let Shenhavan flourish again."

The old king, tears in his eyes, watched in wonder as his people crowded around, finally free of their long fever dream.

Alina became a dragon again in the night, and this time she did not dig but filled holes, giving soil and peace to the exposed roots of an ancient god. She felt the tree in her mind, thanking her, its pain waning, like an injured man drinking soothing silverleaf. When her work was done, Alina stood before the tree, still in dragon form, and she watched as its leaves turned green again, as its trunk brightened, as life and goodness returned to the deity. The people of Bar Luan circled the tree in a great torrent, singing and chanting. Bar Luan was healed.

Alina flapped her wings and took flight, soaring toward the stars. The Draco constellation shone above, and the people of Bar Luan whirled below around their tree, and the moonlight lit the pyramids, walls, and statues of this ancient city. The others, her own people, summoned their magic. They rose as dragons in the night, forty strong, light in their eyes and fire in their mouths. The dragons of Requiem flew into the east, leaving the city of stone. They flew under the stars. They flew to Requiem. They flew to war and to hope and to a new dream.

ISSARI

Issari stood in the ravaged throne room, eyes wide, watching the Demon Queen give birth.

The creature emerged from the womb, still wrapped in the caul. It twisted inside the wet sack, claws tearing at the membranes, teeth biting, cutting free. It rose from the red wetness, unfurling with creaking joints, already the size of a full-grown man. It stood in the muck and stared into Issari's eyes.

All she could do was stare back.

"My brother," she whispered.

It regarded her, dripping wet, its skin gray and stony. It almost seemed to Issari that the creature recognized her, knew her to be its sister. Its jaw was long and pointed, its face hideously deformed, far too long to be human. Wings grew from its back, veined and translucent. But Issari could see her features in it. Her half brother, the son of Raem and the demon Angel, had the eyes of the Seran family—*her* eyes. Large. Green. Not the red, lustful eyes of a demon but the eyes of a mortal.

"My brother," she whispered again, taking a step closer. Across the hall, the surviving soldiers stared with her, hesitating, their swords still raised. Issari kept approaching, and her eyes dampened. "My brother, you're safe here. I will look after you. I—"

The creature opened its mouth wide, revealing rows of sharp fangs. The mouth opened from ear to ear, the jaw dislocating to drop halfway down its chest like a python about to devour a boar. The nephil—a creature born of man and demon— tossed back its head and shrieked. The sound shook the hall. It turned toward its mother. Angel still lay on the floor, her belly deflating, and her son crawled onto her chest and began to suck at the breast, drinking a foul milk of lava and liquid sulfur. Nursing her son, Angel raised her eyes and stared at Issari.

"Behold the heir of Eteer," Angel said. "Behold the future king. Behold—"

"As Queen of Eteer, I command you!" Issari shouted, amulet raised. "Return to the Abyss! Summon your demons to retreat after you. I have seized control of this throne, and—"

Angel laughed. She plucked the feeding creature off her breast and pointed toward the fallen throne of Eteer. Lips smoking, the child leaped, bounded over Issari, and landed upon the seat. He lashed his claws, tearing the throne apart, scattering shards of wood and gold. He looked up from the mess, nostrils steaming, green eyes blazing.

"I do believe that my son has just challenged your claim," said the Demon Queen. "I name him Ishnafel, *Fallen One*. Eteer will be his prize. Your reign has lasted only a few heartbeats, Issari, Queen of Filth." She barked a laugh. "You should have exiled me while you could."

Issari raised her amulet again, though its light dimmed. Shadows were emanating from Ishnafel, cloaking the room, overpowering the glow of Taal. "I will burn you, Angel. Obey me! I still command Eteer's army." She swept her arm behind her, gesturing at the soldiers who still lived. Tanin stood among them, bruised and bloody but still holding a spear and dagger. "She who rules the military rules the kingdom."

Angel grinned and licked her chops. "Oh, sweet innocent child . . . I do fear that a new army now sweeps across the city. Listen, child. You can hear them."

Issari listened and a chill washed her. She heard it. The buzzing rose from outside like a swarm of flies. Human screams rose with the sound. Soon shrieks joined the cacophony, high-pitched and demonic. Inside the throne room, Ishnafel hissed and flapped his wings, rising to hover over the floor.

"Yes, Issari," Angel said. "The nephilim. The army of the fallen ones. They rise and they are my son's to command."

Still covered in mucus, Ishnafel opened his mouth, stared at Issari, and spoke in a hiss. "I . . . will . . . reign."

Issari ran to the window, stared outside, and felt the blood drain from her face. Tanin ran to her side.

"By the stars," he whispered.

They covered the city, rising to bustle like flies, creatures born of demons and mortal women. Many covered the city streets, feasting upon the bodies of their dead mothers. There were hundreds. The blood of their mothers still on their lips, they began to crash into homes, tearing into human flesh, feeding, growing larger. People fled into the streets. Walls crumbled. Blood flowed.

The city fell to darkness, Issari thought. *Now it will fall into the Abyss itself.*

She turned back toward her soldiers. "Men of Eteer!" She grabbed a fallen khopesh. "Follow! Into the city!"

She ran, burst from the doors, and raced down the hill. Her men charged behind her.

Below in the city streets festered the spawn of demons, a shadow covering the land. More kept emerging, tearing their way out of mortal wombs with claws and teeth, taking flight, ready from their first breath to fight for the Abyss. Upon roofs, streets, and corpses, they turned to stare at the army charging toward them. They leered, tongues unrolling, fangs bright, eyes blazing. The creatures clustered together, and their howls rose, shattering stone. Upon a distant hill, the temple columns cracked and fell. The roof crumbled, and dust rose to hide the sun. The water in the canal boiled and turned red. The beasts beat their wings and flew toward the palace.

Issari ran, raising her sword. Tanin ran at her side, spear in hand. Behind them ran hundreds of Eteerians, armor and shields dented and dusty, swords raised high.

Under a veiled sky, upon the foothills between city and palace, the hosts of nephilim and the army of Eteer slammed together with blood, steel, and fire.

Issari had never been a warrior, but this day her sword drank blood.

She fought screaming, lashing her blade, cutting creatures down. All around her they swarmed, dipping from the sky, scuttling up streets, leaping from roofs. Her blade flew, digging through their flesh, spilling their entrails. They were the children of mortals, but she felt no pity for them, and she fought not only for Eteer, not only for Requiem, but for all good people of the overground. Tanin fought at her side, spearing the creatures, and around her soldiers cut through the nephil horde.

"We must fight as dragons, Issari!" Tanin shouted.

She shook her head. "Not while my people die upon the ground."

He grunted, shifted, and took flight. "Fly with me in the sky. Only victory matters now, not honor. Fly and blow fire with me."

He soared, wings beating, into a cloud of nephilim. The buzzing creatures crashed into him, biting his wings. Tanin blasted out flames, torching a cloud of them. His tail lashed. His claws cut into their rotten flesh. They tugged him down, and he crashed onto a roof, cracking the stone, rose again, and blew his fire.

Issari returned her eyes to her own battle. Her soldiers spread around her, swords lashing, and she swung her blade with them, one of them, their queen of blood and light.

The nephilim fought back with a fury. Their maws opened wide, tearing off limbs. Their claws drove through armor, piercing the soft flesh beneath. They bit into faces, chewing, eating. The blood of Eteer spilled. And more kept emerging—three, four from a womb, growing with every bite of meat, until a thousand or more flew, darkening the sky, crashing into walls and columns. The city of Eteer fell, roofs collapsing, trapping souls beneath. Dust and blood covered the ruins.

"Fight for Eteer!" Issari cried. She stood atop a fallen statue, raising her dripping sword. "Rally here, men of Taal, and fight!" She raised her palm, and her amulet blazed into light, raising a pillar toward the sky. "Rally and fight them!"

Tanin flew down toward her. Soot and black blood covered his red scales. "There are too many, Issari! We must flee. Shift and fly with me."

She shook her head, swung her sword, and sliced open a diving creature. Its entrails spilled and its blood splattered her. It crashed down at her feet, writhing. "I will not abandon Eteer."

"Eteer is fallen!" the red dragon shouted back. Blood dripped from a gash on his chest, and scratches covered his scales. "You cannot serve Eteer by dying here. We will find another way."

Shattered bricks, statues, and columns spread around her. Corpses lay among them. One soldier wept, dragging himself forward, his body halved. Another man raced across the battlefield, shouting for his mother. His feet were gone; he ran upon the stumps. Issari's head spun, her heart beat against her ribs, and she could barely breathe. She had never imagined such terror, such bloodshed, such malice in the world. Her entire people crumbled around her—not just her reign but her very race died under the smoke and dust and nephil wings. She had summoned a thousand soldiers from the barracks; perhaps a hundred remained, and still the nephilim flew.

And she knew Tanin was right.

The city had fallen.

Another nephil flew toward her. She sliced off its jaw, and Tanin finished the job, driving his horn into its head. Panting, covered in the creatures' blood, Issari turned her head and stared back at the palace. It rose from the smoke, its columns blackened. Upon its roof he stood, staring down at her with his burning green eyes. Ishnafel—King of the Fallen. Heir of Eteer, a kingdom of darkness.

And so I will flee this day, she thought. *And so my second exile begins. But I vow to you, Eteer, I will return.*

Finally she shifted into a dragon. She rose into the sky, blowing her fire.

The surviving soldiers below pointed and shouted out to her, "Queen Issari, Queen Issari! Do not abandon us. Fight with us."

Nephilim swarmed toward her. She blew her flames, sending them crashing down. She landed back upon the ruins. "Follow, men of Eteer. To the southern gates! To the Spice Gates! Follow!"

She lolloped down the street, claws clattering against the cobblestones, blowing her fire before her to clear a path. Tanin flew above, raining fire upon the buzzing half-demons. Soldiers ran behind, swords swinging, cutting their way through the army of the fallen. Women, children, and elders emerged from homes, weeping, begging for aid.

"Follow, Eteerians!" Issari cried. "To the Spice Gates!"

They ran, soldiers and townsfolk, a life extinguishing with every step. The creatures swooped from roofs and scuttled from alleyways, faster than falcons. Finally the survivors of Eteer, clutching their wounds, reached the archway of Spice Gates, the southern gates of Eteer. Tanin flew above the gatehouse, blowing his fire at the creatures that mobbed him. Issari slammed into the bronze doors, shoving them open, and crashed outside into the plains.

Farmlands stretched before her, and distant yellow hills rose under the veiled sky. Beyond lay the wilderness of Eteer, perhaps some hope for salvation. She raised her paw, hoping to raise a pillar of light, but her amulet was dimmed. Perhaps Taal had no more power over this falling world.

"Run, children of Eteer! Follow my light."

She shifted back into human form and ran, holding the dim light of her amulet, a beacon barely visible in the shadows under the smoky sky. Tanin roared above, and the people followed behind, an exodus from the city of demons, out of ruin and into the wild.

DORVIN

They flew ahead of the rest, scouting the skies, two dragons—green and silver.

"See anything, Dung Beetle?" the green dragon asked. The other dragons—Alina and the survivors of Bar Luan—flew a mark behind them, specks in the distance. Here at the vanguard flew the two warriors of their group.

If you can call the mammoth arse a warrior too, Dorvin thought, looking at Maev. *The damn buzzard only got lucky with the demon wolves.* He growled. *Next time we meet demons, I'll bury her under the corpses I make.*

A silver dragon, he puffed fire her way. "I see only a massive, flying clump of green rhinoceros snot." Dorvin spat out smoke. "No damn demons. I wish I had gone north or south instead. By the the Sky God's hairy nostrils, we fought a damn tree for stars' sake. A *tree*." He growled. "I want to kill demons! Lots of them."

Flying on the wind, Maev smiled crookedly. "You didn't do too well when we met the demon dogs. Your killed only one pup, while I slew three. I don't think you'd fare well with demons. Trees are more of your forte." She gestured down to the forest. "I see a little sapling down there. Want to land and try to defeat it? Just watch out for any sharp branches."

He roared, scattering flames, and banked toward her. He slammed into her, knocking the green dragon aside in the sky. "I can defeat you in a fight!"

She snorted. "Dorvin, you nearly fainted when a mouse climbed on you. I used to pummel men twice your size for a living."

"That does it." He bared his fangs, beat his wings, and raised his claws. "I'll show you who's the true warrior—right now, here in the sky. I can kill many more demons than you. I can kill you. I've slain creatures that would give you nightmares. I—" He slapped her with his tail. "Look at me when I talk to you! Mammoth Arse, what are you doing? Why are you flying away? Stars damn it, you coward, you—"

"Dorvin, you imbecile!" She blasted out fire. "In the east—go on, show me what you've got, Dung Beetle."

He frowned, turned eastward, and his eyes widened. "Well, star spit! Finally."

Three demons were flying toward them—scouts. Dorvin grinned. The creatures were reptilian and limbless, covered in long white spikes. Three forked tongues emerged from each mouth, and feathered wings grew from their backs. Dorvin flexed his claws, preparing for the fight, when Maev darted past him. The green dragon blasted out her fire, flying toward the creatures.

Dorvin growled, unwilling to let Maev beat him at the game again. He beat his wings mightily, shooting after her. The demons ahead squealed, opened their maws wide, and blasted out streams of sizzling liquid.

The two dragons banked, dodging the sprays. Droplets sizzled against Dorvin's flank and he roared; the poison began to eat through his scales, stinging the flesh beneath. He soared, then turned and swooped with the sun at his back. He roared down fire, bathing one of the creatures. The fire washed off its scales harmlessly, but the demon was momentarily blinded. Dorvin lashed his claws, ripping at the beast's wings. He landed upon its back, cutting, biting, until he tore out the creature's neck. It tumbled down toward the plains.

His mouth bloody, he raised his head to see Maev slay another demon. The third and last creature turned to flee.

Maev shot forward, banging into Dorvin and knocking him aside. "Out of my way, Dung Beetle! The last one's mine."

He roared and grabbed her tail, but she whipped it madly, freeing herself, and snorted fire his way. With a slap of her tail against his face, she flew after the fleeing demon.

"Mammoth Arse, stars damn it!" He flew after her, gritting his teeth, and grabbed her tail again—this time between his jaws. He tugged her toward him, flew above her, and slammed his claws against her back. With a kick to her head, he leaped over her and flew onward. His flames roared, roasting the demon. "I win! I slew the last one!"

The creature burned ahead of him, but it still flew. Shrieking, it turned toward the two dragons. Its jaws swung open, and it blasted out more acid. Dorvin and Maev scattered, and the jet fell through the sky. Dorvin darted forward, slashed his claws, and cut deep into the creature's face. Its blood spilled. He leaned in, prepared to bite out its neck.

Something grabbed his tail.

He yowled.

Maev was tugging him backward, away from the dying demon. He thrashed, freed himself, and spun in the sky. By the time he righted himself and flew toward the demon again, Maev had bit out its throat. The creature tumbled down, dead before it hit the ground.

Hovering, his wings scattering smoke, Dorvin turned to stare at Maev.

The green dragon gave him a crooked smile. "I win again."

Dorvin took a deep breath. He spoke in a strained, low voice. "That one was mine. I burned him. I cut him. I was going to finish the job when you—"

"When I won." Maev nodded, her smile widening. "As always."

Something snapped inside Dorvin—something that had been taut and painful since leaving Requiem. He roared. He barreled into Maev, knocking her back in the sky.

They tumbled down in a ball of lashing claws, snapping teeth, and blasts of fire.

"Let go of me!" she roared.

Dorvin refused to, only tightening his grip. Their wings beat against one another. They kept falling. The ground rushed up toward them. The rage flowed over Dorvin. He had spent too many days listening to her taunts, seeing that damn raised chin of hers, letting her strong body, crooked smile, and winking eyes fill his dreams. She was intoxicating, infuriating, impossible, and he didn't release her until they crashed through a tree, tumbled between snapping branches, and fell to the ground. The blow knocked the air out of Dorvin, banged his teeth together, and tugged his magic from him.

He lay on the ground in human form, moaning. Smoke wafted into his eyes. He sat up, wincing and blinking, hoping no bones were broken. When the world came back into focus, he saw Maev back in human form too, struggling to rise. Scratches covered her, and a branch had ripped her tunic.

Dorvin struggled to his feet, stumbled toward her, and swung his fist.

Fast as field mouse—creatures just as horrible—Maev dodged the blow. She leaped up, and her own fist connected with Dorvin's cheek. He crumpled, falling back onto the grass. Before he could rise again, Maev jumped onto him, fists flying. Her knee drove into his belly, and he grunted and couldn't even scream.

"Get off me!" he whispered hoarsely, holding up his arms to protect his face.

She snarled above him, her face rabid. The dragon tattoos on her arms danced as she pummeled him. "I've had enough of your rubbish, Dung Beetle. I—"

He raised his knee into her belly, and she let out a short *oof.* He flipped her over, and she thumped down onto her back. Before she could rise, he leaped onto her, pinning her wrists down. She flailed, unable to free herself.

"Calm down!" he said.

She growled up at him. "Release me now, or my knee drives into your crotch." She raised her knee abruptly, and Dorvin—expecting the pain—loosened his grip and pulled back. She seized the opportunity to slam into him, swinging her fists again. They rolled through the grass, flipped over a fallen log, and began sliding down a hillside, wrestling all the while. Stones and fallen branches jabbed Dorvin, and even as she rolled, she kept attacking him, trying to bite, driving her knees into his sides. Finally they rolled to a halt in a grassy valley between trees.

"That demon was mine," Dorvin said. "You stole it from me. Just like you did last time. Just like you always do—stealing the glory from me." His eyes suddenly stung. "Your family loves that. Your father stole my people from me. Now you keep mocking me."

She snorted, flipped onto him, and pinned him down into the grass. "Grow up and stop whining. Are you a warrior or a little boy?"

"A warrior." He growled. "If you'll let me be one, for stars' sake. It's not easy with you, you know."

"Never claimed it would be."

Dorvin spat out grass. "You're too damn strong, too damn proud, too damn fiery, too damn beautiful, and—"

"Too damn beautiful?" She raised an eyebrow.

His cheeks flushed. "I mean—for a mammoth arse." His tongue felt too thick. "Don't pretend you don't know it! All your mocking smiles, your little winks, your swagger when you walk. You know what that does to a man, don't you?"

She rolled her eyes. "You really are a dung beetle. I can't control that, no more than you can control your pretty eyes or your own smile."

He blinked. "My eyes aren't pretty! They're warrior eyes. They're—" He blinked again. "You think I'm pretty?"

She groaned, still lying atop him, pinning him down. "This is what I think." She leaned down and kissed his lips. "And that's the last kiss you'll ever get from me, so now stop thinking about me like that, and—"

He wouldn't let her finish her sentence. He kissed her in return, and this kiss was deeper, and her tongue flicked into his mouth, and her body softened against his. After what seemed like ages, she pulled back and glared.

"Stop that!" She grabbed a fistful of his hair. "I didn't say you could kiss me. I'm not that kind of woman. I—" She shuddered. "Oh to the Abyss with it." She pulled his head toward her and kissed him again.

Her hands slipped under his tunic and all but ripped the garment off. She stared down at his bare chest. "Stars above, Dorvin, you're skinnier than your sister."

His blood boiled too hot to answer. He grabbed her own clothes and tore them off, leaving her naked above him, then sat up and kissed her again. Her legs wrapped around him, and she tossed back her head, and they rolled back down into the grass. She moaned beneath him, and sweat poured down their naked bodies, and this felt like wrestling too, a thing of passion and groans and heat.

"Damn mammoth arse," he whispered into her ear.

She bit his bottom lip, tugging it. "Dung Beetle."

When they finally flew back toward the others, Alina stared with narrowed eyes, blasting out smoke. Behind her flew the group from Bar Luan, forty dragons strong.

"What happened?" the lavender dragon demanded. "I saw fire and heard roars."

Maev turned to fly at Alina's side. "Three demon scouts." She glanced at Dorvin. "Your brother killed all three. Got to them faster than I could."

The lavender dragon nodded toward him. "Good work, brother."

Dorvin nodded back, silent. He looked over at Maev, and the green dragon winked at him.

Her and her damn winks.

He flew among the others, sneaking glances at her. For the first time, he flew without singing or telling rude jokes. He simply glided silently, remembering the heat of her body against his, her full lips, and the light in her eyes.

JEID

He was standing alone on the mountainside when the demon army arrived.

The others were all inside Two Skull Mountain, celebrating the second day of the great wedding—a day of feasting, music played on lutes and drums, and tribal dances with masks of wood and feathers. Jeid had volunteered to stand here outside the cavern, to watch the southern horizon for an enemy attack. He was not one for celebrations, not since that day his twin brother had murdered his wife, not since his daughter Requiem had died. And especially not today, the day he lost Laira too.

And so he had come here, to watch, to wait, to grieve. As he stood outside, alone, the sound of music and laughter rising from the caves, he clenched his jaw and stared south at the distant rain and lightning, waiting for the demons, waiting for war. Perhaps that was all he had left now—war and death, fire and blood.

"When you arrived at the escarpment, half-dead and trembling, I thought that a new light had kindled in my life," he whispered, eyes dry but throat tight. "I lost so many, but I gained you, Laira. A pure soul. Somebody strong yet fragile, compassionate yet unflinching in her struggle against our enemies. And I love you. You gave me new light, new meaning, new hope. And now you too fade from me."

He lowered his head, feeling like a lovelorn boy. He was King of Requiem, and Laira was a chieftain, and yet he was acting like a foolish boy spurned by a village girl. He would not lose her, not truly. She would wed Oritan, but she would still fight by his side. And he knew that she sacrificed herself for Requiem, not for any love she harbored the chieftain of Leatherwing.

And yet still the thought of her in Oritan's bed soured his belly.

He unslung his axe from his back and was hefting the weapon—an action he often took to soothe himself—when the shadows appears on the horizon.

Jeid froze and stared.

From here it looked like insects rising from a carcass, a cloud of many black spots. Distant sounds rose on the wind—squeals, grunts, screams. A human voice seemed to call among them, and the setting sun glinted on metal. Jeid bared his teeth and narrowed his eyes, staring. Iciness flowed across him.

"The demon army."

They stormed closer, larger with every heartbeat. A thousand of the creatures—still only specks from here—covered the sky like locusts. Jeid's grip tightened on his axe. He remembered the demonic octopus they had fought; four dragons together had barely defeated the creature, and now a thousand of its brethren flew here. For a moment Jeid could only stare, frozen.

Twenty dragons, he thought. *Two hundred rocs and pteros. Against the ancient horde of the underworld.*

It was a fight they could not win.

We're not ready. Stars, we need more time. We need Maev to return with more dragons. We need Issari to ascend to Eteer's throne. His hands shook around his axe's shaft, and a strangled growl rose from his throat. *We cannot win. We must flee.*

The sun set and the stars emerged above. Their light fell upon him, the light of Requiem, and Jeid took a deep, shuddering breath.

"For you, Requiem," he whispered, thinking of his daughter, thinking of the kingdom he would raise.

The demons flew nearer, their shrieks louder now. Jeid turned, ran into the cave, and shifted into a dragon. Light, song, and color filled the great cavern. Pteros hung from ceiling and walls like bats. Rocs perched in alcoves. Tribesmen danced on the cave floor, wearing wooden masks and cloaks of feathers. Laira and Oritan stood upon the stone pillar in the cavern's center; she wore an embroidered garment inlaid with jewels, and he wore his armor of bones. Game cooked upon fires, the smoke wafting out of a hole high above—one of the skulls' eye sockets.

A copper dragon, Jeid flew around the chamber, sounding his alarm.

"Demons! Demons attack. The horde is here!"

The music died. All eyes turned toward him.

After a heartbeat of silence, the cavern erupted.

"Riders of Leatherwing!" Oritan shouted. "Leatherwing, fly!" The chieftain whistled, and his ptero flew toward the pillar, wings beating back smoke, the torchlight blazing against its golden horn. Oritan leaped into the saddle, dug his heels into the animal, and flew out of the mountain and into the night. A hundred other pteros detached from the ceiling and dipped to the floor, and riders leaped into their saddles. The swarm flew after its chieftain.

"Hunters of Goldtusk!" Laira cried. Her roc, the great vulture Neiva, sailed toward the stone pillar. Laira leaped off the stalagmite, sailed through the air, and landed upon her mount. "Goldtusk, fly for Ka'altei! Fly for the glory of our tribe and our god."

The rocs too beat their wings, scattering droplets of oil and spreading their stench through the cave. Riders of Goldtusk yipped upon them, clad in fur cloaks and bronze breastplates. Laira at its lead, the tribe flew out of another exit—one of the skull's mouths.

With the warriors of both tribes gone to battle, Jeid flew above his own people—twenty Vir Requis who huddled below. They were not warriors. They were the exiles of tribes, villages, and wandering clans, people who had come to him for safety, for peace. Now he would have to lead them to war.

He landed before them on the cave floor and resumed human form. They stared back at him, eyes frightened but determined. Three among them were children, no older than ten years old, yet their fire too would be needed this night.

"Vir Requis," Jeid said to them. "People of Requiem. I was a smith, exiled from a village that killed my wife and child. You were farmers, hunters, gatherers, shepherds. You too were exiled. You came to me to find a home, a kingdom where you can belong. You found that kingdom, yet now Requiem is threatened. Now our enemies will crush us just as we rise from darkness. Tonight we will tell them: We will stand. We will fight. We will find our sky. Tonight we fight Requiem's war of independence. Tonight we are no longer hunted and afraid. Tonight we are warriors of starlight."

They trembled. A few shed tears. One of them, a young girl, clung to her mother. But they all stared back at him, and courage shone through their fear. It was Bryn who spoke first.

The young woman stepped forward, her hair a wild red mane, and met his gaze.

"For Requiem," she said. She shifted, took flight as an orange dragon, and soared in the cavern.

Jeid shifted too and the others followed. Twenty dragons, they rose in the cave to join Bryn. Beating his wings, roaring his cry, Jeid—King Aeternum—led them out of the mountain and into the night.

Fire, steel, and the stench of demons filled the sky.

The enemy was close now, not a mark away. Jeid growled and rose in the air, his twenty dragons behind him. He could see the demons clearly now—some scaled, some feathered, some naked and dripping, others dry and lanky, some covered in hooks, others in fur, some limbless, some wingless, all creatures worse than any imagined in nightmares. Upon the beasts, leading the assault, rode a man—the only mortal of the host. He wore armor, and he bore a khopesh, the curved blade of the south. He stared across the darkness at Jeid, and their eyes met.

King Raem of Eteer, Jeid knew. *The Lord of Demons. Laira's father.*

Laira seemed to see the tyrant too. She soared upon her roc to Jeid's right, the western flank of their host. Her seventy rocs rose around her, their riders nocking arrows and howling their battle cries. "Goldtusk, Goldtusk!" The rancid vultures added their shrieks to the din, and their talons stretched out, ready to dig into demons.

"Leatherwing!"

To Jeid's left rose the tribe of ptero-riders, their chests painted white and red, their spears bedecked with feathers and beads. Oritan rose before them upon his mount, chanting for his tribe.

The demons chanted too, their voices mocking.

"Tear off their scales one by one!" one creature cried, a shaggy thing with a warty red head.

"Slay the birds and break the reptiles!" roared another creature, a naked strip of meat beating hooked wings.

Jeers rose among the host.

"We will feast upon dragon bones!"

"We will wear skins of scales!"

"We will drink blood from dragon horns!"

Above them all rose the voice of King Raem, mocking and cruel. "Bring me the weredragons alive. They will beg for death in the courts of the Abyss."

With a thousand cries, the dragons swarmed toward the mountain.

Jeid roared and blew his fire. Around him, his dragons answered his cry.

"Requiem! Requiem!"

The pteros flew from the west, their riders firing spears. The rocs flew from the east, their riders firing arrows. Jeid charged forth, leading the dragons of Requiem, crashing into the host of the Abyss.

LAIRA

My father.

Riding her roc, Laira stared at the host, and her eyes met his. Her heart seemed to freeze within her.

Raem Seran. The man who exiled me. Who hunts me. Who unleashed the terrors of the underground. The man I feared for so long, the man who will kill me if he can.

"Father," she whispered.

He seemed to smile at her from upon his mount—a twisted demon of pink skin, wings stretched tight over bone, and a bloated, vaguely human head. He raised his sword in salute. She doubted he recognized her; she flew as a Goldtusk huntress, not a dragon of Requiem, for in this battle she would lead her tribe proudly. But she knew him. And tonight she knew that to end this war, to let Requiem rise, she would have to kill the man who had given her life.

"Fly to him, Neiva," she said softly, pointing at the man in bronze. She nocked an arrow in her bow. "Fly to him and we will end this."

The roc beat her wings and stormed forward. Around Laira, the other rocs flew too, their riders firing arrows. The demons ahead cackled and stormed forward to meet the Goldtusk tribe.

The hosts slammed together with flashing blades, claws, and raining blood.

Laira tried to reach her father, to cut him down. But the king pulled back, allowing his demons to storm forth. Three creatures flew at Laira, each as large as a dragon and covered in thick brown fur. Red faces grew from them like boils, swollen and sprouting black beards. Their teeth were yellow, their smiles cruel. Their claws reached out, and Laira shouted and fired an arrow. The projectile slammed into one demon before it crashed into her roc, teeth snapping.

Laira screamed, drew her sword, and lashed at the wounded creature. The blade tangled in its thick fur. Its saliva dripped upon her, and Laira grimaced. Her roc dipped in the sky, then reared, talons scratching at the demon's face. Its blood spilled and it shrieked and fell back. Countless other creatures flew all around, moving closer. Laira fired another arrow, and Neiva lashed her talons, and around her dozens of other rocs battled in the sky.

This was Goldtusk's greatest battle. This was the battle that would let Requiem rise or fade from history. This was a battle for more than tribes or dragons—it was a battle for the fate of the world itself, a battle for a world of life and light or demonic darkness.

And that battle raged around her with light, with blood, with arrows and dragonfire. Beyond the tribe, the others fought too—dragons and pteros battling at their own fronts, killing, dying, burning the sky. Flames lit the night. Blood rained and rocs fell around her. Coiling worms the size of whales crashed into rocs, wrapped around them, crushed their bones. Demonic jaws snapped open and closed, tearing tribesmen apart, ripping torsos in two, and gore rained upon the mountainside. Everywhere around Laira the tribesmen fell, and rocs crashed down, and her tribe—and this night Goldtusk was her home, and these were her people as much as dragons—fell and died.

Tonight all memory of Goldtusk might fade, Laira thought, firing her arrows, screaming from atop her roc. *But if tonight we die, then we die with demons.*

"Neiva, fly!" she shouted. "Fight them!"

Her roc was wounded. Gashes thick with bubbling demon saliva covered Neiva. Blood poured from her wings. One of her talons had cracked and dangled loosely. Yet still the great vulture fought, biting, scratching. And demons fell. And demons died.

They can be hurt. She snarled and fired another arrow. *We can kill them. We will kill hundreds of them.*

Her arrow slammed into a coiling serpent, and her roc tore apart a flying blob of slime.

"To the king!" Laira shouted, pointing at Raem across the field. "To Raem! Rocs, rally here. To me!"

The surviving rocs mustered around her, bloodied and weary but still shrieking. The tribesmen chanted atop them. "For Laira! Chieftain Laira!" Their cries rolled across the sky. "For Laira Seran, Chieftain of Goldtusk!"

The surviving rocs—by the stars, barely fifty still lived— stormed forth, crashing into the swarm of demons that hid the world. And there, rising above their rot, she saw him again, the man of bronze. Her father. He met her gaze across the sky, and she saw him gasp, and slowly a grin spread across his face. She could not hear his voice from here, but she could read his lips.

"Laira." His grin widened and he flew toward her, and now his voice carried on the wind. "Laira, my daughter!"

She screamed. She pointed toward him. "Goldtusk, to the bronze king! Slay the king!"

Their arrows fired. Laira dug her heels into Neiva, and her fellow rocs swarmed around her, charging toward Raem.

Hundreds of demons slammed into the tribe.

Jaws tore wings off rocs. Claws lacerated men, tearing through armor. Great tapeworms swallowed tribesmen whole. Flaming demons of scales and lava landed upon the tribe, burning them, feasting on roasted flesh.

"Fly to the metal man!" Laira shouted. "Slay the king!" She fired her last arrow. "Fly to him, Neiva!"

The roc shrieked and flew, but Laira knew the animal was too hurt, too weak. Her blood dripped, and half the feathers had been torn off her left wing. She wobbled as she flew. But Raem was so close now. Laira could see him just a few demons away.

"Rocs, with me!" she cried. But the others too were hurt, surrounded by too many enemies, and more fell every breath.

So I will fight you alone, Father. You exiled me. You drove me to a world of hunger, cold, fear. And now you will taste my blade. She raised her bronze sword high, the same blade that had slain Zerra. *Now this blade will sever your head too.*

He raised his own sword, awaiting her across the battle upon his twisted bat, and his lips peeled back in a horrible smile— a demon's smile.

A cloud of buzzing flies, each the size of a horse, bustled toward Laira. Their faces were humanlike, bloated like waterlogged corpses, gray and leaking. With screeches, they flew onto Neiva like true flies onto old meat.

The roc screamed.

The flies thrust out long, metallic tongues, piercing Neiva's flesh. Blood spurted.

"Neiva!"

Laira swung her sword, trying to reach the unholy insects, but her arm was too short.

"Neiva, fly!"

The roc rose in the sky. The vulture tossed back her head, let out a pained cry, and tried to flap her wings. Two of the demonic flies landed upon one of those wings, bit deep, tugged hard, and ripped the wing off.

The roc tumbled from the sky, flies digging into her chest.

Laira fell with the roc, hair billowing, head spinning. The ground raced up toward them. They slammed into another roc, flipped over, and fell again. The world spun all around Laira— clouds of demons, dragons blowing fire, distant pteros upon the wind, and above them all the stars—the stars of Requiem, the stars going dark behind the smoke and flame of battle.

"Neiva, fly!"

But the roc was already dead, her chest cut open, her wings gone. Laira struggled to free herself from the saddle, but a strap pinned her down. She cried out. They slammed against a demon, spun madly, and kept falling.

An instant before hitting the ground, Laira managed to swing her sword, cutting the strap.

She tore free from the saddle.

She shifted into a dragon.

She soared, a golden beast, blowing fire, roaring her cry.

"For Requiem!"

She fought as a dragon now; Requiem would be her battle cry, her beacon of hope in the darkness. She flew alone; she saw no other rocs. Some other dragons still fought, but they were too distant, and many demons separated her from the Leatherwing tribe. She would face him alone.

A golden dragon, she blew her flame, crashed through demons, and flew toward her father.

ISSARI

They traveled through the desert, thousands of Eteerians, weary and wounded and far from home.

Their city lay in darkness, its halls and homes overrun with the demon spawn. The underworld had risen; a kingdom had fallen. And so here they walked across the dry, stony earth, the sun scorching their skin. They had taken no supplies, had fled their city with only the clothes on their backs. Some walked barefoot, the hot earth baking their soles. Some walked shirtless, the sun turning their skin red. All were parched, their lips dry, their throats tight, their bellies twisting with fear. A thousand men, women, and children. Exiled. Wandering into the deep, southern heat. Demons covered the world, and nightmares haunted their sleep, and only one thing gave the survivors of Eteer hope in the wild. Only one light still guided their way.

The Priestess in White.

She walked at their lead, solemn, her back always straight, her head always high. Her white tunic fluttered in the wind, a simple garment. No golden tassels or embroidery marked her raiment as they had during her days as a princess. No headdress of gold or jewels bedecked her head of raven hair. To a chance observer, she might have, at first glance, seemed like a simple commoner, perhaps the daughter of a milkmaid or a potter. Yet something in her eyes—determined, hard eyes that never flinched from the shimmering horizon—denoted her nobility, her holiness.

She was Issari Seran, daughter of the Demon King. She was a Priestess of Taal, the silver amulet of her god embedded into her palm. She was a daughter of Requiem, blessed with the starlit magic of dragons. She was a leader of outcasts. She was a bringer of hope. She was the shepherdess of a lost flock.

"Bless you, Priestess," said all those who approached her, seeking a blessing, seeking to touch her dusty garment. "Blessed be Issari, True Queen of Eteer, True Daughter of Taal."

She nodded to all those who approached, whispered prayers, and touched them with her silver palm.

"The Light of Taal!" one old man whispered, tears in his eyes.

"Blessed be Queen Issari!" said a young mother, holding her babe. "True Lady of Eteer."

One boy, a scrawny thing clad in rags, approached her on bare feet. He touched her gown—a sign of respect in Eteer—and whispered in awe, "Issari, Daughter of Requiem." The boy's eyes shone. "The White Dragon."

Issari had spent the past few days staring ahead as she walked, rarely removing her eyes from the hazy horizon that shimmered in the heat waves. Now her heart skipped a beat, and she took a closer look at the boy. All others had spoken of Eteer and its gods; this child was the first to mention Requiem, her second home, her land across the sea. The boy was too thin; his ribs showed through tatters in his tunic. His skin was tanned bronze, and dust filled his black hair. He looked like a typical street urchin, one of the many who had once lived in Eteer, aside from his curious left arm. That arm was no larger than a babe's, ending with a hand the size of a walnut.

"You know of Requiem?" she asked him.

199

The child grinned. Despite being half-naked and half-starved, his teeth were remarkably white and straight. "I was a beggar on the canal. I know more than the wisest scholar." He raised his chin proudly. "I watched as you smuggled Vir Requis onto ships, letting them sail north to safety. I watched as you wandered through the city, fighting the demons with your silver hand, hiding weredragons in cellars and attics. They've all left north or died. I was the last." He gave a little bow. "I am Fin, the last Vir Requis of Eteer."

The boy hopped into the air, shifted into an azure dragon, and flew a circle above. The people below pointed and gasped. The boy landed by Issari and resumed human form, eyes bright.

Issari stared at him in disbelief. "If you knew I was saving Vir Requis, if you knew of Requiem, why did you stay in Eteer? Why didn't you approach me for aid?"

He shrugged. "What would I have in the north? Nothing. Would Requiem welcome me, a beggar and thief? Perhaps, though I would only be an orphan there too. In Eteer I knew how to survive, how to hide, how to steal. At least, I did until the demon spawn destroyed our city." He bowed his head. "My life as an urchin is over. Now my life is to follow you, Issari Seran." Suddenly tears filled his eyes. "You are a great leader. You are a great light. We will follow you to redemption. To a new home."

Issari sighed and turned to look at the people walking behind her—haggard, wounded, close to death. She looked at the landscape around her, a lifeless desert, the ground cracked and rocky, the horizons wavering with heat, the sun heartless and beating down on them. Redemption? A new home? What hope could she give these people?

A distant speck appeared in the sky, soon growing to reveal a red dragon, smoke from his nostrils leaving two trails. The dragon circled once above the Eteerian exodus, then landed beside Issari, claws tearing into the cracked earth. Tanin released his magic, returning to his human form, and walked closer to Issari. The bright-eyed young man she had met last winter was gone. Instead she saw a haggard traveler, dust coating his dark hair and weary face. His cloak billowed in the sandy wind, tattered and charred. He had taken a khopesh, breastplate, and shield from a fallen soldier, replacing his old dagger. If not for the stubble on his face and tall frame—Eteerian soldiers shaved their faces and rarely grew so tall—Issari would have thought him a soldier of her fallen kingdom.

"I flew for many marks," Tanin said. "No water. No food, not even birds to hunt. Nothing but dry, cracked earth and stones, and . . . in the south, as you said, a great mountain range, and within it a single pass—a city like a gateway." His face darkened. "Goshar."

Issari nodded. "If any hope remains for us, it lies beyond Goshar's walls. That is where we head."

Tanin gripped the hilt of his sword. "Issari, I urge you to seek another path. Just looking at Goshar chilled me. Cages hung from its walls, dozens of them, men starving inside. Many of the prisoners were already dead, crows feasting upon them. I flew high above the walls, too high for the Gosharian archers to hit me. And what I saw . . ." He shuddered. "Many slaves, Issari. Slaves in great pits, whipped, dying, straining naked in the sun to build towers and great statues larger than ten dragons." He shook his head. "The whole city stank of blood; I could smell it even flying high above. Goshar would be our death."

She gestured around her at the desert. "This desert would be our death. Goshar guards the path through the mountains to the fertile lands beyond. Would you have us die of thirst here, only days away from the desert's end?"

For the first time since she had known him, Tanin glared at her, eyes full of anger. "Would you have us enslaved, broken, chained?" He grumbled. "That awaits us in Goshar, judging by the cages upon its walls. We did not flee Eteer to suffer under another tyrant's heel. We—"

She placed a hand on his cheek. "Tanin." Her voice was soft, and she leaned forward and kissed him. "I would have us survive. I would do anything I could to stop more of my people from dying. Goshar is dangerous, and my father fought wars against its cruel king. But what choice have we? Return to Eteer? Its nephilim would slay us. Wander farther in the wilderness? We would not last long enough to seek fertile lands; the mountains stretch for hundreds of marks. Sail across the sea? We have no ships. We must choose between starvation in the sun or the hope of a vipers' nest. I choose the vipers."

She hugged herself as she walked through the dust. Twelve city-states spread across Terra, the lands south of the sea. Eteer was the northernmost, the realm of seafarers and traders, once wealthy and bright, its arm stretching far across the sea. South of Eteer lay its old enemies. Their lands were dry, their sun blazing, their people cruel, and none among them inspired more terror than Goshar. While Eteer derived its might from the sea, Goshar had become wealthy by guarding the single pass through the mountains, a gateway from the desert to fertile lands. Closest to Eteer among the thirteen, Goshar was also Eteer's greatest enemy; her father had fought the city in several battles, and many of Eteer's sons lay fallen around its walls. Yet without supplies, wandering alone in the desert, it would be death or mercy from old enemies.

They kept walking in silence. Behind Issari, the exiles of Eteer trudged on, the strong helping the weak. Men and women held their children, their elderly parents, their weary friends in their arms. Dust coated all their faces, and their eyes were large and haunted. Several women among them had survived birthing nephilim; they moaned, bleeding, dying, held in their husbands' arms. Night fell and the temperature plunged; the day had been sweltering but in the darkness they shivered, the air colder than any winter in Eteer. The stars burned above, cruel and small and taunting them, piercing their eyes, and even the sight of the Draco constellation could not soothe Issari as she shivered; it seemed too far, unreachable to her, unable to aid her, only able to stare down upon her pain.

She tried to sleep in Tanin's arms that night, but even his body would not warm her, and the sound of his breath would not comfort her. Finally dawn rose, stretching orange and yellow fingers across the sky; that sky seemed vast here, ten times the size it had seemed from her old city. When the light fell upon the camp, it revealed a dozen dead—elders and wounded Eteerians too weary to cling on. They buried them beneath stones, and when the survivors walked again into the south, vultures circled above.

It was the next day, leaving ten more graves behind them, that the Eteerian exodus saw the walls of Goshar ahead.

Issari took a shaky breath, trying to swallow down the horror.

From this distance, she could see little details. The mountains soared like a great wall of stone, covering the horizon, the border of the desert. The range dipped in only one place, a crack in the wall. Here, within this mountain pass, rose the city of Goshar. Its walls were the same tan color as the mountains; beyond them, Issari could just make out the slivers of towers. The people of Eteer pointed, whispering in fear, praying to their gods. As they walked nearer across the rocky earth, more details emerged. Goshar's walls seemed small next to the mountains, but they must have stood twice the height of Eteer's walls; the soldiers upon their battlements seemed small as insects upon the rim of a well. Turrets rose at regular intervals, bearing the banners of Goshar, displaying a nude woman with a snake's head. A gatehouse rose ahead, large as a palace, many archers atop its towers, and reliefs of snakes coiled across its bronze doors. After walking another mark, Issari winced to see the cages Tanin had spoken of. They hung off the walls, dozens of them, their prisoners languishing or already dead within; crows hopped around the bars.

Goshar, Issari thought with a shiver. *City of Bones.*

When she looked down at her feet, she saw the bones there. They spread in a field before her, picked dry by sand and beak. Thousands of skeletons, broken apart, littered the desert outside the walls of Goshar. Here were the bones of her own people, of Eteerian soldiers who had fought this city, who had perished in the heat far from home. Her father had fought two campaigns against Goshar, returning home with tales of triumph, of many enemies slain and towers felled, of the pride of Goshar crushed. Here lay those who had paid for his wars, and still the walls of that old enemy stood; despite Raem's boasts he had never breached these walls, only left fields of death before them. The skulls of her people stared at Issari as she walked by, entreating her, begging her to take them home.

My father could never enter these walls, she thought. *But I must. Not with swords and spears but with my words. If I fail, the thousands behind me will join the dead, just more bones for the sun to bake and the crows to pick clean.*

She looked behind her at her followers, once the proud people of Eteer, now ragged refugees covered in dust and dried blood. She returned her eyes to the gates of Goshar. She took a few steps closer, separating herself from the crowd, and raised her palm. The amulet upon it shone.

"Hear me, Goshar!" she cried out. "I am Issari Seran, rightful Queen of Eteer! I come to speak with your king."

For a long time nothing happened. The guards stared down from above, arrows nocked in their bows, silent and faceless, their helms blank masks. Issari wondered how many of those guards had lost brothers to her father's armies.

If they fire upon us now, and if they slay us, they would only save us from a slower death.

"Open your gates, Goshar!" Issari cried. "I do not come here as a soldier. I am not my father, for he has fallen from Taal's light and has relinquished his right to rule. I am a new queen. I come to speak of peace. Open your gates, City of Stone! I shall enter and speak to your lord, the Abina Sin-Naharosh."

For long moments, silence.

They won't let us in.

Issari expected to feel fear, despair, anguish. Instead she felt rage. Without pausing to think, she shifted into a dragon and soared. Her voice pealed across the land, the howl of a cornered beast.

"Hear me, Goshar!" Her wings beat back the cloaks of the guards upon the city walls. As she soared higher, she saw the city beyond, a land of many tan buildings, towers, and coiling ziggurats. "I am Issari, the Dragon Queen of Eteer, the Daughter of Taal, the Light of Requiem." She blew a pillar of fire skyward. "I can burn your city to the ground and lay waste to your people. My claws can cut through metal, and my fire can melt stone. Resist me and not even your bones will lie here in memory; all of Goshar will become naught but dust. If you do not open your gates and let me enter as a queen, I will enter your city as a dragon raining death. Open your gates to my people, Goshar! Or you will not feel my wrath, for you will die too quickly to feel anything."

She landed back outside the gates, panting, and shifted back into human form.

Tanin raised an eyebrow and spoke from the corner of his mouth. "So much for diplomacy."

Issari raised her chin. "That is the diplomacy of the desert."

For a long time, nothing happened. Then, with a creak and shower of dust, the gates of Goshar began to slide open. Issari gave Tanin the slightest of smiles, then turned to walk into the city. Before she could enter the gates, a dozen guards stepped forward, blocking her way. They wore copper scale armor, and their swords were broad and straight. Horned helms topped their heads, and the sigil of Goshar—a woman with a snake head—was engraved onto their round shields. Their captain approached her, a tall man with a golden snake's head upon his helm. A cloak of many beads hung over his shoulders, and his curly black beard hung down to his belt. He raised his palm.

"Only Issari Seran, Daughter of the Demon Raem, shall enter. Your people will not set foot in the holy ground of Goshar."

She glared at the man. "My people will die out here!"

"That is no concern of Goshar," said the captain. "Many have died outside our walls. Let their bones join the others."

She sneered. "Your bones will be those to litter the desert! Share your supplies with my people or I will burn your city with dragonfire."

The captain stared back steadily, but she saw his fist tighten around the hilt of his sword, saw the fear in him. "You may speak of these matters to the Light of Goshar, our mighty abina, the Lord of the Desert, Sin-Naharosh, blessed be his name. You may follow, you alone, while your people wait outside our walls. If our blessed abina chooses to grant them his mercy, they will be given sustenance."

She gestured at Tanin. "This man will join me. He is my half-brother and will not leave my side." She knew that if she called Tanin her bodyguard, he would be slain as an enemy. If she called him her husband, he would be slaughtered too, freeing her for a possible marriage between the kingdoms. A bastard brother, not noble but still of her blood, would be allowed to accompany her and live.

She turned back toward her people and raised her palm, letting them see the light of her amulet. "Children of Eteer! Wait for me in the desert and do not despair. I will return to you with water for your thirst, with milk for your children, with food for hungry bellies. You have suffered greatly under Raem the Demon King, and you have traveled far in the heat and and cold, but I promise you: I will bring you deliverance. Your queen does not forget your pain. Taal will bless you, my children."

They looked upon her, eyes huge and weary in their gaunt faces. One man cried out, "Blessed be Issari, True Queen of Eteer!"

The others answered his call. "Blessed be Issari, the Priestess in White!"

Her eyes damp, she turned and entered the city of her people's oldest enemies.

RAEM

"Hello again, Laira!" he shouted and laughed. "Hello, daughter!"

She flew toward him, a golden dragon now, but he had seen her human form, and he had laughed at her wretchedness. Issari, his youngest, was a beautiful woman, her hair long and rich, her face fair enough to inspire poems and songs. Her sister, meanwhile, bore the marks of her shame upon her: a crooked jaw probably broken long ago, a frail frame denoting years of hunger, and short ragged hair. She had fled him years ago, and she had suffered for it, and that pleased Raem.

"And you will suffer much more, Laira," he whispered as he flew toward her. "You will grow to miss your exile. Stitchmark will make you more wretched by far."

He grinned to remember Stitchmark, the demon of needles and scalpels and spools, stitching a new face onto Ciana. The young woman was fighting nearby upon her own demon, her new face flushed with her lust for battle. But Laira—she would not become beautiful like Ciana. She would turn into a creature like the bat he rode. Perhaps he would ride Laira too, fly upon her to hunt dragons and ruin this world she fought for.

"Warriors of darkness!" he shouted. "Gather around me. To the golden dragon! Take her alive!"

His soldiers mustered at his sides, a horde of demons of all shapes and sizes, leering, drooling, staring at the golden dragon.

They flew through the darkness, passing through smoke and flame.

Laira flew toward him, howling, her fire blowing. Raem raised his shield, and her flames crashed around it like waves around a tor. Golden dragon and demonic bat slammed together.

Suddenly Laira did not seem a weak, hunted creature but an enraged beast. The dragon's mouth snapped open and shut again and again, ripping at Raem's bat, tearing into the animal's skin. Laira's claws lashed, and more flames blasted from her. Raem's mount screeched, skin lacerated and charred. Raem rose in his saddle, grabbed a spear that hung at his side, and tossed the weapon. The bronze head drove into Laira's back and wobbled like a fork thrust into meat.

Laira roared and Raem grinned.

"Look around you, Laira!" he said. "Look at the battle. You've already lost."

As the dragon howled in pain, Raem gestured around him. The rocs were falling fast; barely any still flew. The pteros, across the fields, were not faring much better. Every moment, demons swarmed upon another one of the beasts, ripping into their leathery flesh. Tribesmen fell from the sky, blood spraying in a mist. The dragons of Requiem fought clustered together, blowing fire in a ring, but even they could not hold back the demon horde for long; only twenty of the reptiles flew here, powerless to stop the hundreds of demons around them.

"It's over, Laira!" Raem said. He grabbed another spear. "You've lost. Return home with me, my daughter. Return home and I will make you a demon in my service."

He tossed his second spear.

The weapon dug into Laira's shoulder, shedding blood. The dragon dipped in the sky.

"Grab her, Anai," Raem said calmly to his mount.

Bleeding and burnt, her eyes shedding tears, the broken woman—stretched and sewn into this creature—reached out her claws and grabbed the golden dragon. All around, Raem's other demons flew in, reaching out claws, talons, tongues, and tentacles, encircling Laira in a demonic cage. Laira wailed and lashed her tail, but she could not break free, and her flames died down to sputtering sparks.

"My sweet daughter," Raem said. "It's time to go home."

Roars answered him.

Raem frowned.

Firelight bathed the sky.

He hissed.

The beat of wings thudded like drums, and cries pierced the night: "For Requiem! For a dawn of dragons!"

He turned toward the west, and he saw them there, rising in a dawn of dragonfire. Dragons. Dozens of them. They rose from darkness, blowing their flames, their scales bright. These were not the dragons that had emerged from the mountain; here were new beasts, and a terrible green reptile flew at their lead.

"Maev!" Laira shouted, tears in her eyes.

The new dragons crashed into the battle like chariots into lines of infantry.

Fire washed over demons. Dragon horns drove into maggoty flesh. Demons fell from the sky, howling, torn apart.

"Slay the king!" Maev shouted, the green dragon who had destroyed Raem's city last winter. "To the bronze man!"

Raem's mount shrieked and released Laira in fright. All around Raem, his fellow demons hissed, flew back, and raised their claws. Some turned to flee.

"Hold your ranks!" Raem shouted, tugging Anai to face the advancing horde. "Stand before them. Fight, warriors of darkness!"

Squealing, half his demons fled from the onslaught of fire. Others, farther ahead, burned and crumbled. The new force of dragons drove like a glimmering spear into the rotted, black flesh of his host, digging toward him. For the first time in many battles, perhaps the first time in his life, Raem felt something cold, overwhelming, all-consuming flood him: fear.

Laira tore free from her captors, and the golden dragon soared to join her brethren. With smoke, fire, and song, the dragons of Requiem crashed into Raem.

MAEV

She had never seen such darkness, such terror in the world.

Maev had fought many demons in Eteer, small creatures no larger than men. She had battled a host of rocs in the shadows of the escarpment. She had faced living nightmares and overcome them. But not in all her years of exile and war had Maev, Princess of Requiem, seen a force of evil like this—a thousand demons, each as large as a dragon, hiding the sky. They were all different—some scaled like her, others flayed, others dry, some rancid, some mummified—but all stared at her, and all flew toward her, and all craved her blood.

"This is more like it!" Dorvin laughed at her side. He roasted a flying worm, slashed a naked bird with two heads, and slammed his tail into a quivering ball of flying fat. "Let's play, Maev. I'm at three already!"

She soared higher, roared her flames, and ignited a cloud of furry creatures with many eyeballs and tails. "Forget counting and just kill them all!" She roared to the dragons behind her. "Kill them all! For Requiem!"

They flew with her: Dorvin, a silver dragon who laughed as he killed; Alina, a lavender dragon, praying as she fought; and forty dragons of Bar Luan, scared but strong, blowing their fire. Ahead, Maev saw them—the others of Requiem. Laira, a golden dragon alone in a cloud of devilry. Jeid, roaring out his clarion call, leading only a dozen surviving dragons against the horde of the Abyss. Rocs and pteros fought here too, but they were falling fast.

For Requiem. For starlight. Maev blew her flames and lashed her claws. *For King and Column.*

"Maev!" Dorvin shouted, dipping toward her. He grinned, blood on his teeth. "Fifteen now! Stop shouting out battle cries and get to killing de—"

A flying python crashed into him. The beast wrapped around the silver dragon and began to constrict him. Dorvin thrashed but couldn't free himself. With a growl, Maev tore into the demonic snake, ripping through its scales, tugging out segments of its spine, and finally freeing Dorvin. She spat out a chunk of flesh.

"And you stop playing games!" She turned to fly eastward, seeking Raem; where had the king gone? "Find their leader. King Raem, a man in bronze armor upon a pale bat. Chop off the true snake's head."

She thought she glimpsed him again, a blaze of dragonfire against metal. She bared her teeth. She had lost sight of the tyrant, but she flew toward that glint, barreling through demons. Dorvin fought at her left, laughing as he bathed the world with fire. Laira joined her and fought to her right, a golden dragon, bleeding, two spears thrusting out of her but fighting still, roaring as she killed. Smoke and flame and rot covered the world; Maev could no longer see the stars.

Perhaps Requiem fell today. Perhaps this dream of dragons, this new kingdom for her kind, would perish so soon after its birth.

If that is so, I will die with it.

A demon landed upon a dragon at her side and tore off his wing. The dragon lost his magic, returning to human form—a young boy, his shoulder blade bloodied. Demons tore the child apart, tearing off limbs and ripping out organs. Ahead of Maev, another dragon wailed as naked, demonic cats landed upon her, biting deep. The dragon became human again and fell as a woman, screaming, silenced when she hit the ground.

Maev roared, refusing to let the horror overwhelm her. There—she saw it again ahead! A glint on bronze. King Raem.

She pointed ahead. "Laira! Dorvin! I see him there."

The golden dragon and the silver one flew up to her, blood on their fangs. They saw it too. Dorvin grinned savagely, and Laira stared with cold hatred. Between them and the tyrant flew a hundred demons of all shapes, each as large as them.

"For Requiem!" Maev shouted.

"For starlight!" cried Laira.

"I bet I reach the king before you, Mammoth Arse!" shouted Dorvin.

The three dragons flew together, wreathing their flames into a great, spinning torrent of heat and light and sound. The blaze crashed into the demons ahead, carving a path, splitting the sea of them. Beating their wings, roaring their fire in a shrieking inferno, the three dragons flew toward the king.

ISSARI

She walked through Goshar, the City of Bones, the ancient rival of her homeland.

Before falling to darkness, Eteer had been an oasis of water and greenery. The canal drove into the city, bristling with sails. Fountains sprouted in courtyards. Gardens nestled outside houses and upon balconies and roofs. Birds had sung and cypress, fig, and palm trees had lined the streets. That city had fallen, but the memories would forever fill Issari, visions of lush beauty and growing things.

Goshar, meanwhile, was a place of stone, sand, and silence.

No birds sang here. No trees rustled in the breeze. Stern, tan walls rose alongside a boulevard, topped with battlements. Archers stood within turrets, staring through arrowslits; Issari wondered if they were watching for invaders or policing their own people. Towering, triangular buildings rose everywhere, shaped like spearheads, their sandstone bricks craggy. Cobblestones covered the streets, set close enough to allow no weed or flower to grow between them. Issari saw wells, silos, and fortresses topped with merlons. Ahead, perhaps a mark away, rose a massive building shaped like the erect, coiling shell of a mollusk; it soared even taller than the Palace of Eteer, maybe even taller than King's Column in Requiem. Even from this distance, Issari felt very small to see it.

She glanced at Tanin, who walked beside her. He looked back, eyes dark. They dared not speak. This city was too silent. The only sound Issari heard was the footfalls and creaks of armor of the soldiers who walked ahead, leading her deeper into the city.

The boulevard reached a round expanse, and in its center rose a bronze statue, fifty feet tall, of a nude woman with the head of a snake. Here was Mahazar, a goddess of fertility and war. Gosharians crowded the square, praying to the statue, and Issari gazed upon them with interest; despite this city's proximity to Eteer, she had rarely seen Gosharians. Both men and women wore white tunics with a single shoulder strap; the garment left half their chests bare, and Issari felt her cheeks redden to see the women's breasts. Most of the men were bearded, and those beards were long, thick, and curled into many tight rings. Their hair too was long, oiled, and curled. Some men were shorter and smooth-cheeked, and they wore metal collars—eunuch slaves. The smell of spicy perfumes wafted toward Issari, mixed with the tinge of oiled metal; everyone ahead carried the same small, curved dagger on their belts.

Past the square and statue, Issari and Tanin followed the soldiers along narrow streets lined with homes, a market where men hawked grains and dried fruit, and a towering limestone temple lined with columns. Ever they moved closer to the Palace of Goshar, that spiral that coiled up into the clouds. A path wrapped around the tower, lined with turrets, like a trail around a mountain. Archways rose along the walkway, leading into the structure. The soldiers led Issari and Tanin onto that coiling path, and as they climbed, she smiled wryly. Tanin and she could have easily flown to the tower's crest, but she thought that one display of her dragon magic had unnerved these men enough for one day.

As they climbed the path around the tower, Issari got a better look at both the city below and the land beyond. Goshar spread for marks around her, just as large as Eteer, a great labyrinth of stone and dust, a painting all in bronze and copper tones. A few scattered palm trees were all the greenery here, and in the north spread the cracked, rocky desert that had nearly killed her people, a desolate land that separated the mountains from the sea.

South of Goshar, however—past the mountain range where the city nestled—spread a land of plenty. The mountains split the world into separate landscapes as clearly as a coast separates land from sea. As barren as the north was, the south was lush. Three rivers crossed the landscape, flowing down from mountain springs. Farmlands and grasslands spread between these blue threads, undulating in the wind. Birds flew in clouds and herds of deer dotted the land. Issari saw many marks of rye, wheat, barley, and other crops spreading into the distance. Several farms spread outside of Eteer, but much of that city's food had come from the sea; meanwhile, Goshar guarded the road to a cradle of fecundity.

The path kept coiling around the tower, lined with many soldiers and turrets, rising into haze. Finally, when Issari was so winded she could barely breathe, they reached a golden archway between two statues of Mahazar. Several soldiers stood here, clad in ring mail, their beards long and curled into rings that mimicked their armor. Here the gatekeepers entered the tower, leading Issari and Tanin into a wide hall. A mosaic spread across the floor, depicting many serpents coiling together. The columns lining the room were shaped as snakes too, their eyes jeweled, their tongues holding burning incense. Many women lounged here, their faces painted, their bodies nude except for many golden bracelets and necklaces. A few women splashed in a pool of steaming water, while others lay upon cushions, smoking from glass hookahs. A cloud of the green smoke hid the back of the chamber.

The gatekeepers—those soldiers who had led Issari and Tanin here—stood at attention. Their captain knelt and cried out, "Blessed Abina Sin-Naharosh, Prophet of Mahazar! Before you, come to beg your legendary mercy, stands Issari Seran, Princess of Eteer!"

"*Queen* of Eteer," Issari said, staring forward with narrowed eyes, struggling to see the abina through the smoke.

A voice rose from ahead, high-pitched and slightly slurred. "Issari Seran! Of course. Tales of her beauty have reached even this tower. Let—" Coughs interrupted the words, following by a hawking sound. "Let her step forth. Let us gaze upon the legendary beauty of our enemy's daughter."

Issari stepped forward, waving the smoke aside, and beheld the strangest man she had ever seen. At first, she almost thought him one of her father's demons. The abina—or king—of Goshar was obese, pink, and bald. He was so large she doubted he could walk or even stand. He lounged upon many tasseled cushions, smoking from a hookah, wearing nothing but a golden blanket upon his lap. What he lacked in clothes he made up for in jewels; golden chains and strings of gemstones hung around his neck, bracelets shaped as snakes with jeweled eyes circled his wrists, and a headdress of topaz and amethysts perched atop his glistening head. His eyebrows thrust out, seemingly the only hair on his body, long as fingers and dyed green. Many golden bowls spread around him, containing sweets, skewered scorpions, and even an entire roast peacock with its bright tail reattached.

Issari walked up toward the abina, head held high. "Merciful Abina of Goshar! My father has abandoned the great kingdom of Eteer, Guardian of the Coast. For many years, Eteer of the Sea and Goshar of the Mountains have fought bitter wars. Let us unite water and rock. I've come to forge an alliance between our kingdoms."

The obese man stared at her. Issari could not decide if his eyes were narrowed shrewdly or simply engulfed by folds of fat. Those small, blue eyes moved up and down her body, and finally the king sucked on his hookah and barked a laugh. "It is told in Goshar, child, that Eteer is overrun. That your father meddled in affairs no mortal should, that the terror he unleashed has toppled his towers. It is said that ragged, starving refugees of Eteer now camp outside my walls, begging for mercy." He snorted, spraying spittle. "You come to forge an alliance? You come as a beggar queen in exile, pleading for a few drops of water and scraps of dry bread."

She bared her teeth and stepped closer. "The walls of Eteer are overrun; it is true. My people have wandered the desert, and they seek aid; that too is truth. My armies are shattered, and I cannot even return to my palace. Yes, I am exiled. But I still have my title. And Eteer still guards the sea. Whether its walls and towers stand does not change that fact. Whether soldiers or demons sprawl along the coast, that coast still leads to an empire of trade." She took a deep breath, her fingers tingling. "I will give you access to that sea. I will free you from your landlocked existence, ever your bane, ever the reason Goshar languished in the shadow of Eteer."

The abina's tongue emerged like a snake from its lair to lick his lips. His small eyes glittered, and his fingers—each one heavy with rings—clutched as his blanket. "Why do I need your title? Your kingdom lies in ruin. I could muster my army, march across the desert, and claim Eteer without your aid."

"And my people, those who survived the demon wars, would never accept you as ruler. At every turn they would resist a tyrant; ever would the blades of my surviving soldiers find the flesh of Goshar. Many of those soldiers wait outside your walls, and they are still armed, still ready to fight. Even should you claim

219

and hold Eteer, defeating both the nephilim who infest its streets and those Eteerians who still survive behind its walls, you would find only a gateway to darkness. Only the rightful ruler of Eteer can seal the doors of the Abyss. My father has forfeited that claim; it is now mine. Let us join our forces! The remnants of my army and the might of yours. My claim to Eteer and your leadership. Together we will recapture the coast, slay the children of demons, seal the Abyss . . . and rule together."

Saliva dripped down the king's chin to land on his chest. He leaned forward in his cushions with a sticky sound. "So you suggest a marriage. I've offered King Raem to wed you before; he replied by laying siege to my walls."

Issari closed her eyes for a heartbeat and took a deep breath, steeling herself. "I offer myself to you."

She heard Tanin give a strangled sound behind her, and Issari lowered her head. She knew that she must do this. She knew she must sacrifice herself to save Eteer, to save her people. She would not love her husband, but she loved Eteer, and she loved Tanin, and she loved her people; this was how she would save them.

She caressed the amulet embedded into her hand—her mother's amulet. *I do this for our home, Mother. For our people. We are daughters of Requiem, both of us, but so are we daughters of Eteer. And I do this for you, Sena, for your memory, for the love I have for you, for the love you had for our fallen home.*

The obese abina slapped his hands together, jiggling his rolls of fat. He mouth opened in a grin, and sweat dripped down his red cheeks.

"Excellent! We shall be wed at once. Tir-Kahan! Step forth, Tir-Kahan! I add another jewel to my treasure. This one will be the crown of my collection."

A man stepped forward from the smoke. As large as Sin-Naharosh was, this man was thin; he was almost skeletal, his skin stretched over his bones. Like most Gosharians, he wore a white tunic that left half his chest bare, and Issari could see his ribs. A thin white beard dangled from his gaunt face, and a crown of gilded bones—they looked like human finger bones—nested upon his head. The amulet of the goddess Mahazar hung from his neck. The talisman was so large and heavy, the man walked with a stoop. In his gaunt hands, Tir-Kahan held a clay tablet engraved with cuneiform writing.

Armor clanked behind her, and Tanin approached. He leaned close and whispered to Issari, voice urgent. "Issari, don't do this. There are others ways. The women here . . . look at them." He held her arm. "Let us return to the desert if we must."

The skeletal priest stepped forth, reached into a pouch, and pulled out a writhing snake. The animal hissed, tongue darting, and Tir-Kahan held it forth. Before Issari would react, the snake struck, biting her neck. She let out a cry and reached to the wound; her fingers came away bloody.

"The great goddess Mahazar has tasted the blood of Issari Seran!" the old priest announced. He turned back toward his abina, the lounging Sin-Naharosh, and brought the snake close to the man's sweaty chest. The serpent struck again, biting into the flesh. The old priest spoke louder. "Blood is mixed with blood, blessed with the bite of the serpent. Mahazar, Queen of Snakes, Goddess of Goshar, blesses this union. Blessed be Issari, wife of Sin-Naharosh!"

Tanin stepped closer to the king, and his hand strayed toward his sword. His face reddened. "Wait a moment! You mean they're married already? That's not a marriage ceremony. I refuse to—"

221

The king sighed and waved his hand dismissively. "Guards, drag this man away." He puffed on his hookah. "Keep him alive for now, but keep him out of my sight."

Soldiers stepped forth, drew their swords, and approached Tanin. The young Vir Requis drew his own blade and snarled. "Stand back! Stand back or I'll burn you all. I do not accept this marriage." He sliced the air with his blade. "I warn you, stand back!"

Across the hall, the nude women gasped and chattered. Soldiers shouted at Tanin, the priest sang prayers, and Sin-Naharosh laughed and tossed sweets into his mouth.

Issari shouted over the din. "Do not harm my half-brother! Sin-Naharosh, I will honor our marriage, but do not harm him! I—" She gasped as soldiers stepped forth and grabbed her arms. "Release me! Sin-Naharosh, what is the meaning of this?"

One soldier twisted her arm. Another kicked her behind her knee, forcing her to kneel. She shouted as the soldiers brought forth chains. Before she could react—before she could even summon her magic—one soldier slapped a metal collar around her neck. Another bound her wrists behind her back. Her magic filled her, and she tried to shift, to become a dragon in this hall. Scales rose across her, yet as her body began to grow, the chains and collar tightened around her, shoving her back into human form.

"Tanin!" she cried.

He had begun to shift. Wings grew from his back. Claws lengthened from his fingers. Before he could complete the transformation, a soldier swung a club. The metal weapon slammed into Tanin's scaly head with a crack. His magic left him, and Tanin fell to the floor, only a man again. Soldiers leaped onto him, punching and kicking, and bound his arms and legs.

"Drag him away!" Sin-Naharosh said, laughing as he chewed his sweets. "Toss him into the dungeon." He wiped crumbs off his chest. "Toss the girl among the others."

Issari screamed and struggled as the guards pulled her away from the throne. Her heels dragged across the mosaic, and her chains clattered. The other women of the hall looked at her silently, their eyes full of pity. They lay upon tasseled cushions, on the ledges of pools, and upon giltwood beds, nude and jeweled and scented of sweet perfumes. For the first time, Issari saw what the hookah smoke had previously obscured. Every woman here was chained. These were not simply wives; they were slaves.

The voice of the gatekeeper, the man who had led Issari to the palace, rose ahead. "What of the Eteerians outside our hall?"

Sin-Naharosh snorted, nearly invisible now behind the green smoke. "Bring in whoever is strong enough to serve as a soldier or slave. If you find the women attractive enough, give a few to your men." He sucked in more smoke and coughed. "Leave the rest outside to perish. The vultures must feed too."

Terror pounded through Issari. Her limbs trembled, her belly froze, and her heart thrashed against her ribs. "Sin-Naharosh! You will pay for this treachery. You will burn in the light of Taal!" She raised her amulet, but its light seemed so dim in the smoke; it barely shone for more than a few feet.

"Treachery? I fulfill our deal." The obese king waved smoke aside, coughing. "I married you as you wished. And I will conquer Eteer as you wished too. Your kingdom, like your body, are mine."

She screamed. The guards knocked her down among the slaves, attached her chains to a column, and walked away. Issari leaped up, tugging at the chains, trying to free herself. The smoke flowed thicker, engulfing her. She saw nothing but the swirling green clouds. She heard nothing but the cruel king laugh.

ALINA

"Shine upon me, stars of Requiem," she prayed. "This is Requiem's birth. This is Requiem's greatest hour of need."

Tears shone in her eyes to behold the evil engulfing her. She flew among only forty other dragons, perhaps the only children of Requiem in the world. Before her the demons seemed endless, covering the sky, hiding the mountainsides, hiding even the light of the stars. Did those stars still shine upon her? Alina had spent her life worshiping those heavenly lights, the Draco constellation that had always guided her way. Today she could not feel that guidance. Their light had led her here—from her tribe, to Requiem, to Bar Luan, and here to their great battle above Two Skull Mountain—but even their light could not pierce the darkness that had flown from the south.

"Please, my stars. Do not abandon your children."

A skeletal creature flew toward her like a dragon stripped of all muscle and fat, beating decrepit wings stretched with brittle old leather. Its jaws opened wide, lined with many teeth. Alina tried to burn it, but her fire washed over the dry bones harmlessly. The creature slammed into her, clattering, snapping its teeth, cutting her with its claws. She screamed, her lavender scales cracking under the onslaught. She cried for aid, but none would answer; her brother flew ahead with Laira and Maev, and the dragons of Bar Luan were battling their own demons. The creature's teeth drove into her wing, and Alina shouted out to her stars.

I've never killed before. I don't know how to fight. I—

The creature's claws grabbed her throat. Her blood poured.

I am a dragon of Requiem. Today we are all warriors.

She swiped her tail, slamming it against the skeletal beast. One of its ribs snapped, and it released her and howled. With a hoarse shout, Alina drove forward, crashing into it, and lashed her tail again and again. Its spine shattered, raining segments. Blowing smoke, she grabbed the creature's neck in her claws, twisted, and tore off its head. She tossed it down, and it slammed into another demon—this one a slimy worm the size of a whale. She roared down her fire, burning both severed head and the creature beneath it.

Alina growled, teeth bared, and stared from side to side at the flying demons. "And so, with darkness around me, I will cast my own light."

The demons flew toward her and her people. Behind her, her fellow dragons raised their flames. Demons and dragons slammed together with crashing fire and blood.

And Alina killed. Her teeth tore through demon hides. Her fire blazed over creatures of nightmare. A bloated thing, its belly swinging, buzzed toward her, and she disemboweled it with her claws. A great, naked fowl with three necks swooped above her, beaks pecking. She blasted it with fire, then bit into the charred meat, tugging out its innards. A pale demon covered in spikes and hooks slammed into her, cutting her leg, and she clawed madly, shattering its armor, cutting the softness beneath. Blood coated her scales and teeth, and she became a feral thing, a beast herself, a creature of retribution. The starlight had faded and her own darkness claimed her.

"For Requiem I kill," she said. "For Requiem I will become this beast. For Requi—"

An arrow whistled and slammed into her shoulder.

Alina yowled.

She beat her wings, but they felt so slow, so heavy. Pain pulsed from her shoulder across her body, digging like insects crawling through her veins. Her heart pounded. Haze covered her eyes. She looked up, struggling to stay aloft, to see the young woman flying toward her.

The woman held a bow, and a quiver of arrows hung across her back. She wore a cotton tunic, a fur cloak, and patches of bronze armor. She rode upon a buzzing insect as large as a dragon, its many eyes burning with inner flame. The strangest thing about the woman, however, was not the demon she rode but her face. Stitches surrounded it, as if she wore a mask of skin. She flew toward Alina, nocking another arrow.

"Fly to me, reptile!" the woman called down to her. "I am Ciana, Slayer of Dragons. I wear a new face after the fire of Requiem burned me. Now I live to see your kingdom fall."

She fired a second arrow.

Alina tried to dodge the missile, but the first arrow still blazed in her shoulder; she thought that poison covered its head. She managed to flap her wings once, but she only rose a few feet. The second arrow drove into her leg, and new pain exploded through Alina, and she dipped a dozen feet in the sky.

She managed to stay afloat through sheer willpower. Tears in her eyes, Alina looked up at the young woman. Ciana hovered above in the haze, riding her buzzing insect.

"You don't have to do this, child!" Alina said. "You don't have to fight for him. You don't have to fly with evil. You—"

Ciana fired a third arrow.

It slammed into Alina's neck.

Poison flowed through her, the world spun, and Alina fell from the sky.

She crashed against one demon, tumbled over him, flapped her wings once, then slammed into the mountainside. The arrows in her body snapped. The shock knocked the magic out of her. She shrank, taking human form again, and lay moaning upon the mountain in her druid robes. Her blood stained the lavender fabric.

Before Alina could rise, the demonic insect swooped toward her, wings buzzing, eyes spinning. Wreathed in firelight, Ciana leaped from the saddle, landed gracefully upon the mountain, and held a sword to Alina's neck.

Alina froze, staring up at the woman.

Ciana trembled, and her lips peeled back into a snarl. Her eyes burned and leaked tears. "Where is Tanin, the creature who lied to me, who tried to sneak into my bed?" Her tears splashed down, and her sword shook. "Where is Jeid, the King of Reptiles, the one who burned me?"

Such pain in her. Alina winced. *Such grief, such rage.* She had never seen a child so lost, so broken.

"We never meant to hurt you, child." Alina pushed herself onto her elbows, her blood still trickling. "I'm so sorry for how you suffered. Let me help you. Let me pray for you. I can heal the pain inside you, can—"

Ciana drove down her sword, piercing Alina's thigh.

Blood spurted and Alina screamed.

"You will be silent, creature!" Ciana twisted the blade. "All you creatures do is lie. You took my face. You made me somebody else. You will all die here this night, and I will laugh and spit upon your graves."

Alina grimaced, crying out in pain, the sword in her leg. "Listen to me, Ciana. You don't have to fall to evil. Look above you. Look at the demons that cover the sky, that spread across the world. Is this what you fight for? A world of demons?" She reached up a shaky hand. "You need not do this. You can find another way. You can be forgiven."

Tears streamed down Ciana's cheeks, collecting on her new face's stitches like dew on cobwebs. "It's too late for me. Too late. When Jeid burned me, he burned all compassion from my soul. When he took my face, he took my heart too. And now I will do the same to you." Ciana knelt, driving her knee into Alina's belly. She tugged the sword free from Alina's thigh and brought it to her face. "Now I take your face. I will peel it off, creature, and leave you alive and screaming."

Alina tried to summon her magic, to become a dragon again, but she had lost too much blood. More blood was flowing from her thigh; she thought an artery was cut. Poison from the arrows still flowed through her. Her magic eluded her, and she could only raise her arms weakly, uselessly trying to shove Ciana off.

The blade pierced the skin under her ear.

"You made me do this," Ciana said, trembling. "You made me who I am."

She moved the blade, cutting a line from Alina's ear down to her chin.

Her blood dripped, and Alina tried to rise but could not, and she cried out to her stars, but she could not see their light, only the face of her enemy, a face stitched onto a broken soul.

My own soul will rise, Alina thought. *My soul will fly to the stars. If you can hear me, stars, grant me death now.*

Light blazed above, but it was not starlight. Fire rained. A silver dragon swooped and roared. The demonic insect, Ciana's mount, tried to rise and fight, but the dragonfire crashed into it. It crumpled.

Ciana leaped to her feet, bloody sword in hand, and spun around. She raised her arms in defense, a useless gesture. The dragon's claws drove into her chest and emerged bloody from her back.

Lying on the mountainside, her lifeblood dripping away, Alina winced and her heart twisted, for even now she had not craved Ciana's death.

"Alina!" The silver dragon shook his claws, sending Ciana's corpse tumbling down the mountainside. Dorvin released his magic, resumed human form, and knelt above Alina. "Stars damn it. Alina! Can you hear me?"

She smiled weakly at her brother. She raised her hand and touched his clean-shaven cheek. "Even as war burns the world, you still shave every morning, you vain thing." Her tears flowed down to her smile. "You're going to drive Maev crazy, but you'll make her happy too."

"*You're* going to drive *me* crazy." He tore off a strip of his cloak and bandaged her leg. "Talking like that, like you're not going to be here? Hush your big mouth." Yet she saw the dampness in his eyes, the tremble in his fingers. "Falling down and getting wounded like that . . . Are you sure we're related?

Damn it, Alina." He pressed more cloth against the wound on her neck. "Once this war's over, I'm going to kill you."

Her eyelids fluttered. He was too late; she knew that. She had lost too much blood, and her pain was fading now. "I'll look after you." Her voice was but a whisper. "I promise you, Dorvin. Always. I will look down upon you from the stars, and I will bless Requiem. My light will always shine with you."

His tears flowed freely. He pulled her into his arms. "I told you to hush your mouth! You just have a few scratches on you. You're talking as if you're dying or something." He held her close. "I'm not going to let you die. I've always looked out for you."

"And now you'll look after Requiem." She clutched his hand. "You are a warrior of Requiem, a defender of our people. Remember that always. In Requiem's gauntlet, as fire rains and our blood spills upon the mountain, I name you Eleison, an old word in a forgotten tongue. It means mercy, and I pray now to the stars to show mercy to Requiem, to let her rise from flame into a great kingdom of starlight."

He held her close, whispering into her hair, begging her not to leave, but Alina knew it was her time. This had always been her time to die. A young child learning of the stars, a druid leading her people to Requiem, a priestess freeing the captives of Bar Luan, a warrior in a battle of demons—she had always been meant to travel this path of darkness. This path led her to gates of starlight, and Alina smiled because she could see them now, shining above—the stars of Requiem. The Draco constellation emerged from clouds, and its light warmed her, welcoming her home. And she saw them above—great halls woven of starlight, their many columns bright, a vision of the Requiem that would be, the Requiem those she had led here would build.

"It's beautiful," she whispered. "It's so beautiful."

Her brother held her close, and she closed her eyes. She let his warmth comfort her, and she let a new kind of magic flow through her and lead her down a new path.

LAIRA

Her father laughed upon his demon. "Your friends abandon you, Laira! The silver dragon has fled."

Laira glared and blasted fire his way, but she was down to sparks; they scattered off his armor. Dorvin had darted off, calling for his sister. Jeid still fought across the battlefield, surrounded by demons. Only Laira and Maev faced the King of Eteer. The battle raged around them, a sphere of rocs, pteros, and demons. Here, in a pocket of smoke and fire, they fought alone.

"Fancy the left side, Laira?" Maev asked. Smoke rose between the green dragon's teeth. "I'll take the right."

Laira beat her wings and smiled thinly. "Let's dance."

The two dragons, gold and green, charged.

Raem laughed upon his demon. Scattering what fire remained within her, Laira flew toward her father's right flank. The king's mount reared and lashed its claws, and Laira was forced to pull back, to snap her teeth, to try to claw her way forward. The demon was larger than her, a twisted thing of skin stretched across too much bone. The demon's head was its worst deformity—it looked like a human head, waterlogged, swollen, its eyes leaking tears. But the creature's claws still lashed out, tipped with metal. One claw drove along Laira's chest, shedding her blood. She screamed and clawed back, tearing at the creature. She ripped through its skin and hit bone. The demon barely seemed to feel the pain; it had no blood to shed.

Laira growled, rose higher, and swooped, trying to reach Raem in the saddle. He raised his shield, and her claws clattered against the bronze disk. He rose in the sky, knocking her back, and his demon turned toward her, teeth snapping.

On the king's other side, Maev was attacking, but the demon's tail was whipping madly, holding her back.

"Is this how you dance?" Raem asked, laughing. When Laira swooped again, Raem swung his sword. The khopesh bit into Laira's foot, and she roared in pain. The demon's tail slammed into Maev's neck, piercing her skin; the green dragon cried out, suddenly sounding very young, and crashed down onto the mountainside. At once a horde of demons, massive slugs covered with white spikes, landed upon her and began to bite. Maev flailed upon the mountain, rolling down the slope, struggling to tear off the creatures.

Still flying, bleeding and winded, Laira tried to attack Raem again. His swinging sword and his demon's claws held her back.

"And so we fight alone, Laira." He smiled thinly. "Everyone has abandoned you. Your friends are gone. Your king cannot reach you. Your mother is dead." He stroked his demon's hair. "Do you see this creature? She was human once. I will turn you into a similar demon."

Terror pounded through Laira. She did not fear death, but to linger in mockery of life, never dying, always serving her father's cruelty . . . that she could not bear. The demon wept even as it attacked; perhaps some part of its broken mind still clung to memories of its old self. That fear gave Laira the strength to charge again. She slammed into Raem, snapping her teeth, raining her last sparks of fire onto his armor.

He laughed as he fought back, cutting her. His demon's wings entwined with her own, and for a moment they flew as one creature, some conjoined twin, their limbs locked together. Teeth dug into Laira's chest, and her father's sword cut her again, and they tumbled through the sky, a ball of scales and skin and metal. The world spun madly. Locked together, the dragon, demon, and king fell toward the mountainside, rolled through a cave, and entered the shadowy cavern within.

The women and children of Leatherwing and Goldtusk still stood within. They fled from the battling beasts, scurrying into alcoves on the walls. Locked into a ball, Laira and the demon slammed into the great stalagmite rising in the center of the cavern. It cracked and tipped over. Half the pillar, the throne on its crest, drove down and slammed into the cave floor with a cloud of dust. The impact tore Laira and the demon apart. Laira kept spinning, crashed onto the floor, and could not rise.

Laira's wings beat, too weak to lift her back into the air. Her tail flailed. She managed to blow a spurt of fire, but it wasn't enough to stop her enemy. Raem hovered above her atop his demon. The creature's wings blasted Laira with air. Raem gave a sharp, shrill whistle, and with a flutter of insect wings, a dozen motley demons buzzed into the cavern to join him. All hovered above Laira, leering with red eyes, their tongues drooping. Some were furred, others feathered, and some inverted, their exposed organs pulsing. One among them looked like a beetle with human arms, and from each of its fingers grew a tool—scalpels, needles, spools with thread, bone saws, and other instruments. Laira yowled and tried to rise, but demons spat upon her, their globs of saliva hitting her like stones, knocking her back down onto the cave floor. Stars floated before her eyes.

"And now, Laira," Raem said, smiling down from his beast, "your pain begins."

Dragonfire blazed.

A roar echoed across the cavern.

With a clatter of copper scales, engulfed in smoke, Jeid flew across the chamber and barreled into the demons.

The creatures scattered. Some crashed down onto the cave floor. The copper dragon roared, a sound that shook the cave, and the walls undulated in the heat waves rising between the great king's teeth. Jeid Blacksmith—King Aeternum, Lord of Requiem—blasted his fire. The jet shrieked, blue in its center, washing over the demons and crashing onto the cave walls. The inferno blazed across the chamber, the sound deafening, the heat almost intolerable. Laira lay on the floor, gazing up at the holocaust, and for a moment she saw what the humans hunted, what Raem feared—a dragon in his full glory and might, a beast of sunfire and fury.

"Jeid!" Laira called out, tears in her eyes.

The demons crashed down, charred with dragonfire, cut with claws, leaking their innards.

All but Raem's mount. The demonic bat, too lanky to burn, rose from the blaze, skin peeling off her bones. The King of Eteer still sat upon her, the fire clutching at his cloak. His arms burned, wings of fire. But still Raem laughed as he soared, head tossed back, wreathed in the flame.

"So this is Aeternum, King of Reptiles!" Raem raised his sword. "You too will join Laira in the courts of the Abyss."

Jeid landed beside Laira, raised his head, and roared again. The cave shook at the sound. Cracks raced along the walls. Laira struggled to her feet, still in dragon form, half the size of the coppery beast. The two dragons raised their heads, staring up at the demon fluttering above.

"Requiem rises," Laira said.

Jeid smiled crookedly. "With a pillar of fire."

The stone pillar had fallen in the cave. Laira and Jeid roared their flames, the streams wreathing together, rising in a new pillar, a column of dragonfire. The shrieking fountain crashed into the demonic bat.

The creature plunged down.

Laira and Jeid stepped away from each other, and the bat crashed down between them, charred down to bones. Skin peeled off its head, and its hair had burned off. It was still alive, its organs exposed and still pumping. One of its eyes had melted. The other eye met Laira's gaze. Laira winced, the pain of that eye worse than arrows or demon teeth. There was gratitude in that eye. The creature opened her mouth and whispered.

"Thank you." Relief flooded the demon's face. "Thank you."

Its eye closed and its organs deflated.

For a long moment, silence filled the cave. Then a trembling voice spoke.

"Please. Laira, please." Raem rose, covered in soot and blood. His sword was gone, fallen in the battle, and deep gashes bled upon his legs. His arms were burnt, the skin peeling away. He tried to run, but Jeid's foot slammed down, blocking his escape. Raem turned toward Laira. "My daughter. Mercy."

Still a golden dragon, Laira growled. She stepped closer to Raem, leaned down above him, and bared her teeth. "I have killed many before. I slew Zerra, the chieftain who spent years hurting me, the chieftain you bought with bronze. I killed many of your demons. And now, Father, I will kill you. You turned me into a killer. You called me a beast, but I was a daughter to you, an innocent child you sent on a path of blood. Your own fear became true, and yes, now I am a monster. You made me one, and this monster will be your death." She roared, the sound pounding against him, her breath flattening his skin against his skull. "In the name of Requiem, in the name of my brother, in the same of all those you hurt, I end your life now."

She leaned down to bite.

"Laira, please!" he shouted, raising his arms in front of his head.

Her jaws snapped shut around his arms, severing both at the shoulders.

Raem screamed.

Blood sprayed from his stumps. Laira spat out both arms, tasting his blood. Raem still stood before her, shouting hoarsely, face pale.

Laira bellowed and leaned in to bite again.

Her father turned and ran.

"Stitchmark!" the tyrant cried. "Stitchmark, help!"

One of the demons—the creature with tools growing from its fingers—had survived the inferno of dragonfire. Its shell was cracked and leaking, and its face was burnt, but it still buzzed forward, wrapped its legs around Raem's torso, and lifted the maimed king. The demon soared, insect wings beating with a fury, and began to fly toward the cave exit.

Fast as a crocodile leaping from water, Jeid lunged upward and snapped his teeth. His jaws closed around Raem's dangling legs. Blood showered and Jeid spat out both legs. Raem screamed again, a horrible sound, high-pitched, almost demonic. Stitchmark flew faster, holding its lord. Raem bled from four stumps, only his torso and head remaining. Jeid snapped his jaws again, trying to catch the king, but Stitchmark flew out of the cave too quickly, bearing the dying, mutilated wreck of a man.

Laira beat her wings and took flight, chasing her father. Jeid flew at her side. They burst out from the cave into a sky full of demons.

"Where is he?" Jeid shouted.

Laira whipped her head from side to side, seeking her father and the creature Stitchmark. Too many demons still flew here, and smoke hid the moon and stars. She couldn't see Raem through the clouds of enemies.

"Grizzly!" rose a cry. A green dragon came flying toward them, blood seeping through cracks in her scales. Maev spat out a chunk of demon flesh. "Father, the demons are fleeing! Victory is ours!" She grinned.

"Hunt them down!" Laira shouted. "Burn them all!" She beat her wings mightily, flying back into battle. Jeid and Maev flew at her sides.

The demons, once a thousand strong, had lost many; hundreds lay upon the mountainside, burnt and lacerated. Pteros, rocs, and dragons kept crashing into them, tearing more apart. The unholy horde, their leader gone, seemed to lose all will to fight. Screeching, they flew south, leaving the mountain, crying out for their missing king.

The alliance of dragons and tribes gave chase. Laira blew her fire, roasting demon after demon. Her claws and fangs tore the creatures apart. The dragons of Requiem flew around her, dozens strong, their flames lighting the night, burning the creatures, and raining down onto the fields. Surviving tribesmen of Goldtusk and Leatherwing flew with them, firing arrows, their beasts catching and ripping demons apart. Rot and blood fell upon the world as the demons fled.

"Slay them all!" Laira cried. "Let none escape. Kill every last one!"

For long hours they flew in pursuit, hunting demons, chasing them in the darkness. The horde broke apart. Creatures flew every which way. Some landed in the forests and fled between the trees. Others sank into rivers. And ever the fire of Requiem lit the sky, illuminating and burning them.

"Where are you, Father?" Laira asked, flying over fields, seeking him, burning whatever fleeing demon she saw.

He was dead; he had to be. She knew that. She knew no man could survive that injury, the loss of all four limbs. He must have died within moments. Almost certainly, he lay dead back at Two Skull Mountain, hidden among other corpses upon the mountainside. Yet still Laira flew over hills and valleys and forests, hunting demons, seeking him.

Dawn rose, painting the sky and land red. Sunbeams fell between the clouds like pillars of fire. The dragons of Requiem—thirty had survived the slaughter—flew around Laira, gliding on the wind, the sunlight on their scales. Jeid flew at Laira's right side, eyes narrowed, and smoke rose from his nostrils.

"He's dead." Jeid grunted. "The last demons fled or perished. Let us return to Two Skull Mountain and seek what survivors we can."

Laira wanted to keep flying, to keep hunting, but Jeid was right. They had not seen a demon for an hour now, but perhaps some demons still remained at Two Skull Mountain, and perhaps some of their people—Vir Requis or tribesmen—lay wounded, needing aid. Reluctantly, the dragons turned in the sky. They flew back to a mountain covered in blood, shattered bones, and the corpses of men and demons. The fallen Vir Requis were almost indistinguishable from the dead tribesmen; in death they had returned to human forms.

Gingerly, Laira landed upon the mountainside beside Dorvin. She lowered her head, folded her wings, and shifted back into human form. She knelt, the pain almost too great to bear.

Dorvin looked up at her, eyes red. He held his lifeless sister in his arms.

"She gave her life for Requiem," the young man said, voice choked. "She was a brave warrior, but she was more than that too. She was a healer. A priestess. A great light." He lowered his head, and his tears flowed. "She was the dearest person I knew."

Jeid approached them, back in human form. The gruff, bearded man knelt by Dorvin and placed a hand on his shoulder. "Through Alina's sacrifice, Requiem rises. We are victorious."

Victorious? Laira looked around, seeing so much death. Half of Requiem had fallen here; sixty dragons had flown to war, and thirty lay mangled and burnt upon the mountain. Many warriors from Goldtusk and Leatherwing lay among them, their bodies crushed, and dozens of the great beasts—rocs and pteros—lay dead among them. Everywhere the corpses of demons rotted.

This is no victory, Laira thought, looking at the few survivors. *There is no joy here. This is only a shred of hope.* The wind blew against her, scented of blood and ash, and she shivered. *We won a battle, but more fear than ever fills me today.*

She closed her eyes, seeing her father again, hearing his cruel words, biting off his arms, staring frozen at the creature Stitchmark. They were still out there, maybe still alive, maybe still seeking her. A few survivors were chanting for victory, but their voices sounded too small, too weak in this endless world of despair. Kneeling in blood, Laira hugged herself and lowered her head.

RAEM

Buzzing.

Clatters and whispers.

Sawing and spinning and trickling.

Raem floated through a dream of sounds, lights, and shadows. The creature hovered above him, a beetle of the sky, a god of bone and metal and spinning eyes. Glass lenses moved on copper rods, up and down, forward and back, magnifying and shrinking those peering white eyes. The creature's tongue hung low, and its voice chattered, and always its fingers probed him, hurt him. Fingers of scalpels. Fingers of saws. Fingers of needles. Fingers of spools, the thread around them spinning madly. Beyond this demonic physician spread dark clouds and streams of light, rising and falling suns, nights and days dancing, creaking trees, clouds of pain.

He laughed and bucked, wriggling, trying to rise, to move his limbs. Nothing but stumps. Nothing but pain.

"An abomination." His spittle flew as he laughed. "Look what they did to me. But I still live. I live!"

The insect above him only chattered in its tongue, tools moving in a fury. Dead demons spread around them in the forest, their limbs severed like his own—tentacles, insect legs, claws, strewn around, piled up, leaking. He wondered if his own limbs were among them. He wondered if Laira had swallowed his arms.

He wondered if they still moved inside her, grabbing at her innards.

"Stitchmark heal you," the insect buzzed above, its tools dipping and rising, cutting and sewing. "Stitchmark bring back your limbs."

The sun set and rose, the trees moved, rain washed him, and the shadows of a fever dream danced like demons.

Finally in a pale dawn he rose.

He looked down upon his body, then tossed back his head and laughed in the sunlight.

New limbs grew from him. His left leg was that of a great bird, ending with a yellow talon. His right leg was furry and thick, ending with a hoof. His right arm was that of a lobster, its claw clacking. His left arm was now a long, wriggling tentacle.

"You should have used human limbs, Stitchmark!" he said, still laughing, tears flowing down his cheeks.

The demon buzzed and hovered before him. "Human limbs are weak. They rot and fall off. The limbs of demons I gave you, and they made you strong."

Raem took a step. The furry leg moved forward and the hoof pushed into the mud. He took another step. The talon stepped onto grass. He raised his arms, the lobster claw clacking, the tentacle writhing. He was an abomination. He was a demon. He was strong.

"You cannot stop me now, Requiem." His body convulsed with his joy. "You took my arms, Laira. You took my legs, Jeid. You made me so much stronger. I rise greater than ever before! I am Raem Seran, King of the Abyss. The bones of dragons will bedeck my new hall!"

Sweat drenched him and he trembled with weakness. He stumbled toward Stitchmark, climbed onto the creature's armored back, and pointed his tentacle to the south.

"Fly, Stitchmark. Fly to Eteer. Our army has fallen but we return home in glory."

They flew, the world streaming around them, skies streaked with many clouds, beams of light like dragonfire, wilted forests, gray seas. They left the north, this realm of dragons, this realm that had purified him, that had cleansed his soul and turned him into a demon, into a great king of the underworld. He was half-starved, mad with thirst and fever, pale and thin but still laughing when Stitchmark carried him back into Eteer, his wondrous city.

"Beautiful Jewel of the Coast." He gazed upon his city with damp eyes. "Fair Crown of Taal." It was an ancient city, perhaps the oldest in the world. It was a beacon of civilization in a world of chaos. It was a hive of demon spawn, shattered bricks, and the birth of a new nation.

His children had been born; today they were all his children. The nephilim perched upon the shattered walls and broken roofs of Eteer, gazing at him with wide, lit eyes. Half demons. Half mortal women. Fallen Ones. They were the size of men already, their skin rotten, their wings leathery and warty. Fangs grew from their mouths, long as daggers. Their sweet, rancid smell filled Raem's nostrils, and he smiled. They had destroyed his city, the lovelies; few buildings remained standing, and the skeletons of many mortals littered the streets. From the ruins rose his palace, one of the few buildings that still stood. Its gardens were gone. Its columns were blackened. The engravings of old gods had been scratched off its walls; the spirals of the Abyss now dripped upon them, painted in human gore.

Stitchmark took him to that great palace, and Raem walked into his hall, his horse hoof thudding, his talon scratching. When he passed by his statue—one of the few statues to have survived the war—he gazed upon that proud, stone king and laughed. He saw a noble man, clean-shaven, his limbs muscular, his body pure. When Raem looked down upon his body, he saw a creature more glorious by far, a creature more than a man. He kept walking, heading toward his throne.

Angel lay here, her body long as a dragon, her wings draped around her. She gazed at him with eyes like embers. Like a serpent, she coiled around his throne. The seat appeared to have been shattered, and strings of skin and veins held it together like flesh growing over broken bone. Upon the throne sat a nephil, its eyes large and green, its body raw and wet.

"Our son," said Angel. "Ishnafel."

Raem approached slowly. He reached out his new left arm, and the writhing tentacle brushed against Ishnafel's cheek.

"He is beautiful. He is my heir."

When Raem tried to remove his son from the throne, the nephil hissed and snapped his teeth. His fangs drove into Raem's new arm, but he felt no pain. He placed the prince in his mother's grip. The child nursed at the stone breast, the lava flowing down his throat. Raem sat down, leaned back in his throne, and lovingly gazed upon his family.

LAIRA

Laira stood in the dawn before the communal grave below the mountain. Boulders topped the hill of crumbly earth, one per vanquished life. Over a hundred souls lay buried here at the foothills, Two Skull Mountain forever watching over their rest. Tribesmen of Goldtusk. Tribesmen of Leatherwing. Many of their mounts, dear Neiva among them. Grass rustled around this hill of mourning, and birds sang overhead. The sky was clear, the air fresh, but forever this would be a place of grief for Laira.

"Goodbye, Neiva," she whispered, the wind streaming through her hair and fur cloak. "Goodbye, my husband."

She lowered her head, the pain grabbing and squeezing her heart. She had married Chieftain Oritan to forge an alliance, to bring aid to Requiem, not for love. In his bed, however, she had found the bud of that love, found a man who was strong and mighty yet gentle, loving, kind. She would forever remember how he had gazed into her eyes years ago, treating her—a mere servant—as an equal. And she would never forget marrying him, sharing a life with him if only for a day.

Goodbye.

She turned from the grave to look at those standing behind her. The tribes of Goldtusk and Leatherwing, down to half their size, watched her with solemn eyes—men, women, children. The wind ruffled hair, feathers, and fur cloaks. All were silent, staring, awaiting her words.

The world was so silent, Laira didn't even have to raise her voice for them all to hear.

"I am Laira, Chieftain of Goldtusk, Daughter of Ka'altei. I am Laira, Widow of Oritan, Chieftain's Wife of Leatherwing. Today I stand before a united tribe, and you await my commands." Her throat felt too tight, her eyes too dry. "I came north as an Eteerian exile. I suffered for many years as a slave. I rose to lead your tribes, to become a huntress, a warrior, a chieftain. Flying with you has been an honor I will never forget." She took a deep breath, collected her magic, and rose into the air as a golden dragon. She spoke louder. "Yet today, as we celebrate our victory and mourn our loss, I must choose a home. I must choose one path for my heart. Today I am not Eteerian nor a chieftain." She looked at Jeid; he stood across the crowd in human form, looking at her with gentle eyes. She spoke softly, more to him than to anyone else. "Today I am a daughter of Requiem." She looked back at the tribesmen. "Choose a new leader amongst yourselves. Fly as one tribe, and I pray you find your own sky. Mine lies above the forests of Requiem and the marble column that rises in the starlight."

She rose higher in the sky, letting the wind flow across her, fill her nostrils with the scent of the free air, and billow her wings. The other dragons rose around her. Thirty remained alive, no more. Thirty souls to forge a kingdom. Thirty souls to birth a nation. Jeid flew at her side, the largest among them, the sun bright against his copper scales. Maev flew at Laira's other side, solemn and silent.

Behind Laira, every other dragon held a body in his or her claws.

Fur cloaks shrouded the dead, the fallen Vir Requis. In death they had regained human forms, their magic forever gone, their lights forever dimmed. Laira looked at them—survivors and fallen. She met Dorvin's gaze, and he stared back at her with wet, red-rimmed eyes. In his claws, the silver dragon held the body of his sister, of the druid Alina, and Laira felt lost, for the guiding light of Requiem had fallen dark.

They flew on the wind.

They left the mountain and tribes behind. They sailed over swaying plains, rolling hills, silver rivers, and misty forests of birches and maples. They flew through day and night until they saw it ahead—King's Column rising from the forest. The heart of Requiem.

They landed on a hill, the column rising in the horizon, a golden pillar in the sunset. And here they dug more graves. And here they mourned a loss too great to bear. By the graves of Requiem, a young dragon slain too soon, and Eranor, the first priest of starlight, they buried their new dead. And now her tears did flow. Now Laira wept, kneeling before the graves, her hands upon the soil.

"I don't know how I can go on without her," Dorvin said, voice choked. The young man's cheeks were pale, his eyes haunted, his cheeks covered in stubble. "She was the light of Requiem, a beacon sent from the stars to guide us home. To guide me." He lowered his head. "Goodbye, Alina, my sister. I love you."

Her golden hair still stained with the blood of their battle, Maev approached Dorvin. The tall, gruff woman, perhaps the greatest warrior in Requiem, embraced the young man, and her eyes dampened. She kissed Dorvin's cheek and whispered comforts into his ear, and the two stood upon the grassy hill, the wind in their hair, holding each other close.

As Laira stood here, she felt more than loss for their dead. Many lights had gone out; two were missing.

"Where are you, Issari, my sister?" Laira whispered. She had already lost a brother; to lose her sister too would a pain she could not bear. "Where are you, Tanin, Prince of Requiem?"

The two had gone south to claim a distant throne. They had never returned. Laira looked south as if they would appear upon the horizon as she waited, a white dragon and a red one, a sister and a prince, the two she needed with her here. It was a dream, perhaps a fool's dream, and deep inside her Laira feared that they had fallen too, that their bodies would remain across the sea, leaving her always doubting, always empty, a shell of who she could have been.

Return to me. Please.

As she gazed at the horizon, she thought she saw a dragon there, a vision, a wish woven into a daydream of her sister coming home. Laira's breath caught in her throat. She narrowed her eyes.

She turned to Jeid who stood beside her. "Jeid, do you see it?" Her eyes dampened. "A dragon from the south."

He nodded. Laira shifted and took flight. She flew toward the distant figure, hope kindling inside her. Issari! Issari returned! She—

No.

Laira felt her heart freeze and shatter within her. The dragon flying toward her wasn't white like Issari. His scales were a pale blue, the color of robin eggs, and one of his legs was too small, barely larger than a human leg. The young dragon—he was even smaller than Laira—panted in the air, smoke puffing out from his nostrils in short spurts. He seemed close to exhaustion, and his scaly skin hung loosely over his bones.

"Requiem!" he cried out. "I seek Requiem. I—"

His eyes rolled back and he dipped in the sky. His magic left him, and he became a human boy clad in rags. He tumbled toward the ground. Laira raced forward and caught him in her claws.

She descended, shifted back into human form, and held the child in her arms. He gasped for breath. Jeid landed beside them, claws digging ruts into the hill, and also returned to human form. Others joined them, surrounding the child. The boy lay in Laira's arms, his skinned tanned brown, his eyes black, his frame almost skeletal. His left arm and hand were small as a babe's, hanging loosely from his torso.

"Have I . . . have I found Requiem?" He licked his dry lips, drank from a gourd Jeid held above him, and coughed. "I flew from Eteer. I seek the land of dragons. The land of my people."

Laira stroked the boy's hair. "You found Requiem, my child. You found your home."

Tears filled his eyes. "She told me it would be here. The Lady in White. The Daughter of Taal with the Silver Palm."

Laira's breath caught in her throat. "A Silver Palm? Do you mean an amulet embedded into her hand?"

The child nodded. "A holy woman. A seraph from the sky. Issari." Tears streamed down his face, drawing lines through grime. "With her was a great Prince of Dragons. They entered the desert, and they will bring light to the world. They will deliver us from darkness. They will heal the sky."

His eyes closed and he fell into slumber, and Laira held him close, and a hint of hope, a flutter of light like a firefly on a moonlit night, filled her breast. So many had died around her. So many nightmares filled her mind. But her sister was alive and Laira laughed, her tears of relief falling onto the child she held.

JEID

Beneath the marble column, the birches rustling around them, King Aeternum wed his bride.

They had no druid to join their hands. Eranor had fallen; so had Alina. But night had fallen and the stars shone above, reflecting in the marble of King's Column, and holiness filled this place, and Jeid knew this marriage was as real as the starlight, the marble, and the heat of dragonfire.

He had no fine cloak, no bright armor, no garments for a king. As always, he wore his shaggy old furs. As always his hair was too wild, his beard too long, his weapons too coarse. He did not feel like a king today, only like Jeid Blacksmith, an outcast from a village, a broken man hiding in a canyon. He looked at the people who gathered before him in the night, holding clay lanterns, the few survivors of Requiem. They all stared at him, the light painting their faces, and in their eyes was love for him, devotion to their king.

I took the name King Aeternum, he thought. *A noble name. The name of a great leader to be remembered for eternity. But I still feel like Jeid. I still feel lost.*

The pain swelled inside him, the pain of all those who had fallen. His wife, slain by the cruel Zerra. His father, Eranor, who had fallen defending the escarpment. His daughter, little Requiem, whose name now lived on in their kingdom. So many others, the people he was supposed to lead, the people he had brought here, the people he was so scared for.

Doubt might fill me, he thought, *and too much fear for any man to bear, but for them I will be King Aeternum. For them I will be the leader they need.*

The crowd parted, whispering and bowing their heads, and from the darkness she emerged—his bride.

When Laira had first come to him, she had been only half alive—starving, wounded, feverish, a fragile thing barely clinging to life after years of abuse. He had watched her grow into a warrior, then a chieftain, and now before him he saw a new Laira. He saw the woman he would forever fly with, the light he would join to his. She walked toward him, smiling softly, staring at her feet. She wore a fur cloak and a necklace of beads, attire as humble as his, but she was beautiful to Jeid. A garland of flowers crowned her head of raven hair; that hair, once sheared short, now grew down to her chin. When she reached him, she looked up at him, her eyes huge and green and lit with starlight. Her lips—slanted from an old injury—parted, and she whispered to him, her voice so low only he could hear.

"I have loved you since I first saw you, Jeid. I will love you forever. Always will we fly together."

He kissed those lips, and the people raised their lanterns around them, and the lights glowed like the stars.

The dragons of Requiem worked through the summer, flying to the mountains in the north, cutting out stones, carving, building. Around King's Column they laid down more tiles, and more columns rose, sisters to the first pillar of their kingdom. Porticoes rose among the birches, soaring hundreds of feet tall, forming the skeleton of what would become a palace, the heart of a nation.

As the palace grew from the forest, so did their number.

The first new dragons arrived on a clear summer night with no moon, a husband and wife from the eastern plains. Three days later, on a warm evening, seven dragons flew in from the distant, snowy north where no plants grew and ice formed the walls of homes. By the summer solstice, a hundred dragons flew above the halls of Requiem, a hundred souls no longer lost, blessed by their stars, joined together.

The palace was not yet complete; only half its columns stood, and no roof topped them. The winds blew into the hall, and birch leaves scuttled across the marble tiles. It would still be many moons, perhaps many years, before the halls of Requiem shone in all their glory. That did not stop one Vir Requis, a young hunter with dark eyes, from spending that summer carving and polishing, working an oak into a throne of wood, its branches and roots coiling to form its shape. On that summer solstice when Requiem welcomed its one hundredth dragon, Dorvin took his creation into the hall of his king, and he placed the throne upon the tiles between the columns.

"The Oak Throne of Requiem," the young man said to his king. He bowed. "Every king needs a throne."

Jeid looked at the young man and smiled. Dorvin had first come to him bursting with rage, ready to fight the world. Today Jeid saw a solemn warrior of Requiem, wise and strong. He placed a hand on the young man's shoulder.

"Your sister gave you the name Eleison, an ancient word for mercy. I will sit on this throne you carved me, but you will always stand at my right-hand side, a noble son of Requiem, first among her warriors."

Dorvin raised his head, and his eyes shone with tears. "I will forever fly at your side, my king."

In the light of summer, the forests green and the sky clear, King Aeternum sat on his throne and gazed upon his kingdom— the columns that rose around him, the rustling birch trees, and the mountains that grew beyond. His family stood at his side. Laira, his wife, the light of his heart. Maev, his daughter, the beacon of his soul. Dorvin, a young warrior who had become like a son to him. They stood with him in his hall, and some of his pain, some of his loneliness, eased to see them with him. He was not alone. When he raised his eyes to the sky, he saw the others there, a hundred dragons beneath the sun.

Yet two lights were missing, two holes inside him.

I pray for you, Tanin and Issari, Jeid thought. *Return to us.*

He rose from his throne, shifted into a dragon, and took flight. The others flew at his side—a bride, a daughter, a brother in arms. They flew higher, circling around the sun, and gazed down upon their kingdom. Laira sang softly as she flew, her golden scales bright in the dawn.

"As the leaves fall upon our marble tiles, as the breeze rustles the birches beyond our columns, as the sun gilds the mountains above our halls—know, young child of the woods, you are home, you are home." Laira's voice rose and the others sang with her. "Requiem! May our wings forever find your sky."

The story continues in . . .

REQUIEM'S PRAYER

Dawn of Dragons, Book Three

NOVELS BY DANIEL ARENSON

Misfit Heroes:
Eye of the Wizard (2011)
Wand of the Witch (2012)

Dawn of Dragons:
Requiem's Song (2014)
Requiem's Hope (2014)
Requiem's Prayer (2014)

Song of Dragons:
Blood of Requiem (2011)
Tears of Requiem (2011)
Light of Requiem (2011)

Dragonlore:
A Dawn of Dragonfire (2012)
A Day of Dragon Blood (2012)
A Night of Dragon Wings (2013)

The Dragon War:
A Legacy of Light (2013)
A Birthright of Blood (2013)
A Memory of Fire (2013)

The Moth Saga
Moth (2013)
Empires of Moth (2014)
Secrets of Moth (2014)
Daughter of Moth (2014)
Shadows of Moth (2014)
Legacy of Moth (2014)

KEEP IN TOUCH

www.DanielArenson.com
Daniel@DanielArenson.com
Facebook.com/DanielArenson
Twitter.com/DanielArenson

Made in the USA
San Bernardino, CA
18 December 2016